LET SLEEPING CATS LIE

Miranda's cat, Thorpe, lay purring in its sleep. Miranda smiled and said, "The poor dear is exhausted. I doubt if a bomb could shock him into wakefulness."

At this, Lord Adam Brand smiled a different kind of smile, and asked, "Shall we find out?"

Magic—Miranda had no other explanation for this total bombardment of the senses, this feeling of utter defenselessness as Adam swept her into his arms and hungrily pressed his lips on hers. Undone by a kiss that seemed to plumb the depths of her being, Miranda tried to understand the nature of a spell that seemed to sap the strength from her bones, and caused an explosion of contradictory reactions, cold and hot, light and darkness, as her consciousness seemed to shatter and rebuild itself.

The cat might not wake, but Miranda had—and every fiber of her being was crying for more. . . .

THE
WOULD-BE
WITCH

—⁓—

by

Rita Boucher

A SIGNET BOOK

Chapter 1

It was just before sunset when the coach slipped into the shadowed mews behind Jermyn Street. From his perch on the driver's seat, Adam, Lord Brand, surveyed the deserted stretch of small gardens and stables. As he had hoped, the equipage excited little notice, being almost indistinguishable from a common hired carriage in this busy part of London. Only a knowing eye could discern the true nature of the vehicle, built for speed and maneuverability, and none but a savant would see the traces of a mud-concealed crest or the powerful horseflesh disguised beneath a carefully applied layer of dirt.

Nonetheless, when the Marquess of Brand halted the carriage, he made certain that he was well out of sight. The rear exit of Professor Guttmacher's Hall of Wonders was perilously close and it would not do to take chances. Word of the bet last week at White's had spread. Rumor had it that half the Ton was now attending Guttmacher's demonstrations, if only to be present when Lord Brand finally fulfilled his pledge to unmask the erstwhile professor as a fraud. Although the large crowds and publicity would serve Adam's purposes, the fanfare had also made matters deucedly difficult. Guttmacher's confederates would do their utmost to keep his nemesis from the hall.

"Adam, I cannot believe that you intend to go through with this absurd masquerade," Lawrence Timmons said as his nephew climbed into the cab and discarded the concealment of broad-brimmed hat and driving coat. " 'Tis foolish beyond permission—to go through all this for a wager. And you will

not be the only one to suffer should you fail. I hear that Lord
Ropwell has wagered a thousand pounds upon your success."

"So, he thinks to tow himself from Fleet on my coattails,
does he?" Adam said, his square jaw jutting in a frown, as he
pulled a dressmaker's box from beneath the seat. "I would
think that a patron of charlatans like Ropwell would make his
bets against me instead of in my favor. There is not a necro-
mancer in Town who has not seen that man's face."

"I wonder what he will use for payment should you lose?"
Lawrence asked with a chuckle. "'Tis said that Ropwell's
debts nearly rival Prinny's. No wonder at all then, that he is
trying all avenues in his search for the family jewels. Apparently, his wife secreted them somewhere before her death,"
Lawrence informed him.

"They say a good deal more than that," Adam added, an
amber spark of anger tinging his brown eyes. "'Tis galling
that a bounder like Ropwell might profit far more than I from
this bit of business. Even if I win, I am still financially the
loser. The hundred pounds that Lord Sedgewick wagered will
not even cover my costs." He removed the lid to reveal a vo-
luminous silk gown. Lifting it gingerly by the shoulders,
Adam shook it out in a rustle of pea green. "Madame Felice
charged nearly as much as Sedgewick bet just to create this to
my specifications."

"And swore you to secrecy, no doubt," Lawrence sighed as
he struggled to slide the gown over his nephew's head. The
younger man's height, well nigh to six feet tall, made the
cramped confines of the carriage an extremely poor choice of
dressing room.

A muffled laugh was heard. "Actually, the modiste looked
upon it as a most excellent challenge. 'Eef I can make the
seigneur look like une femme, then every chienne in town
will flock to me,'" Adam said, mimicking the seamstress's
heavy accent, his tousled Apollo finally emerging from a
fount of white ruffles at the neck. Carefully, he worked his
arms into the sleeves and pulled the front in place "Well?"

The older man sat back in his seat to eye his nephew critically. For the first time, he began to believe that they might
carry off the charade successfully. Although Adam wore full

evening dress, not a trace of Weston's work was visible; even the snowy fall of immaculate linen vanished beneath the swaths of lace. Madame Felice's creation was a marvel of deception, its padded folds transforming the marquess's masculine frame into that of an aging female. That cunningly fashioned facade of sagging charms and strained seams was virtually indistinguishable from the figures of those ample matrons who presided over many a fashionable salon and ballroom.

Still, though the garment contrived to stoop those broad shoulders and conceal his athlete's physique, there was nothing frail and feminine about the Marquess of Brand. Those chiseled features, the aristocratically sculpted planes of chin and cheek, were undeniably male. Without careful artifice, Adam's face would not pass muster as that of a crone, the expression in his eyes being the only exception. There was something in those brown depths that was far too old for a man who had not yet passed to the twilight side of his thirties, Lawrence thought sadly. Perhaps that was the reason behind Adam's insane and dangerous stunts; his nephew had never had much of a chance to be young.

"You put me in mind of Great-aunt Sophronia," Lawrence remarked with a rueful shake of his gray head. "Ugliest woman that ever walked on the face of the earth. I had never remarked the resemblance till this moment, somehow. 'Tis the gown, I suspect; her taste was almost as hideous as her phiz."

"I think it rather becoming," Adam retorted, batting his thick lashes in a parody of femininity. "Will you fasten up the back, please?"

"As becoming as a pair of Hessians on a rooster," Lawrence grumbled, fumbling with the row of buttons. "Damme, I never thought to spend my graying years playing abigail to a thirty-four-year-old man. How do you mean to shed these togs when the time comes?"

"The front is very lightly stitched," Adam explained, reaching beneath the seat to unearth an elaborate wig. "All I need do is rip it away and step out of the skirts. Then Herr Guttmacher—or Bob Taylor, as his mama named him—will be exposed for the charlatan that he is. Taylor is as much a graduate of the University of Heidelberg as I am king of Prussia. The flash houses of Covent Garden were the only schools that he can honestly lay claim to."

"You do realize that it may not be all that simple to get into the hall," Lawrence cautioned, reaching to tuck a stray wisp of his nephew's chestnut hair underneath the powdered curls. "As we passed, I saw a burly fellow out front, an apostle of the Fancy, by the look of him. The fighter was giving a careful eye to anyone walking through the door."

"I know." Adam chuckled as he took up a mirror and pulled a hare's foot from the powder pot on the cushions. "Herr Taylor has posted only one lookout this evening, when there were three bruisers there searching the faces of the crowd yesterday. It is far better than I expected. Likely, Taylor believes himself safe. Heaven knows that I have told everyone from the potboy to the archbishop that I fully intend to be at Lady Enderby's entertainment tonight. He does not expect me."

"Really, Adam, it would be most unkind of you to cry off at this late hour," Lawrence exclaimed in dismay. "I should have realized that something was havey-cavey when you agreed to attend Hester's gathering. Always saying that the Lady Enderby's hair outweighs her wits. Well, I won't have it, I tell you. Hester's husband is a dear friend of mine for all that his wife is something of a widgeon and she is in alt at the thought of you gracing her table. She has even secured the services of Astley's new magician, a Monsieur Sirloin or some such."

"That is Barone, with an 'e', not as in 'baron of beef,' Uncle," Adam chuckled. "There will be meat, I daresay, but if I know Lady Enderby it will not be on her table. No doubt she and her fellow ewes have gathered a flock of eligible little lambs with no more than a 'baa' and the current state of the weather for conversation. In all honesty, I tremble at what Lady Enderby has in store far more than I fear anything that Taylor might try." Adam feigned a shudder and touched his glowering companion lightly on the shoulder. "Have no worry, Uncle. I have no intention disappointing your friend Hester. I will be there, if only to meet Barone. The magician and I have a bit of business to discuss. We might be a trifle late, but we shall have a tale to tell in compensation for our tardiness. Ouch!" He grimaced as he maneuvered the hairpin to anchor the wig fully in place. "Damned thing must weigh ten stone," he muttered, patting the curls into place. " 'T'was no wonder that Grandmama Lawrence was plagued by perpetual megrims."

"The lice were none too pleasant either, as I recall. There were veritable hoards of them in those old perukes. Occasionally even a mouse or two," Lawrence added acerbically.

Adam turned, his hand rising involuntarily in search of a sudden phantom itch until he saw the older man's lip quirk upward. "And you dare call me unkind. Now I shall imagine all manner of vermin running about my skull for the balance of the evening."

"Serves you right, boy, for cozening me into this," Lawrence grumbled. "I shall account you lucky if a mere megrim is the only consequence of tonight's lark. 'Tis the two-legged vermin that cause me to worry. If the half of what you have said about this fellow Taylor is true, he will not take this humiliation in good grace."

"That is why I want you to leave as soon as I make my move," Adam said, all traces of humor vanishing from his countenance. Dipping a finger into a tin, he skillfully spread a waxy substance to simulate the tracks of wrinkles near his eyes. Next came rouge, applied with the heavy hand of a woman with failing eyesight. "Wait for me at the reins, as we planned, in case there is a need to make a rapid exit. In fact," he reflected, taking a brush from the Chinese box and dabbing it in carmine, "maybe you ought not to come in with me at all."

"Nonsense, might as well be in for a pound as a penny," Lawrence said, then drew an awed breath as he took in the full effect of his nephew's disguise. "I cannot credit it! You are the image of Great-aunt Sophronia!"

The devil danced in Adam's eyes, and his baritone dropped to a crone's cackle. "Aye, Nevvy, a gel in Drury Lane taught me a thing or two about painting the face."

"And knowing you, I suspicion that you taught her a thing or two in return," his uncle retorted. "I would say that you look at least a century old."

"La, not a day over eighty!" Adam declared, slapping him playfully on the hand with a folded fan. "So, ye think I'll do?"

"Your own father wouldn't know you," Lawrence assured him.

"That is significant of nothing, I fear." The merry light in the marquess's eyes was suddenly extinguished, causing him to appear almost as aged as the facade he effected. "I was much as a stranger to him for the most part. After Mama died, I think that Father scarcely saw me at all. When our paths would cross in Brand Manor, he would seem almost startled, as if he could not quite place me."

"You must remember how deeply he loved your mother. Her death was a mortal blow," Lawrence said softly. "Their affection was like nothing I have ever seen before or since. Your father was somehow incomplete without my sister, like a drifting ship that had lost its anchor. As for me, I miss her still. Helen and I had always been very close."

"I know. I loved her, too, for all that I was well aware that Father would forever be first in her life," Adam said, trying to keep the bitterness from his voice. With deliberate care, he placed a patch near the cleft of his chin. "But you and I went on living, dealt with our grief. Sin though it might be, I almost wish that the smallpox had killed Father, too. Heaven knows, he might as well have been in the grave with her. Perhaps then he would not have . . ." Adam choked back the words and shook his head, picking up a lacy mitt and jamming his fingers in blindly.

"Here, allow me, Aunt Sophronia, before you rip those gloves to shreds," Lawrence said, giving the young man's wrist a gentle squeeze, offering what comfort he could with that small contact. Two pairs of brown eyes met, mourning the immutable past; then Adam shook his head and grinned.

"Shall we go, Nevvy, and see if Professor Guttmacher can cure what ails me?" Adam asked, his tones rising to an old woman's pitch. With the handle of his ivory cane he pushed the carriage door open. "Way I hear it, the man's wonderful electric machine can cure everything from the flux to the French disease. A miracle worker, they say."

"Ah, but can he cure a broken heart?" Lawrence asked as

he alighted and offered his arm. "For if he can mend that fragile organ, then he is indeed a man of miracles."

Adam gave an indignant "Harumph" as he plodded along in a humpbacked hobble. "Ain't no remedy for that, Nevvy. 'Tis nothing but a fool's malady anyhow, since it only strikes those who place their hearts in the keeping of others. Haven't given mine yet, in my lifetime. Don't intend to, neither!"

"Poor Aunt Sophronia," Lawrence murmured as they turned the corner and mounted the steps. "To have a whole heart at your age. Well, even with your advanced years, there is still hope." He answered Adam's hooded glare with a smile and pulled two one-pound notes from his purse. "I was just telling my dear aunt that there is hope for her," he told the doorkeeper, placing the entry fee in the man's outstretched paw.

"Aye, guv," the hulking seneschal agreed heartily. "'Ope for everybody, s'what th' perfesser 'as ter offer. Why t'other day, th' perfesser made a cripple walk what counnent walk afore. Yer auntie won't be needin' 'er stick, sir, nor yer strong arm afore th' night is done. Mark me words, she'll be walkin' on 'er own."

"Or mayhaps even running," Lawrence commented in a dry undertone as they entered the velvet-draped chambers of Guttmacher's Hall of Wonders.

The setting sun gilded London, painting brick and stone with a warm glow. Windows winked in the last sparks of day and even the dull Thames was temporarily a reflected ribbon of light.

"I vow, it almost looks beautiful," Miranda Wilton said, azure eyes sweeping the horizon beyond the carriage window. "Look, Mama, there are the houses of Parliament. Is it not fine, the way the rays strike the glass? One can almost fancy them huge diamonds."

"There are no diamonds in Parliament, not since Pitt the Younger departed that pile of stone," Lady Wodesby said sleepily, peering out from under the wide brim of her hat. Her pert nose wrinkled in disgust. "By Hecate! Is that the Thames

I smell? 'Tis hard to credit that this is the same river that runs past The Wode."

"Like a huge chamber pot," Miranda said deliberately, watching her mother's expression.

"And then they wonder why the catch of fish has dropped of late. Were I a finned creature I would be swimming for Oxford with every ounce of strength in my tailbone," Lady Wodesby murmured, still half asleep.

"The state of the Thames is minor compared with the crime and the noise that occur on its shores," Miranda added, trying to keep her lips tightly in line. Usually Mama would have been able to read any change of expression easily, but in her current state, she was not nearly as wary. With a bit of luck, Mama might be led into some revelation. "'Tis a marvel that anything or anyone would choose to visit London."

"Much less live here," her mother agreed, her lids drooping. "Were it not for Bond Street and Monsieur Doucet's Herb Emporium, there is not a . . ." Lady Wodesby's eyes widened as she realized that there was a hook hidden in Miranda's innocent baiting. Knowing that she was nearly caught out, the older woman shoved the arms of Morpheus aside.

"Why do you not continue, Mama?" Miranda asked sweetly, leaning back in her seat. "I believe you were about to say, 'There is not a person or place that is worth the trouble to harness the horse or the price of the tolls.' That is your customary line, I believe, whenever you are forced to go to Town." Silence was the only answer, but there was something in her mother's eyes. A silky swath of Miranda's strawberry-blonde hair came unpinned, momentarily obscuring her vision, but by the time she had smoothed it away, that fleeting expression was gone. Still, she refused to give it up. "Sometimes, I suspect you would rather be burnt at the stake than have to endure an evening of idle chit-chat."

"Here, allow me," Lady Wodesby said, moving to sit beside her daughter. Deftly, she removed Miranda's pins and began to repair her daughter's coiffure. "It would not do to arrive in Town looking like a ragamuffin."

Miranda stifled a sigh. With her mother at her back there was no hope of catching her out by reading her expression.

"With Macadam's roads, London is but half a day from The Wode, yet I can count on one hand the number of times you have visited Town since Papa's passing. You have gone to a great deal of trouble to retain this reclusive life of ours, declining every overture or invitation. Until tonight. I find myself wondering why."

"Lady Enderby is a dear friend," Lady Wodesby said, struggling valiantly against the tide of conversation.

Miranda arched a sandy brow in doubt. "Are we speaking of the woman you once styled as 'Hester the Hopeless'?"

"I do hope you will not use her given name this evening," Lady Wodesby said weakly, brushing the last of Miranda's loosened knot firmly into line with her fingers before coiling it with a skillful twist and fixing it in place. "Such familiarity would mark you as hopelessly ill bred."

"I believe you once said that if Hester's thoughts were pounds and pence, she would not have enough in her purse to visit Vauxhall." Miranda turned to face her mother and repressed an exultant smile. No one else would have seen the signs of agitation, but wrinkling in the corners of the eyes, an almost imperceptible thinning of the lips told Miranda that she had hooked on the truth. Relentlessly she reeled her mother in. "It was during my Season, if I recall. 'No more wit than a woodcock' were the words you used to describe her."

"Your recall is extremely selective," the lady said, rallying a lame attack. "Lady Enderby and I were quite close in our schoolroom days. She is a perfectly convenable woman and she knows everyone worth knowing."

"So now we get to the meat of the matter," Miranda said, her lip slipping into a lopsided smile.

"I have no inkling of what you are trying to imply," her mother said as she returned to her seat, avoiding her daughter's piercing look.

"Really, Mama!" Miranda said, taking an exasperated breath. "You know my meaning full well. Ever since that letter from Aunt Titania last month, you have been brooding about—"

"I do not 'brood'." Lady Wodesby's eyes flashed topaz.

"Did she have a foretelling?" Miranda dared at last to ask

the question that had been troubling her. "Did she see something for Damien?"

The older woman shook her head, the shadow in her eyes clearing for a moment. "No, my sweet, you need not fear for your brother. Tania's visions show nothing of import and Damien is quite charmed. He is far safer than any man in Wellington's army may be. I only wish that he were here."

"As do I, Mama. I thought that you might be asking Lord Enderby to use his influence with the Regent, so that Damien might be a bit less in harm's way," Miranda said.

"You know full well that Damien would not thank me for meddling with his Fate, much as I might want to."

The two women sighed in accord, their thoughts racketing along with the clatter of the carriage wheels.

"If it is not Damien, then what is vexing you?" Miranda asked, as they crossed the bridge. "What did Aunt Titania say?"

Lady Wodesby hesitated. There was no choice but the truth or prevarication. Although Miranda lacked the family talent, she could detect a lie as soon as it was uttered. "Your aunt was dreaming of the family, as she occasionally does this time of year. There were typical signs and omens—nothing terribly specific, of course. Cousin Delia will be delivered of a healthy boy when her time comes. There is good fortune in store for Uncle Seth; I suspect his investments on the Exchange will bear fruit. Unfortunately, as you know, foretellings are rather vague when it comes to people of the Blood. But Tania did see an image of you . . ." Her voice trailed off.

"What did she see?" Miranda asked.

"A bride . . . Tania saw a bride," Lady Wodesby said, her voice rasping.

"*Me*?" Miranda asked, not quite daring to believe her mother's tight nod. "Could it be that Martin will finally come to the point? I was hoping, but considering my years—"

"You are only six and twenty," Lady Wodesby's tones rose indignantly. "That scarcely renders you an ancient."

"Nine and twenty," Miranda corrected, her eyes shining as she allowed herself to dare a dream. A husband. A family of her own. "Certainly old enough to place me quite securely on the shelf as far as the world is concerned, but if Aunt Titania says I am to marry—"

"Not Martin Allworth," her mother snapped.

"Was there anything specific in Auntie's prediction?" Miranda asked, watching her mother carefully. "As you say, when it comes to those of us who share the Blood, Destiny is often ambiguous."

The older woman shook her head. "Nothing definitive. I read the cards for you immediately of course, as soon as I heard. Though, as you say, the messages they reveal for our family members are often deceiving, a wedding for you, my love, is a distinct possibility. But 'tis my opinion that you will not marry Allworth," she repeated.

"Are you certain that Martin is not the man?" Miranda asked, knowing full well that there could be no lies or prevarication when it came to the cards.

"No." Her mother's reluctant answer was barely above a whisper. "But your brother would never allow it, Miranda. Allworth is an Outsider."

"Damien will have no choice but to reconcile himself to Martin," Miranda said. "Especially since he is the only one who is likely to ask for my hand. I cannot understand why you dislike him so. He is considered quite handsome and his bloodlines are excellent."

"I have heard equal recommendations for a horse," Lady Wodesby snorted. "And I daresay you might find more intelligence in a good Thoroughbred then you would in Sir Martin Allworth. By comparison, Hester is a veritable Athena in wisdom."

"Martin is a man of few words," Miranda said, her lips pursing into a straight line.

"And those precious few that he utters, his mama places on his tongue," Lady Wodesby retorted. "An echo of a man, if ever there was one, petticoat ruled—"

"Now I begin to understand." Miranda tilted her head, skewering her mother with a look. "This sudden urge to visit Town and put up the knocker at Portman Square after nearly a year's absence. You knew full well that Martin and his mother had invited us to dine with them tonight. And we had to decline because of your prior engagement. How did you manage to arrange Lady Enderby's invitation upon such short notice?"

"I had received Hester's request for our presence weeks before Martin's mama decided that your dowry and name might be a sufficient inducement for an alliance," she replied with a sniff. "Especially now that his pockets are to let."

"Temporarily," Miranda said, startled. "But how did you know of Martin's financial troubles?"

Lady Wodesby looked everywhere but down at the basket upon the floor.

"Thorpe! I should have known," Miranda fumed, catching the cat's calm, green-eyed gaze. "He was eavesdropping again."

"You do not imagine that I would allow you to be unchaperoned," her mother said. "I cannot help it if Martin is careless with what he lets slip before the servants."

The mottled feline mewled plaintively.

"There is no need to defend me, Thorpe," the older woman declared, "nor to excuse yourself. If anyone owes an apology, it is Miranda, for she knows that we both want the best for her, and Martin Allworth is certainly far from the best."

"I shall not apologize to Thorpe, Mama." Miranda closed her eyes and took a deep breath, trying to stem the sudden tightness in her throat. Mama simply did not understand the realities of the situation, Miranda told herself. Lady Wodesby's world was governed by a different set of rules. "Mama," Miranda began, blinking back the tears. "Martin may very well be the best that I can do. My Season has long past and though my fortune and face were well enough, the Wodesby name was a burden I could not overcome."

"Our heritage? A burden? Were it not for a Wodesby, Arthur's court in Camelot would have failed utterly," Lady Wodesby's chin rose in indignation. "Our lineage is more exalted than that of that trumped-up mad Hanoverian that sits upon the throne."

"And how many men are knowingly willing to take a descendent of Merlin to wife unless they themselves are of the Blood?" Miranda asked. "What manner of husband would wish a woman whose power surpasses his own?"

"Yet you would consider Martin?"

"In my case, there is nothing to fear." Her words came steadily, but the pain in her eyes could not be masked. "I am a cripple."

Thorpe let loose a furious hiss.

"There is little use pretending otherwise, Thorpe." Miranda calmly gave voice to long-held conviction. "I may be the Keeper of the Scrolls, but everyone knows that the post is no more than a sugar-tit to keep a child from crying."

Lady Wodesby protested. "Why, those records were little more than a dragon's nest when you took charge. Spells, potion receipts, and craft journals all mixed higgledy-piggle with the records of maledictions and remedies. Now every proceeding is duly registered and the histories are in excellent order. Just last month Morwenna Gwynn discovered that charm to prevent cave-ins among the arcanum and it is only due to your organization."

"A librarian or skilled secretary would have been more than equal to the task," Miranda said with a sigh. "It is far past time for the acknowledgement. There is not a shred of magic in me."

"You are an excellent seer of character."

"When one is well trained in the arts of facade, it takes no more than shrewd observation to see beyond artifice," Miranda countered relentlessly. "For all that Papa was the Chief Mage of Albion, I will never be a witch like you are, or have as much power as Damien can summon with his little finger. Everyone among the Seven Covens has been kind, but even they cannot hide the pity in their eyes when I attend spring rites and stand round like a dead stick of hazel. I cannot foretell, or make rain, or even charm the simplest of warts. The Deck is but pieces of pasteboard to me. Is it any wonder that there is not a man among the Coven families who would offer for me, in spite of the fact that I am a Wodesby of The Wode?"

A tear spilled from the corner of Lady Wodesby's eye. "I have tried, my dear, as has every member of the family. There is not an incantation or charm that we did not wield. When you came to your woman's blood and nothing changed, Papa and I even attempted to wake the Grandfather of Us All on your behalf, but he did not answer us."

"You risked rousing The Merlin?" All weeping was forgotten in horror. More than one had died attempting to break the spell that Nimue had used to place The Merlin in eternal sleep. Some had lost their powers entirely. "Mama! You should never have taken that chance."

"I would go back to The Merlin's Tree again if I thought that it might help you," her mother said as Miranda slipped into the seat beside her and clasped her hands. "You are my daughter."

Those four words held a wealth of love, yet Miranda could not let the matter rest. "There is only one means to fulfill Aunt Titania's auguring, Mama, and that is outside the Blood. Martin will be quite biddable; he will let me continue my work because it holds no interest for him. In fact, there is no need for him to know about the Families at all. If I am to marry an ordinary man, it might as well be Martin."

" 'Ordinary' encompasses a considerable field and Martin is definitely at the most unexceptional end of the range," Lady Wodesby commented. "But if he is your fate, there is little that I can do to change it, much as your brother and I might object." *However, if there is any means by which I can deter you from disaster,* she added silently, *then by The Merlin, I shall.*

"We are horribly late," Lawrence fretted, all but hauling his nephew up the stairs of the Enderby house on St. James. "Hester will never forgive us if we have spoiled her dinner. It is a shame that your quarry turned sick tonight and could not fleece his flock."

"Of course, I shall explain that I am entirely to blame," Adam said, drawing off his gloves as they stepped into the entryway. "All those deuced buttons on that damned dress, and all for nothing in the end."

The butler stifled a grin as he took his lordship's hat and greatcoat, hurrying to announce the final guests to her ladyship, then lingering to hear his lordship's explanation.

"Lawrence!" Lady Enderby exclaimed as the two men reached the landing. "We were just about to go in to dinner."

"Forgive me, Lady Enderby, it was my fault, a sartorial matter," Adam began, mischief in his eyes. "Buttons are—"

"He found a button missing and there was naught to do but change," Lawrence broke in, flashing his nephew a warning look. "His valet all but wept. No less than a dozen cravats wasted, too! Brummel is to blame for setting so high a standard."

"Indeed, he goes too far," Lady Enderby agreed. "They say his valet polishes his boots with champagne."

"Ah, if Brummel could have but seen me earlier, he would have laughed himself silly," Adam added, heeding a warning dig from his uncle's elbow. "In consideration of my charming hostess, I had no choice. Forgive us for delaying you."

"Well," Lady Enderby preened at the compliment as she rushed them into the company. "There is no harm done, I suppose, but I must introduce you to—"

"Lawrence!" The silver-haired woman exclaimed as Lady Enderby brought Adam and his uncle to her side.

"Adrienne." Lawrence smiled in delight. "I would not have allowed this young scapegrace to detain me had I known that you were coming out from hiding."

Lady Enderby breathed a relieved sigh. "So you are already acquainted?"

"Old friends," Lawrence replied warmly.

"Certainly older than we would care to admit." Lady Wodesby chuckled.

"Then I shall have dinner announced." Lady Enderby bustled away, leaving the latecomers to fend for themselves.

"My daughter, Miranda," Lady Wodesby said, drawing her forward.

"This cannot be," Lawrence said. "You look barely out of the schoolroom yourself, Adrienne. 'Tis impossible for you to have a daughter old enough for a Season."

"You always were the most shameless of flatterers, Lawrie," Lady Wodesby declared, fluttering her fan like a young miss. "Is this your son?"

"Alas, I never married. Would that Peter had not secured

your hand first, it might have been different, of course. This is my nephew, Adam."

"Helen's son? The resemblance is remarkable; certainly he has her eyes and the Timmons chin," Lady Wodesby observed, taking the arm that Lawrence proffered and strolling with him toward the supper room.

"And Miranda is the very image of . . ." Lawrence's voice drifted back.

"How discomfiting to be disassembled piece by piece," the young woman said. "And then be discarded altogether. I know nothing beyond your Christian name, sir."

There was honesty in her eyes, Adam decided, although it was difficult to believe that there was a matchmaking hen in London who had not supplied her chick with such vital information. But then, upon further examination, it was apparent that Miranda was not the downy fledgling that his uncle had supposed. Those newly hatched girls could not hide their lack of experience, even though they affected the feathers of the world-weary. Not a one in the flock would have dared to venture a conversational sally upon being abandoned with half an introduction. Yet this young woman did not seem the least bit atwitter at being left in his company.

"When did you arrive in London, Miss . . .?" Adam asked.

"Wilton," she supplied. "Is my lack of Town bronze so apparent? Or did I leave some straw hanging in my hair?"

Twenty? Twenty-five? Perhaps older? Adam found it hard to determine with any certainty. Not an Incomparable, by current standard, her lips too wide to be in vogue, the blue of her eyes too like a summer sky to fit the current icy ideal. Clearly she had gone without a parasol and bonnet too often; the sun had lightly toasted her skin and bleached the blonde of her hair to the color of ripening wheat. In her favor, fortune had blessed her with one of those countenances that seemed immune to change. At seventeen or seventy, Miranda would draw the eye. But while her prettiness might capture a man's notice, it was her piquant expression that would arrest his attention. Her face was unfashionably alive with interest and amusement.

"No straw," Adam said, "not even a bit of chaff."

"Then what gave me away as a country greenling?" she asked. "My gown? I fear it is some time since Mama and I last visited Madame Felice."

"Not at all, Miss Wilton." Adam hastened to assure her. "Madame Felice's creations are of that rare type almost beyond style, as modish next Season as they were last. That shade of emerald is an excellent choice for you." To his delight, she turned an adorable shade of pink.

"I hope you do not think that I was fishing for a compliment, sir," she murmured.

"Ah, but you should, Miss Wilton, if only to avoid being revealed as countrified. You must fish assiduously for flattery, affect an air of outright boredom, and never, never, under any circumstances, blush at anything you hear. To do so shows a lack of sophistication."

"And such cynical sang froid is valued above all," she remarked, her lip curling in a combination that conveyed both distaste and amusement. "I begin to recall why I prefer the country life, Mr . . . ?"

"Chapbrook." Adam gave the family name and waited for a reaction, but there was not so much as a glimmer of recognition in those depths of blue. It was too bad of him not to say more. Inevitably, she would find out that he was the Marquess of Brand. Yet he could not resist the omission. "And why do you favor field and farm? I had thought that every woman longs for routs and levées and balls that last till dawn."

"Oh, I love to dance," Miss Wilton said.

Adam shook his head. "Tsk . . . tsk . . . Miss Wilton, the hay is showing."

"I find dancing . . . tolerable," she murmured in lofty tones.

"Much better," Adam approved. "But you still would rather be in the hinterlands?"

"There is far more freedom there, Mr. Chapbrook. In Town, I cannot so much as gallop my horse without some biddy running to tell Mama that I am making a scandal of myself. There are always eyes watching, searching for some sin that may provide a tidbit of gossip."

"Rumor has ever been the grist for society's mill," he agreed, suddenly conscious of surreptitious glances, whispered words behind the screen of fans, an eddy of ominous undertones beneath the flow of conversation.

" 'Tis almost a tangible force, this social cannibalism. They fete you, feed you, then eat your reputation for breakfast," she said lightly.

Although her tones were mocking, Adam detected an underlying tinge of bitterness. Wilton? Wilton? There was a nagging familiarity to the name, but try as he might, he could not bring forth anything from his memory. The announcement of dinner precluded any further exploration in the mines of recall, but eventually, he knew, the nugget would come to the surface. "May I escort you to the table?" he asked, offering his arm.

"Would the confession that I am ravenously hungry put me beyond the pale?" Miranda asked, astonished at her own audacity as they strolled to the table. In the past, she had found it necessary to supply no more than a sentence or two before relinquishing the reins of conversation. Most men were well content to steer the subject to themselves and remain there.

"Absolutely," her partner informed her. "Young women subsist on nectar and ambrosia. Occasionally, in tribute to their hostesses, they may allow a few morsels of food to pass their lips."

"How much constitutes a morsel?" Miranda asked. Never before had she enjoyed this bantering back and forth with a stranger. It was almost like talking to Damien, except that she was quite conscious that this man was not her brother. Though he was not quite as tall as the lanky Damien, he was still somewhat broader built. Solid muscle rippled beneath the tight-cut sleeves of his evening jacket—no padding there, she would wager. Nor anywhere else; his closely tailored attire left no room for doubt. "If a morsel consists of less than a fair cut of beef, I fear that I may be about to disgrace myself."

"Then as it appears we are seated next to each other, I shall guard my plate," he whispered solemnly, as she took her seat to his left. "Lady Enderby is not known for the generosity of her table."

Her answering grin caught him off guard. Not a social snicker, nor a simpering polite gesture, but a wide expression

of pleasure transformed her face. Suddenly, Adam felt the
corners of his mouth stretching dangerously upward, well beyond the bounds of the urbane smirk that polite society
deemed proper. He was precariously close to outright laughter. However, it appeared that poor Miss Wilton was already
one foot over the edge. Her shoulders were trembling, and her
bottom lip was gathered mercilessly beneath her teeth. For a
few seconds, it appeared that she had succeeded in barricad-
ing it in, but the gate could not be held.

Ringing with delight, the melodic sound of Miss Wilton's
laughter floated across the room. Quizzing glasses glinted in
the candlelight as all eyes focused on the spectacle of honest
emotion. Among the stares and glares, there were few smiles.
Beyond the bland façades, he sensed the cold calculation of
predators scenting blood. They would make her suffer for this
compliment to his riposte, unless . . .

Adam began with a tentative chuckle, his deep baritone
joining in counterpoint to her delicate alto. Little more than a
look at Miss Wilton's face was necessary for hesitant mirth
to graduate into genuine laughter. The sparkle in her eye
proved to be an irresistible inducement. As their voices
twined in a humorous duet, Adam found himself forgetting
about the other people at the table, losing sight of everyone
but the girl in the emerald dress, the pulsing dance of the
long, slim column of her throat, the gleam of her hair like a
sheaf of wheat satin wrapped in a nimbus of light. Even as
the gale diminished and the last gasping chuckle faded to an
echo, Adam could not shake this bewitching sense of com-
munion.

"Will you not share the joke, Lord Brand?" A high-pitched
voice broke the spell.

"Forgive me, Miss Bellgrave," Adam said, using the
process of being seated to shield his befuddlement. Unless he
could gather his wits, his aching side would be for naught. "It
was the type of humor which builds itself sentence by sentence," he explained to his other seatmate, and by way of
raised voice to the rest of the table. "I could not hope to repeat
the effect again, nor would I. I fear I have discomfited Miss
Wilton entirely too much." His apologetic glance swept the

company. To censure Miss Wilton, they would have to condemn him as well. Luckily, the Brand title and newly restored fortune sufficed to put him well above reproach. Just as he had hoped, the buzz of table talk began anew interspersed with the rattle of china as the first remove appeared.

Chapter 2

Maddening though it was, the deity of decorum demanded that Miranda speak to Lord Quimby, who was seated on her left. A few words about fences and foxes were all that was needful to send that elderly master of the hounds jabbering about the woeful state of the hunt. Not more than a nod or a sympatheic murmur was necessary to keep him on the conversational trail, while her own thoughts were free to wander far afield. How could she have so lost herself? Had not her ill-fated Season been lesson enough? What was it about Mr. Chapbrook—no, Lord Brand—that had induced her to forget everyone else in the room? Caused her to lose her hard-won wariness?

The turtle soup was thin and foul tasting and Miranda found herself near to choking as her glance met Brand's. Brown eyes, rich and dark as earth, ripe with secret promise, spellbinding . . . the thought gave Miranda a start. Sorcery? Was her mother so desperately set against Martin that she would dare to enspell her own daughter?

Miranda cast a look toward Lady Wodesby. However, the older woman's attentions were fully directed at Lord Brand's distinguished-looking uncle. A compulsion so powerful required tremendous concentration, so it was scarcely possible that Lord Brand was the locus of intense witchcraft. If there was a spell working, the source must be within the man. How else could this untoward attraction be explained?

Brand? Chapbrook? Though neither name brought immediate magical association, Miranda sought within herself, tracing through the tangled web of relationships within the Seven Covens. The names and lines of descent of the Families were well known to her. Indeed, the complexities of kinship were as much a part of her education as the first simple incantations.

Unfortunately, the DeBretts of Mages had been about the only thing that Miranda could conjure, requiring neither talent nor craft, only the gift of an excellent memory. But try as she might, she could recollect no Brand scion anywhere on the branches of The Merlin's Tree. Surreptitious study revealed nothing more than the skill of an excellent tailor whose handiwork displayed Lord Brand's physical attributes to advantage. Tight black superfine stretched over well-defined lines that were obviously solid sinew. His fingers were long and well shaped, but bare of the talisman ring that was as much a part of an adult mage's attire as smallclothes. Yet if there was no sorcery afoot . . . ?

A clammy hand came to rest on her knee, interrupting her jumbled thoughts. Quimby! From the smile on the old satyr's lips, he knew full well that she would not dare risk yet another scene. But as the crabbed fingers crept slowly up toward her thigh, her father's voice echoed in her mind.

"The first rule of magic, my love, is belief. It is far simpler to work a spell in concert with Nature's intent than against her. Sometimes, one can even charm a credulous subject without the risk entailed by the use of magic powers."

Miranda forced a smile, modulating her voice carefully so that only Quimby could hear. It would seem that at least some part of her training might finally be of use. "Your estate is in Devon, Lord Quimby, is it not?"

"Aye, my dear. Perhaps ye'd care t'come and see it one day." The lord leered, mistaking her composed demeanor for complaisance.

"No doubt you were acquainted with my Great-aunt Ceres, Lady Le Fey." The hand's crawling invasion halted as Miranda continued. "She was a notorious beauty, they say." Her lips curled upward, but there was deadly purpose in her eyes as she trapped Lord Quimby with a basilisk gaze.

"L-Lady Le Fey," he stuttered. "Your aunt?"

"On Mama's side, of course. They say I resemble Auntie, not in looks, but in *other* ways," Miranda said significantly.

"It is quite a reputation to live up to, as one might well imagine."

Lord Quimby nodded dumbly.

"I doubt the tales could all be true, though. There are so many stories that it is rather difficult to credit them all. And some seem much too absurd to be real." Miranda went on with a sigh. "Nonetheless, Mama vows that they are entirely authentic, especially about Lord Ratherton and Aunt Ceres. Mama was but a babe in arms at the time, but she was not the only one that I have heard it from. Apparently, Ratherton was a notable rake, one of those disgusting creatures who was not above forcing his attentions when they were unwelcome. Did you know him, Lord Quimby? You *are* of an age."

Once more the lord nodded and from his ashen expression, Miranda determined that the rumors about Ratherton were not entirely unknown to the elderly lecher. It was time to shoot the bolt home. "Perhaps you can confirm if it was all invention, milord? Mama claims that his lordship dared to lay an unwelcome hand on Aunt Ceres. Auntie laid a curse for the insult and part of him just shriveled away, the legend goes. For some reason, Mama never said which piece, though." Miranda tapped her cheek thoughtfully as she paused to let her words take effect. Suddenly, her thigh was unencumbered. "I always wondered if it was trespassing fingers; were Lord Ratherton's digits in any way unusual, milord?"

Lord Quimby shook his head and stared down at his hands, both of which were now trembling visibly upon the table.

"I thought it was a fabrication," Miranda said, her voice as frothy as new-poured ale. "But then one can scarcely go and ask Ratherton's children or grandchildren. That would be intolerably rude."

"Ain't none," Quimby said, his voice shaking. "Ratherton died without issue, for all that he'd had a quiverful born on the wrong side of the blanket before he offended Le Fey. Wife left him, said that he couldn't—" He halted, recalling the company.

"How very sad, but entirely coincidental, I am sure," Miranda said, schooling her expression to the proper mixture of innocence and regret. "Still, it is a most curious tale, do you not think so?"

Lord Quimby did not answer. He was staring downward as if his gaze could somehow pierce through the table linen. His chair was precariously close to tipping him into the lap of the lady on his left. It was all Miranda could do to keep from bursting into laughter, but she had already made that error once. Rarely did she make the same mistake twice.

Having thus secured her left flank, Miranda returned to the conundrum of Lord Brand. Had her judgement failed, she wondered? So much for her vaunted powers of discernment. Never before had she given her trust so quickly. But then, no man had ever clouded her senses with such dispatch. Still, Miranda was reluctantly forced to allow that Lord Brand's omission of his identity might have been deliberate. How could she have been so foolish as to forget society's spiteful diversions? If she had addressed him as "Mr. Chapbrook" within range of Honoria Belgrave's ear . . . Miranda suppressed a shudder. Ample opportunity had been available for him to enlighten her. Yet he had not. But if humiliation had been his intent, why had he had rescued her from her faux pas when he could very well have enjoyed the spectacle of her twisting in the wind? A puzzle indeed.

Adam was done for the moment with his offering upon the altar of manners. Miss Belgrave had subjected him to a discourse on the present paucity of fashionable company in Town. After suffering several threadbare on-dits about Prinny and surviving a soliloquy on the state of the weather, he finally allowed himself to return to Miss Wilton.

"Well, *Mr. Chapbrook*," she said sotto voce.

Irony was unmistakable in the arch of her brow and the distinct emphasis she put on his name. Miss Belgrave, he recalled, groaning inwardly. His impulsive charade was over. Certainly, it was well within Miss Wilton's rights to be affronted at his omission; she would have been the inevitable butt of scorn had she gone about calling him "Mr. Chapbrook."

"It was not my intent to deceive you, Miss Wilton," he said

in soft tones echoing her own. There was something discomfiting in her direct blue gaze, as if she were assaying every word for truth. "I was going to tell you that I am cursed with the title of marquess," he added.

"Cursed?" she asked, momentarily taken aback. "Was this recently done? I have heard of no maledictions registered against any English marquess. There are some rather old French banes pending, but nothing locally." Even as she spoke, she wanted to bite her tongue. What in the world had caused it to run so loose tonight? She turned her indiscretion into a semblance of a jest. "However, I do begin to suspect that there might be some minor household curse upon the Enderbys, at least upon the kitchen."

Her earnest expression prompted an appreciative smile. This humorous reaction was far beyond his expectation. Miss Wilton would do very well at the card table, Adam decided, for despite the utterly ridiculous nature of her declaration, her demeanor was entirely serious. "The title and all it holds can be a curse in and of itself," Adam felt compelled to tell her, even though he was convinced that she would not understand. "It has been such a long time since anyone other than my uncle has actually talked to Adam Chapbrook."

The last trace of frost in her eyes melted instantly.

"The Marquess of Brand being a very lofty individual. I see. How very lonely that must be. Yet," she added with an impish quirk of her lips, "being a marquess does have its uses. It seems with a title for your whip, you can make the Ton prance as neatly as the trained horses at Astley's. My thanks, milord."

If Adam had possessed a quizzing glass, he would have used it then and there to test his accuracy of his observations. Surely, the woman could not be so perceptive as to discern how he had brought the other guests to rein by means of a laugh. Yet, there was no denying the quiet amusement now glinting within those wide pools of azure. He felt transparent, as if she could somehow see into the very core of him, a sense both strangely exhilarating and somewhat frightening. Only when the footman leaned forward to refill the empty glass did Adam realize that he had drained his goblet completely. How-

ever, there was no wine strong enough to explain this sudden
sensation. Hastily, he cast about for something to say, seizing
upon her mention of the famed amiphitheatre.

"Speaking of Astley's, I understand that out hostess has
prepared some prime amusement for us this evening," Adam
said. "The management of the amphitheatre has just imported
a conjuror direct from Napoleon's court. Lady Enderby has
convinced Monsieur Barone to favor us with his presence
tonight."

"Do you think that he might be able to transform this soup
into something edible?" Miranda asked, placing her spoon at
the side of her still-brimming bowl with regret. "I would give
him credence if he could make it worthy of ingestion."

"That *would* require a magician," Adam agreed, watching
as the footmen took the covers from the next remove. Stingy
meat hid shamefully beneath a skimpy layer of sauce. With
diminishing hope, he surveyed the other nearby offerings, but
they were either unrecognizable or inedible. Miss Wilton
wrinkled her nose in eloquent dismay, somehow contriving to
make the childish gesture seem delectably charming.

"Well, milord, it appears that I am doomed," she said with
a sigh. "If I expire of starvation before the evening is over,
please tell my mama that I blame her for my untimely end and
fully intend to haunt her for it. It is she who dragged me here
against my will."

"Come, come, Miss Wilton," Adam said, trying to recall
when he had last smiled so much. "Think of it this way: Our
conversation will not be much curtailed by the need for chew-
ing. However, if you do achieve the state of wraithdom tonight,
you might have a few words with Monsieur. He claims to speak
to the spirits more often than Brummel consults with his tailor."

Miranda's snort could not quite be entirely contained. "And
this Barone fellow has the audacity to claim to be Napoleon's
conjurer?" Unfortunately, she was well aware of the true identity of France's preeminent mage, a rogue cousin whose inclination toward the forbidden powers had caused the French Du
Le Fey to disown him entirely.

"So Astley says," he told her, delighted by her tone of
skepticism. Women, for the most part, tended to be of the

gullible sort, ready to believe in those who shrouded their illusions in mysticism. "Although his appearances in London have been few, Barone has already developed quite a formidable reputation. His skill is renowned."

"Would this conjurer's talents by any chance extend to loaves and fishes?" she asked mournfully.

"Nothing so pedestrian, I am sure, Miss Wilton. Are you back to your stomach again?" And a most admirable stomach it was, he noted, flat and firm, with no trace of corsets. A curious pendant of Celtic design dangled from the column of her throat, the single emerald dipping into the modest dècolletage of her gown as she spoke. "Recall that you are a lady."

"Yes, yes, I recall. Nectar and ambrosia. An excellent idea, milord; as soon as dinner is ended I shall remove myself to the garden and partake of the flowers. That is my only hope if the sweet course fails me," Miranda said. "Surely, no chef could so thoroughly ruin an entire meal. But until then, I pray that you provide me some distraction, or I might just chew up the linen. Tell me more about this Barone. What else does he do, other than babble with the beyond?"

"He claims to be a reader of minds, as well as a conjurer."

"Do I detect doubt in your voice, milord?"

"You do indeed, Miss Wilton," Adam said. "I take it that you share my skepticism?"

Miranda nodded, lifting her fork and rearranging her food upon the plate in order to avoid his scrutiny. She had already slipped up on the matter of the curse and even the talk of conjurer's magic might cause her to blunder. Among her folk, such weighty affairs were naught to jest about, but then for a brief moment she had forgotten that he was not of the Blood. Never before had that happened with an Outsider, not even with Martin. Unfortunately, she could not explain to Lord Brand why her disbelief went well past mere incredulity. To do so would be to risk his scorn, for to him the reason would seem entirely preposterous.

Barone was a fraud, of that she had no doubt. No true Reader would willingly walk among untrained minds, his or her own thoughts exposed naked to all. To suffer that unspeakable intimacy, to risk breaking the fragile bond between body and soul for the sake of mere amusement, a few pieces of gold? The notion would be laughable were it not already obscene beyond measure, a mockery of the Gift that could ultimately destroy both the reader and the read, if used so lightly.

"He is quite adept, although I have not yet discovered how he performs his mental feats," Adam admitted. "But I shall. I am something of a professional skeptic, you see. In fact, I've done quite a bit of study on the fine art of chicanery."

"Have you, milord?" Miranda asked, racked by sudden uneasiness. "Toward what aim?"

"The exposure of fraud, Miss Wilton," he said, his voice hardening. "It is my aim to unmask those who prey on the credulity of innocent people, to lay bare the perfidy of the ones who sell counterfeit cures and sham hopes with promises of false magic."

"You describe many a mountebank, sir, and more than a few physicians, I fear," Miranda said, making a feeble effort at levity.

"Unfortunately, there is sometimes scarcely a noticeable difference between the two," Adam said, the corner of his mouth rising ruefully. "But I must admit 'tis not the quacks that irk me so much as those who purport to practice magic and claim congress with the spirits. The manner in which those necromancers trade upon emotion and sully all that is sacred is absolutely beyond sufferance."

Miranda took shelter in silence, although she knew that it was a flimsy haven at best. It was sheer chance that Lord Brand did not already know who she was. An accidental glance in Quimby's direction sent the old roue cringing to the farthest corner of his chair. Seemingly, the only selection was betwixt Scylla and Charybdis. Brand would either fear her for her heritage or mock her as a liar.

"I am sorry, Miss Wilton," he apologized, misinterpreting her sudden withdrawal. "'Tis a most reprehensible tendency of mine, this inclination to preach. No wonder there have been so many Chapbrooks who decided to take the collar and surplice."

"A family of priests and ministers?" Miranda took a sip of wine, but found it nearly impossible to swallow.

"By the score. How else could we Chapbrooks possibly atone for the regiment of rogues that we set loose upon an unsuspecting world? Luckily, I was never bound for the Church since I am a heathen at heart, holding to no religious credo. But then, there is not much in this world to put faith in these days, is there?"

Four glasses of wine upon an empty stomach. Though Adam knew that he was not even upon the borderline of tipsiness, it was still the only explanation that he could muster for letting his tongue slip its reins. Although he had never made any protestations of public piety, neither had he ever before made the error of any candid professions of doubt. Until now, of course . . . Only Uncle Lawrie was aware of his beliefs, or rather the lack of them.

Miss Wilton absently picked up her fork, convincing Adam beyond doubt that he had passed well beyond the pale of acceptability. When she actually took a bite of Lady Enderby's mysterious meat dish, he became absolutely certain that his heretical statements had driven her into shock. No other explanation would suffice for the politely shut expression that clouded a face that moments before had been an illuminated book. Now, suddenly she was silent, intent on this suicidal abuse of her palate.

Succumbing to cowardly impulse, Adam used the excuse of the next course's arrival to return to Miss Belgrave. Perhaps while she prattled, he might think of some way to resurrect the corpse of enjoyable repartée.

Brand's words had indeed affected Miranda; she felt an unexplainable sense of loss. He believed in nothing, neither above nor below. How could she entertain the hope that a self-confessed skeptic, a man closed to all belief, would even attempt to understand that real magic might exist?

However, the likelihood that Lord Brand might react with an open mind once he learned that she was of witch Blood born was none to nil. But more shocking still was the fact that she had even pondered any manner of disclosure. In the past, such frank revelations had almost inevitably resulted in disaster for witchkind. Despite the fact that no witch had been burnt in England for three-fourths of a century, many of the Blood still cowered in hiding, some even going so far as to deny their special inheritance. Not that Miranda blamed them; she had met far too many Quimbys to believe that the world was ready to embrace the practitioners of magic.

With Brand's attention occupied elsewhere and Quimby effectively quelled, Miranda was left alone to chew on her thoughts. Unfortunately, they were even more difficult to digest than the food. Far wiser it would be to steel herself against this strange attraction. Like a bitter potion, Miranda forced herself to remember the stacks of accounts and journals chronicling the near-devastation of witchkind. They awaited her at the Wode, all of them yet to be catalogued. A grim task it was, one that she feared that she might never be able to complete. The scale of suffering was so overwhelming that a mere perusal of the opening paragraphs was almost beyond bearing. Would the name "Chapbrook" appear upon those tattered pages figuring among the scourges of witchkind? She wondered. But even that bleak possibility proved no talisman against the sound of his voice. A devastating shiver slipped along the length of her spine and she found herself drowning in the dark of his eyes.

"Miss Wilton, have you succumbed to starvation or is it the taste of that unidentifiable stuff on your fork that has stopped your throat?"

Miranda recalled herself to the present, trying not to melt at Lord Brand's smile. "My apologies, milord. I must have been woolgathering," she said stiffly.

Adam's stomach rumbled in complaint. "That was most cruel; the mention of wool immediately associated itself with the word mutton, which my imagination promptly roasted to a turn. Though I confess, at the moment even an allusion to knitting might cause my mouth to water." He waited for the dimple to appear in the corner of her mouth, but there was not even a faint trace of humor to be found. Apprehension had replaced the laughter in her eyes. He told himself that a mind so puritanical could not possibly appeal to him. If the mere mention of a deviation from orthodox thought could so disturb her, then he would do well to give Miss Wilton ample distance. However, this sensible inner discourse did little to alleviate a strange sense of loss. "Knitting connecting to yarn, leading back to wool . . . "

"And from thence to mutton. Yes, I follow," she said, her voice distant. "Then your salvation may be at hand, Lord Brand. I believe the sweets have arrived, an apple tart from the look of it and a cake that would seem almost passable by its appearance."

"And a plum pudding," Adam commented, taking an experimental taste. "Excellent! Might I recommend the pudding, Miss Wilton?"

"No, thank you, milord," she said softly. "I suddenly find that I am no longer quite as hungry as I was before."

The ladies had withdrawn, but Adam decided to decline the opportunity for cigars and port, preferring to catch a glimpse of Barone's apparatus. Locked doors were easily dealt with and Adam slipped quietly into Lady Enderby's ballroom. The gilt chairs were so tightly packed that there was barely space for movement. Yet, Adam noted, a rather substantial distance separated Barone's impromptu stage from the spectators. Less than a third of the candles upon the chandeliers were lit. Either their hostess was practicing economy or the Frenchman preferred venues that were dimly lit. The latter was the more likely.

Not a soul was in sight, so Adam silently stole to the front of the room, evaluating the conjurer's props with an expert's eye. An array of coins, cards, and kerchiefs adorned the top of a table draped heavily with black velvet.

"*Arretez, Monseigneur!*" A hulking man garishly garbed as an Arabian scuttled forward to stand before the table, his hands crossed over his chest in a position that made it clear that he was prepared to use more than words if Adam came any closer. "*C'est très dangereuse.*"

"One must not meddle with the forces of magic, eh?" Adam replied, his eyes narrowing as he searched the man's face. "Philippe? Philippe Rubelle? Is that you beneath the face paint?"

"Adam, *mon ami*?" The man's face split into a grin. "*Incroyable*! I was mistaking you for a *gentilhomme*. Never did I think to see you again this side of hell. Always I was wondering why the body was never found. They lock you in shackles, they put fire to the hut, but all they find after is the chains, nothing more. If they did not believe you *le diable*'s disciple before, they did after. And all because you refuse a comtessa's favors. Was there ever such a fool?"

"I have always preferred to be the one who does the choosing, Phillippe, nor did I care to be just one more link in the lady's chain of Lotharios."

Philippe laughed. "Me, I have never been so discriminating. To be some wealthy *femme's* kept man would suit me well, but I have yet to find one who would keep me. Still, you seem to have done adequately for yourself, Adam, despite your strange ways." He shrugged philosophically, surveying his friend's attire from his patent pumps to his elegantly styled Apollo. "An interesting notion, to perform in evening clothes, but the fit, it is too close. Where do you put the pockets? Not an inch to spare on that evening coat and those trousers, to that I would swear." He rolled his eyes heavenward as he gave the seam of Adam's jacket an experimental tug. "*C'est impossible*! To conceal so much as a chick under that second skin would take real magic."

"I still can produce some surprises," Adam said facetiously. Phillippe had always been known more for his sheer physical power and mechanical skills than his wit. Obviously, the possibility that Adam might be a guest had not yet dawned on him. That might well work to advantage. "Been with Barone long?"

"But half a year. After our fiasco in Italy, I return to France, travel for a bit with Torrini, keep his automaton in repair. Then I think maybe to perform on my own." His turban slid precariously as he shook his balding head in gloom. "A mistake! The quickness of hand I have. The props I make. But the savoir-faire—non. I lack your finesse. You, you had but to look at the audience, and poof! You know what they wish, they eat from your hand. Me, they pelt with old fruit." He busied himself under the drapes. "So, I sell what is left of my props. Now, I fashion tricks for Barone, automatons, special compartments. The man pays well and he knows my worth."

"Has he got anything unusual?" Adam asked, slipping behind the cabinet.

"A few pieces of my handiwork. I have made him a delightful automaton, a ballerina. A marvel!" Philippe bragged, picking up a cage of doves from the corner. "But for the most part, there is little that you have not seen before. Barone is an excellent showman."

"Napoleon's personal conjurer? A mere showman?"

Philippe gave a humorous bark. "We did perform once for the emperor."

"And the Sight Beyond Sight?" Adam asked. "How is that done?"

Philippe wagged his finger. "Ah, *mon ami*, even if I knew, I could not say, of that you are aware. An assistant who speaks too much is soon out switching cards on street corners. But in truth, Adam, I tell you, I cannot tell because I do not know how he does it. The blindfold, I show you." He took up a large fold of black silk and put it over Adam's head. "You can see nothing?"

"Nothing," Adam confirmed, his voice muffled.

Philippe drew it off. "Sight, he has none. The audience, its members cannot possibly be known to him. Yet when Madame Barone holds up the objects, he says if it is gold or silver, ruby or diamond, even, often as not, what the item is. Every time, he is correct. I swear to you, it is almost enough to make me believe that the spirits speak to him."

"But not quite?" Adam asked, dropping the mask and marking it surreptitiously with dust from the floor before picking it up, folding it.

"When you have seen what I have seen?" Phillipe gently smoothed the feathers of a bird before placing it in its special compartment. "How can one believe?"

"Ever try explaining to a woman that you have seen too much to quite believe in anything at all?" Adam asked, picking up a deck and toying absently with the pasteboards.

"Women? Eh, they are natural believers, *les femmes*. Distract them with bright colors and smoke and they will never see how they are manipulated," Philippe said, closing the door of the cage and setting it aside.

"Not all women are so credulous, at least about illusions," Adam said, his thoughts returning abruptly to Miss Wilton.

"Oho! So at last there is a female who sees through you, eh?" Philippe crowed. "Long have I waited for this day."

"I was speaking in the abstract," Adam said,

"You cannot trick a trickster." The large man emphasized his point with a dig of the elbow. "Who is this wonder, eh? Part of your act?"

"You know how I feel about entanglements," Adam said, rubbing his suddenly sore rib. Abruptly he changed the subject. "I have heard tell that your new master has arranged to contact Lord Pelton at midnight tonight."

"So?" Philippe shrugged eloquently. "What of it?"

"Pelton has been dead these ten years past," Adam said, his tone turning to ice. "His widow is barely one foot out of Fleet."

"Then the woman, she is a fool," Philippe said quietly, opening a hidden catch and replacing a wilted concealed rose with a fresh one. "So that much has not changed, I see. You still pursue it, Adam, after so many years, this hatred of the mediums. When I think of all the money we could have made! The grief you caused Roselli over that affair with the dead soldier and his *père*. After Roselli taught you half your magic! But no, you could not keep your nose out of it."

"I gave Roselli fair warning not to cheat that old man. Poor fool, he was so desperate to talk to his lost boy. The conjurer would have taken his last sou. He was a fraud."

"Are you not? Are not we all? Beguiling the eyes, lying to the senses. Pah!" He waved a hand in disgust.

"I never claimed to perform wonders," Adam said.

"But did you ever go before an audience and say, 'Mesdames and messieurs, I am a charlatan. What you will see, it is falsehood'?" Philippe asked, his voice shaking in anger. "This dirty part of the business has never been to my liking, that you know, but still I think it does some good. How much is it worth to ease the soul, eh? A chance for a grieving old man to say what he left unsaid during his son's lifetime, a few

comforting words to help ease a widow's pain. What harm
does it do, Adam? I ask you."

Adam sighed. "We have been round and round this argument before, my friend, and it is far too complex a subject to
reprise now. Suffice it to say that I have not changed my feelings. In fact, in the normal course of things, I would give
Barone no warning before I strike." Adam fanned the ordered
deck, presenting the cards face up; he shuffled, reshuffled,
and showed them again, the sequence unchanged. "But since
we are old comrades, I will allow you to alert your master.
Tell Barone to leave Lady Pelton be and to keep his tricks
confined to Astley's. It will go hard with him if I hear word of
any sèances. And be assured, Philippe, I *will* know."

"But if not Barone, another, perhaps less kind, maybe more
greedy charlatan, would pluck your widow. Besides, what
could you do to stop him? Challenge him to the duel?"
Philippe clucked and shook his head.

Adam smacked the cards to the table with a thud that
caused the doves to coo in alarm. "A duel? In a manner of
speaking, I suppose one might call it that. If Barone plays his
spirit games with Lady Pelton, I will reveal him for the fraud
that he is. He may fool the public with impunity on stage in a
legitimate fashion. However, if he begins to ply the necro-
mancer's lay and claim to raise the dead, I *will* ruin him."

"Ah, you always were a great talker, *mon ami*. For that the
audiences loved you. But you talk to Philippe Rubelle now,
and so, I will warn *you*. Barone has much money. He has
many friends, powerful friends who would make certain that
an unknown magician like yourself would vanish. Any chains
that will bind you at the bottom of the Thames will not be
breakable; *comprends-tu*? So stop with this nonsense,"
Philippe said, clapping him on the shoulder with a friendly
paw. "Now, I will go and tell Barone that another act precedes
him, yes? He will not be pleased that the Lady Enderby did
not say so, but I tell him you will be an aperitif to whet the appetite of the audience. Who knows? Maybe Barone will like
you and we will once again work together, eh? Bring your
equipage and I will move our box back to give you room."

Adam grasped Philippe's arm. "I am quite serious, my

friend. Tell Barone that the Marquess of Brand will hound him if he so much as crosses Lady Pelton's threshold. Your snug job will disappear and you will be back on street corners fleecing the flats at three cards or 'Find the Lady.'"

Philippe guffawed. "Ah, Adam, Adam! You are the noblest of liars. A carnival performer, a second-rate conjurer who never had more than the price of a baguette in his pocket . . . The Marquess of Brand! If you are Brand, then I am the king of France!"

"I was *not* second-rate!" Adam said, pulling a gold piece from behind Philippe's turban and flipping it to him as the sound of footsteps began to herald the arrival of the audience. "Keep the guinea; you may soon have need of it."

"*Stupide!* You did not bother to lock the door!" Hastily, the man covered the exposed part of the table.

"Relax, Philippe," Adam said as he saw his uncle peering into the room. "There is no need to act as if your mistress's husband is knocking at the bedchamber. My uncle knows more than he would wish to about the accoutrements of conjuring, and the ladies who accompany him are also friends."

"I thought this was where you had likely disappeared to, Adam," Lawrence's voice echoed in the ballroom. Cautiously, he made his way through the maze of chairs with Miss Wilton and her mama following close behind. "I was just telling Adrienne and her daughter about your odd predilection for the company of conjurers and tricksters."

"Certainly an unusual hobby for a marquess, milord," Lady Wodesby said. "But then I must confess some fascination with the subject myself."

Philippe's eyes bulged at the use of the title.

Adam chuckled softly. "Remember, Your Majesty, that comfortable employment by French monarchs is rather scarce these days." As he went to secure a seat in the front row beside his uncle and the ladies, the marquess hummed the *Marseillaise*.

Chapter 3

Adam stifled a yawn. Despite his familiarity with the conjurer's bag of tricks, raving descriptions of Barone's talent had served to build Adam's anticipation to an unusual peak. However, the Frenchman's skills had been grossly overstated. His presentation was better than average, but he made more than one clumsy slip in the execution of tricks that were well-worn routines. Not that the audience had noticed, naturally. Philippe's automaton made a charming appearance, but beyond that, Barone's minute hesitations and maladroit slips soon made the business on stage pall. Instead, Adam amused himself by observing Miss Wilton. Once again, she utterly defied his expectations.

Almost every face in the room wore the same vapid expression of open-mouthed wonder, gasping almost with one breath as Barone produced doves and coins from seemingly nowhere, made instruments play apparently untouched, and faultlessly predicted which card their charming hostess would take from the deck. However, Miss Wilton was a spectator of the type that was the conjurer's worst nightmare.

Her keen gaze swept the stage, refusing to be directed by Barone's skilled diversions. The sardonic crinkle in the corners of her eyes as the magician reached into a hidden pocket, the cynical upturn of her lip as the Frenchman palmed a card, served to convince Adam that she was viewing the performance with a connoisseur's awareness. In her concentration, she had inadvertently gravitated closer to him and he could smell her perfume, a scent that was somehow both light and intoxicating. So intent was he upon her that he nearly missed

the sight of Barone fumbling a simple pass. Her brow rose in
sheer disbelief. Adam's eyes met hers in mutual amusement.

"Napoleon's conjurer, indeed," he whispered.

"If so, Wellington cannot fail," she replied, her smile falter-
ing as she reminded herself of their conversation at dinner.
Physical attraction, Miranda acknowledged, was a powerful
natural force but certainly nothing magical. Other than that,
there could be no common ground between them. Not for the
first time, Miranda felt a terrible loneliness. She had one foot
in two worlds but was part of neither. Her heritage gave her
glimpses of untold marvels, a power that illuminated mind and
heart.

For her, there could never be contentment in the illusions
that lent awe to the lives of everyday mortals. But more tragically, never would she know the joy of true magic. Was this
how Lucifer had felt down in the depths, knowing that heaven
was above him but forever beyond his reach? Automatically,
she applauded as Barone slid aside the disguised door in the
tabletop and let loose a flight of doves. Madame Barone made
her entrance.

"*En maintenant, mesdames and messieurs. Nous presentons*
Sight Beyond Sight," Madame Barone announced. "A remarkable demonstration of the cerebral skill."

It took no reader of minds to sense Miss Wilton's withdrawal. She shifted in her seat, firmly reestablishing the space
between them. Though her eyes were focused upon the stage,
her mind was clearly someplace where he could not follow.
There was sorrow in her eyes, a deepened blue darkness that
he recognized as pain.

"Milord Brand?"

Adam was shaken from his musings. Barone's wife stood
before him, black silk shining in her hand. A quick glance revealed his dusty fingerprints at its edge. It would seem that the
blindfold was not the key to the trick.

"You will be kind enough to verify zat through ze mask,
you cannot see?" she asked, venom in her look.

Barone's eyes gleamed with wicked amusement. Who better
to ask for the seal of sanction than Britain's premiere skeptic?
In the wing of the improvised stage, Philippe gave an apolo-

getic shrug. It seemed that his message had been passed on, Adam thought, as he tried the mask on to the titters of the audience. The challenge had been offered and the duel begun. "It is quite blinding," Adam admitted, drawing off the sack but not returning it. Instead, he walked up to Barone. "If Monsieur will permit?"

Surprisingly, the performer made no protest. In fact, there was a definite smugness about him as Adam placed the mask. Adam leaned closer, on the pretext of adjusting the fabric. "Phillipe gave my warning," he said in precise undertones. "Do you go to Lady Pelton's?"

"Mind your business, Monseigneur." Although his reply was muffled his anger was clear. "And I will mind mine."

"Then be damned, Barone," Adam said, his fingers tightening the drawstring ruthlessly. "You will soon be back to performing for pigs and fishwives on market day." He leaned closer as if to examine his handiwork even though he was certain that there was no way that the conjurer could twist his head in order to see. "I will give you ten minutes to think it over. If you change your mind, use the name Beelzebub in your patter."

"I'll see you in hell first, Monseigneur."

"Doubtless, Barone, you will be one of many who will be there to greet me," Adam said before reluctantly returning to his seat. No switch of mask had been contemplated, it would seem. The key to the trick was obviously elsewhere, but what was it? Madame went among the audience, as individual after individual pulled out some item. Barone stood well away from his table of shams, beyond any touch or whisper from a concealed confederate.

Miss Wilton's attention had returned to the stage; her face was a study in concentration. She, too, it appeared, was trying to discern Barone's method. Her eyes ricocheted from the magician to his wife, searching for some sign, some means of communication.

The minutes ticked away as baubles were proffered and correctly identified, one after another. Collusion with members of the audience was unlikely. Luminaries of the Ton such as Lord Alvanley, the Princess de Lieven, and Mrs. Drummond-Burrel were hardly the type of individuals who would cooperate with a common showman's deception.

"I am holding in my hand, Monsieur?" Madame Barone's interrogative was delivered in a monotone drone.

Barone hesitated dramatically, his head tilted upward as if listening for a spirit voice. "Ah, gold, they tell me. Holy gold. A gold crucifix, Madame."

It was extremely well done and maddening beyond measure. Under less pressing circumstances, Adam would have simply chosen the expedient of attending several of Barone's performances. Usually, it took no more than two or three observations to unravel the most complex of tricks. But there was no time for such lengthy maneuvers, not if he wished to prevent tonight's séance.

As the ten-minute limit passed without Beelzebub being invoked, Adam focused on Barone and his wife, examining every possibility, but try as he might their technique was beyond his detection. He castigated himself for not examining the mask more closely. Had he missed a hidden seam perhaps? Somehow, Adam had to get his hands on that mask again.

His heightened senses detected a sudden shift. Miss Wilton was no longer leaning forward. She was now sitting back in her chair, her expression composed and satisfied. *She knew.* Adam was prepared to swear upon it. Somehow, Miss Wilton had identified the technique that the Barones were using.

"How?" He leaned toward her and whispered the single word.

She knew exactly what he meant. "You look too much. Listen," she commanded. "Hear what he hears."

Obediently, Adam closed his eyes, observing only with his ears.

"Ask the spirits what they see," Madame said.

"They say silver, with . . . a jewel . . . yes! . . . yes! an emerald."

The audience whispered excitedly; another success. Footsteps then Madame's lackluster tones. "What is seen for you now in my left hand? Then tell what I hold in my right."

"Silver," he replied without hesitation. "In the left hand, silver. And gold . . . a gold snuffbox in the right."

The gasps of the audience were like a goad to Adam, forcing his eyes open. Increasing complexity in a trick was a sure sign that Barone was building to his finale. There was no time to waste. "I surrender, Miss Wilton. Please give me a clue."

"Key words, milord. 'Hold' always means gold. 'See' is inevitably silver," she explained, her eyes shining with excitement. "Their code is fairly intricate, indicating any number of objects and their descriptions in a few words. Various names for spirits correspond with certain jewels. For instance, the sapphire necklace she has in her hand now; I would wager thirty guineas that she uses 'fairy' and 'hold' in her phrase."

"Can the fairies tell you what is being held here?" Madame Barone asked.

"Thirty guineas, Miss Wilton," Adam said, wanting to embrace her then and there, but he put aside that appealing thought for the future. It was time to lend to the business at hand.

His smile dazzled Miranda, warming her in a blinding glow of admiration. However, that flush of heat quickly dissipated as Lord Brand rose to his feet.

"Madame," he called, digging into his pocket. "I have an object for your husband to identify."

"But of course, milord," Madame Barone said, hurrying to his side. "Will you give it to me, *s'il vous plaît?*"

"If you please, Madame, I would prefer to hold it," he said, shielding a gold watch and fob from her view.

"But it is necessary for the spirits to see," Madame protested.

"Very well," Adam said, moving closer to her. "What if *I* reveal my trinket to the spirits, will that suffice?"

"It is most irregular, Monseigneur. The spirits, they are accustomed to me alone."

"Very well, Madame, if all that is necessary is for you to show the item to your *corps d'ether*, then do so." With a show of reluctance he handed her the timepiece. She held it aloft, but her look of triumph was cut short as Adam's hand clamped firmly over her mouth. The spectators snickered as the silence lengthened.

"Well, Barone," Adam called. "The spirits can see it now.

Do have them tell us what your lovely wife is holding in her hand."

"You disturb my ethereal guides, milord," Barone declared.

"What a charming way to speak of your wife, Monsieur. An ethereal guide, how very delightful. Name the object she holds, Barone."

The conjurer's hands began to shake. "I must consult with other forces since my spirit friends have momentarily deserted me. I fear that I must invoke the powers of Beelzebub."

"In Lady Enderby's ballroom? Tsk, tsk, and she a churchgoing woman." Adam shook his head, trying to keep his hold tight enough to evade Madame's teeth. "I am afraid that would never do. Besides, we all know that the devil is rather busy in London these days, so appeals to him will do you little good now."

"Perhaps Beelzebub will have mercy upon a poor magician." Barone's voice rose to a pleading whine. "If not for me, for the sake of Philippe."

In the corner, Philippe's hands were clasped together prayerfully. Adam relented. "Perhaps so, if Satan cannot have mercy upon his own spawn, who will?" Adam said, withdrawing his hand and returning to his chair. "Maybe if I am seated, your spirit guides will return."

Madame Barone's expression was murderous, but her tones were steady as she spoke. "What do I hold in my hand, husband?"

"The spirits, they are returning, my dear. They were very worried about you and they send their apologies."

"How very touching," Adam commented, trying to catch Miss Wilton's eye, but her attention seemed firmly fixed forward.

"You are holding a gold watch, they say," Barone declared.

"'Husband' must be their code for 'watch,'" Adam observed after the conjuror's wife returned his timepiece with a scowl. "A true performer, the Madame. Didn't miss a beat and the show goes on."

But there was no reply from the seat beside him. The presentation progressed rapidly to its close and the Barones took their bows. "I must thank you, Miss Wilton," he said, as the audience applauded. "My wits had entirely deserted me."

"As well as your decency," she said, turning at last to regard him, her fury colder than the North Sea. "Had I known your designs, sir, I would never have given you a clue. You very nearly ruined Lady Enderby's entertainment, not to mention the featured premise of Barone's performance. He may be less than a perfect trickster, but he did not deserve the death blow that you so very nearly dealt his career. How could you bully entertainers who were doing nothing more than earning their bread by providing a harmless diversion?" she sputtered, under cover of the clapping. "So, milord, since you have proven your superior knowledge, is it now your intent to rip off Barone's cape and show us all the secret pockets! I vow you must have been the type of little boy who took pleasure in pulling the wings off of butterflies."

Such was his reward for good deeds, Adam thought glumly. A public denunciation of the Barones would have been an infinitely more effective warning to all other would-be swindlers. Now his standing with Miss Wilton was somewhat lower than a salamander's stomach. But he cheered himself with the knowledge that she would surely understand once he explained matters. He would then, in all modesty, wave aside her apologies and her praise. Perhaps she might even consent to a drive in the park.

Lady Enderby waved her hands for silence and the crowd gradually quieted. "Our evening of magic is not quite ended. We are privileged tonight to have among us a most talented individual, a dear friend. Many's the autumn night I recall sitting before the fireside at Miss Morehead's select seminary. The young girl who is now Lady Wodesby would read her cards for us all and I must say that everything that she had predicted for us came true."

As the crowd murmured, Miranda stole a surprised sideways look at her mama. After all the scoldings about the misuse of magic that she and Damien had endured, their mother had dared to use the Tarot as a parlor pastime.

"I was young, dear," Lady Wodesby quietly answered her

daughter's unspoken question. "And now it appears that I may be about to pay the price for those youthful indiscretions."

Miranda could almost feel the stares boring into the back of her head as their hostess went on cataloguing Lady Wodesby's successful predictions. A masculine snort of contempt jolted her from her self-consciousness.

"A pasteboard reader, Miss Wilton! I have heard of this Wodesby Witch."

Miranda fortified herself with a deep breath before turning to smile sweetly. "Have you really?" she asked Lord Brand, with a coquettish sweep of her lashes.

Oblivious to her strained delivery, Adam's native caution drowned in a sea of deep blue. "Indeed, the woman is notorious, and no better, I am certain, than the Gypsies who prophesy the advent of tall dark men for every spinster."

"A teller of fortunes once said that my fate was tied to a man who was handsome and clever," Miranda said.

"By chance, some of these predictions do come true." Adam's voice deepened. By heaven, she was flirting with him. How fortunate that females were fickle. Her anger seemed forgotten. Handsome and clever, indeed! "However, as Lady Enderby says, Lady Wodesby is reputed to be more than a teller of fortunes. But perhaps I ought not to say that she is a witch. She might well turn me into a toad."

"A tempting thought, to be sure, but doubtful. Unfortunately, due to the difficulty of the spell involved, there are few documented cases of human beings transformed to amphibious creatures." Miranda sighed. "However, to transform a toad like you to a human being, now that would be witchcraft indeed. You may be handsome, milord, but at present, I find you a rather poor excuse for a man."

Adam could not quite credit his ears, but Miss Wilton's countenance was thunderous. And then the reason for her anger presented itself with painful clarity.

"Would you favor us, Adrienne?" Lady Enderby asked, coming to stand before Miss Wilton's mama. "Please say that you will give us a reading."

"I fear I have not brought my deck," Lady Wodesby protested weakly.

"I anticipated that possibility," their hostess trilled, motioning a waiting servant, who brought forth a silver salver and presented it to Lady Wodesby.

Upon it was a cheap set of pasteboards of the kind that any fair-day fortune-teller would use, the twenty-two Trumps that comprised the Major Arcana. Of the Minor Arcana, the cards used to foretell detail, there was no sign at all. Miranda watched anxiously as her mother touched the cards. Surely she would not consent to this public travesty. But Lady Wodesby's doubtful countenance changed to one of deep thought. As she examined the pack, Miranda's alarm grew. Those eyes, so like her own, gradually took on the jewellike lapis hues that marked the seer. Her mother had crossed the bridge into that Otherwhere, Otherwhen, the distant shore where the sands of the present were pounded by the waves of the future. And when she smiled, it was clear that the bliss known only to those of the Blood had kissed her. Even before she spoke, Miranda knew that the decision had been made.

"Of course, Hester, I shall read, but only for one. And I shall do the choosing," Lady Wodesby said, her words floating. "I shall need a table and two chairs, at once."

"I had hoped . . ." Lady Enderby began with a moue of disappointment, but quieted with a wave of Lady Wodesby's hand.

"She must be a sorceress, indeed, to silence Hester so easily," Lawrence whispered in admiration.

But Adam made no reply. His focus was entirely upon Lady Wodesby as she moved majestically through the crowd, her graceful glide making the appearance of treading on air. An atmosphere that was a peculiar mixture of trepidation and anticipation was almost palpable. Eager hopefuls shifted forward in their seats while the fearful withdrew to the farthest corner of their chairs upon her approach. She was a masterful artist, Adam conceded, as she paused in seeming consideration. She waited, as if consulting with some unseen advisor, then went on, building expectations to a fever pitch.

All at once, Adam was distracted by a meow at his feet. A mottled ginger tom raised its sleek feline head. How in the world had a cat gotten into Lady Enderby's ballroom?

"Thorpe?" Miranda whispered. "What ever are you doing here? Return to the carriage, immediately."

"Your familiar, Miss Wilton?" some devil made Adam ask.

"My mother's, actually," she informed him with a chilly look. "To the carriage, Thorpe," she demanded once again, but the animal remained firmly at Lord Brand's feet, placing an imperious paw on the man's patents.

"Really, Thorpe, this is the outside of enough," Miranda hissed.

"It would seem that he is not heeding you," Adam said with a soft chuckle. "If you would allow me, Miss Wilton."

"He will scratch you dreadfully, milord. No one but Mama—" But the marquess had already drawn the cat into his arms. Miranda's mouth nearly fell open in amazement as Thorpe suffered his head to be stroked in the manner of a common alley animal, letting out a decidedly contented, pedestrian purr.

At the sound, Lady Wodesby turned with a startled stare. Hurriedly she made her way back to the front of the room to stand before Lord Brand. "But of course," she spoke a trifle absently. "It should have been obvious. Thank you for bringing him to my attention, Thorpe. You may go now."

With a "Meoowrrrr" that somehow put Adam in mind of "Yes, milady," the cat jumped from his arms and padded from the room with the dignified gait of a superior servant, his tail and head upraised.

"I shall read the cards for you, Lord Brand," Lady Wodesky said, inclining her head like a queen conferring a boon.

His Uncle Lawrence kicked him on the shin. The older man's warning frown emphasized his none-too-gentle hint that a polite decline was in order. "Perhaps, milady, you might want to seek out someone who is more interested in your . . . er . . . skills."

Lady Enderby was aghast. A scene of monstrous proportions was looming. Certainly something had to be done. She was quite convinced that the infamous incident about to unfold in her very ballroom would surpass the night when Lord Selby had nearly challenged Lord Herrinsward to a duel over Charity Wentworth. Never in her most perfect fantasies had she conceived of anything so utterly delightful. The rigid metal of the foremost naysayer in England tested against the flinty heiress of ancient magic, with all the Ton as tinder for a marvelous conflagration. If only Lord Brand did not ruin it entirely. Lady Enderby stepped into the breach.

"Now, milord," she said soothingly. "Lady Wodesby said that she would do the choosing and 'tis clear that her cat chose you."

"The beast was only seeking out those known to him," Adam protested. "Doubtless, the cat would have gone to anyone sitting next to Miss Wilton."

"I must say, Lord Brand, that this is most unsportsmanlike of you. You should be glad of this privilege," Lady Enderby declared with a martial gleam in her eye. "Especially given your most public interest in the realms of magic. Do not tell me you are afraid of what Lady Wodesby might say?"

He was doomed. Lady Enderby had laid him low by invoking the sacred credo of sportsmanship, but her final imputation was a dastardly blow. By no means could he refuse without seeming both hypocrite and coward.

"Very well, Lady Wodesby, but I feel it only fair to warn you that I do not place any credence whatsoever in this folderol," Lord Brand said as he rose and walked up to the front of the room.

"That is of limited importance, milord," Lady Wodesby said graciously as she seated herself in one of the chairs. "Although the reading would be somewhat easier if you were a believer."

"Is that what you intend to claim then, Madame?" Adam asked, his words dripping skepticism. "Even before you start, you hedge your bets by implying that your interpretations might be inaccurate due to my feelings."

"Nothing of the sort, Lord Brand," Lady Wodesby said, inclining her head to indicate that he should sit down. "The cards will reveal as little or as much as they wish. It is only a matter of the energy that *I* must expend to seek the answers if you close your mind to the possibility of what they may say." She closed her eyes and held the cards in her hands, frowning as she attempted to accustom herself to the unfamiliar deck. Then she handed the cards to Lord Brand. "Look at them; touch each one."

"This is absurd."

"Do you wish me to have the excuse of failure because you refuse to play this game by its rules?" she asked archly.

Reluctantly, Adam received the deck into his hands, examining the garishly drawn pictures. He had more than a passing familiarity with the Tarot. His many encounters with the false prophets of the pasteboards had provided him with a fair acquaintance with the Tarot's iconography. With grudging obedience, he handled each card, marking a few surreptitiously under cover of close examination. No telling if that information might prove useful, but at least it gave Adam a small sense of control over the situation.

The tawdry painted Sun, an unsmiling bearded hermit, the Wheel of Fortune, the macabre face of Death, each was minutely bent or impressed with the imprint of a nail until the last of the twenty-two, the Hanged Man, came into his hands. The poor fellow, dangling upside down by his foot with his eyes wide open, roused odd feelings of sympathy. As Adam surveyed the expectant faces of the crowd, he felt as if he, too, were suspended for humiliating public display.

"Enough?" he asked.

Lady Wodesby nodded. "Shuffle."

Adam obeyed. Candle glow touched the rings on her hands as she received the deck once again. Her fingers moved with swift grace, touching everything with a jeweled aura that seemed to soften the harsh colors. A trick of light, nothing more, Adam decided, blinking.

"Past, present, near future, far future." She indicated clusters of face-down cards representing each. "Self, others, dreams, and fears. Choose."

Following her pointed direction, Adam chose from among the cards, deliberately seeking the Hermit.

"So you take cynicism as your symbol," Lady Wodesby said, tacitly telling him that she was well aware of his effort to fix the draw. "Loneliness is your companion and bitterness has driven you inward."

Generalities, words that could apply to most of mankind, so it was not surprising that they struck a chord. Yet as they moved on, Adam was impressed by the manner in which she matched the cards with shrewd assessment. Without doubt, Lady Wodesby was the most skilled card-turning charlatan he had ever come across, though most of the information that she "revealed" was public knowledge. Finally, Adam could stand the charade no longer; the "oohs" and "ahas" of the spectators irritated him beyond bearing.

"Specifics, milady," he demanded. "You say nothing here that half of London does not already know."

Lady Wodesby raised a dark eyebrow. "It will be difficult, Lord Brand. 'Tis usually the Minor Arcana that is used for the divination of the esoteric. Normally, I carry my decks with me; however the small reticules that are de rigeur for the evening can hold nothing of use. My cards are at home."

"How convenient," Adam said, not bothering to conceal his derision. "Shall we draw this gammon to an end, milady?"

"I said that it would be difficult," Lady Wodesby said stiffly, "not impossible. All the Arcana are in my mind, sir."

"Mama, no!" Miranda rose, concern writ plain on her countenance. "Is it not bad enough that you must work against his disbelief? No matter what you say, he will still find some way to make you appear the liar. Without the proper tools, the strain upon you could—"

"Hush, my dear," Lady Wodesby said, "I do what I must."

Miranda was instantly silent at the final "must." Obviously, a compulsion of some kind was at work. Her mother could no more discontinue the reading than she could cease breathing. Nonetheless, if anything happened, Brand would be to blame. She cast the marquess a look of disgust.

Adam groaned inwardly. Miss Wilton obviously believed in her mother's magical fiction, and like as not Lady Wodesby had fooled herself as well. True charlatans were relatively simple to deal with. Uncover their trickery, reveal them as frauds, and the vermin scurried back behind the wainscoting from whence they came. But there was no means of convincing those who truly placed credit in their own magical capacities. They would hang upon any excuses, seize upon any questionable rationale when their so-called powers failed. If Lady Wodesby's reading were to continue unsatisfactorily, she had already paved the path of blame by placing fault upon the cards and his attitude. Yet having cast down the gauntlet, he had no choice.

"We shall continue if you will, but I ask you to forgive me if I reveal what you would have wished to remain private," she said.

"You have my permission," Adam said with a dismissive wave of the hand.

Lady Wodesby's eyes closed as she fixed the forty cards of the four suits in her mind. The faces of the Queens, Kings, Knights, and Pages, with their accompanying symbols of Wands, Cups, Swords, and Pentacles, materialized in thought. Mentally, she shuffled them, dealt them, before raising her lids to gaze at Lord Brand. "Choose," she whispered softly. "They are arranged in four rows representing past, present, near future, and far future, for the sake of simplicity. Ten cards are in each column. Choose two to begin."

"First row, second and third card," Adam said.

"Knight of Wands. Knight of Swords. You and your father. He is the source of your bitterness, milord. You have never forgiven him for dissipating the family fortune. In his desperation, he chose the help of frauds in an attempt to pierce the veil of death. But his worst sin was to cut you off in his pain. How very sad."

"Second row, fourth card," Adam said quickly, before she could go on. How the devil had she cut so close to the truth? She smiled cannily, as if she knew the reason for his haste.

"King of Pentacles. Battle, milord; you have challenged a most dangerous man. I see a needle and thread. A tailor? I do not understand, but it is quite significant. The forces of lightning contained in a bottle. This tailor fears you, seeks to destroy you."

"Perhaps Weston is after him for his bill?" Lord Ropwell called from the audience with a snicker.

Adam scowled the man down. Lady Wodesby did not need any further excuses of interference from the spectators, should her performance be deemed a failure. All the world knew that Guttmacher was out for his blood, but Adam could swear that only himself and the Runners were aware of that charlatan's Cockney origins and the fact that his name was Taylor . . .

Adam himself, the Runners and . . . Uncle Lawrie? It was entirely unlike his uncle to be so indiscreet. Yet there was no other possible explanation. The woman had without doubt pumped Uncle Lawrie during dinner, with the object of making Adam appear a fool. Bottled lightning indeed.

"Third row, fifth card," Adam said, deciding that the near future was safer than the past or present.

"Ace of Swords. Conflict. I see a . . ." Her voice dropped weakly. "A . . . threat of death, milord, against you and someone else. Quickly, choose another card in the row."

"Seventh card."

"Page of Cups, the female aspect. A woman is also at risk. There is threat of magic here, strong magic . . . No," she whispered, her stricken eyes meeting his. "I see the hand of death involved, but I cannot say who he will take. Spirits are at work, a ghost could kill . . . There is peril to all, Page, King, and Knight . . . if only I had my own cards to hand! Perhaps the Major Arcana can help."

Unbidden, Adam turned a card on the table.

"The Empress!" Lady Wodesby hissed, her aspect blanching. "By Merlin, I had feared as much. Milord, henceforth you are under Wodesby protection. Whatever we may do to prevent this disaster, we shall. By the Blood, I swear it!" With a sigh, she closed her eyes and slumped back in the chair, drooping like a wilted orchid.

"Mama!" Miranda rushed forward in alarm to kneel beside the stricken woman.

"Shall I get a vinaigrette?" Adam asked. "Or call a physician?"

"No!" she said. "You have done quite enough for this night, milord. Neither sal volatile nor the attention of quacks will remedy exhaustion of this magnitude. Lady Enderby, if you would be so kind as to instruct your footmen to assist my mother and have our carriage brought round."

"But of course, my dear," Lady Enderby said, all concern now that the evening had come to a better finale than she could possibly have hoped. "But you cannot go alone with your mama in this state."

"My nephew and I shall escort her home, milady," Lawrence

declared, ignoring the marquess's skeptical look. "It is the least
we can do."

"*You* are kind, sir," Miranda said, favoring Adam's uncle
with a harried smile. "However, I assure you that Mama will
do best without the presence of *disagreeable* influences."

"I quite understand. My nephew is sometimes quite disturbing. Nonetheless, I would not feel comfortable without assur-
ing Adrienne's safe journey home." Lawrence bent to take a
limp hand and chafe it gently.

"Of course, Mr. Timmons, you will be most welcome," Miranda said, touching her mother's pale cheek. "However, I am
sure that Lord Brand must have other plans. No doubt there are
abundant magicians to malign, and fortune-tellers to ferret out
here in London tonight."

"Actually, the séance that I had planned to attend tonight
has been abruptly canceled, Miss Wilton. Monsieur Barone,
for some untold reason, has abruptly decided that it was not
worth his while to fleece Lady Pelton of her last pennies."

"What in the world are you talking about, milord?" But before he could answer, Miranda's mother moved slightly.

"My dear child," Lady Wodesby called weakly, her eyelids
fluttering.

"Mama, rest now. We shall have you home soon and I shall
brew you a tisane," Miranda said softly.

"You must be . . . wary, my love. Vigilant . . . until we can
fully . . . fathom the source . . . of danger . . ."

"We will, Mama. Now let us take you to the carriage and we
shall be home in a trice," she said, brushing back her mother's
hair with a smoothing hand.

Lady Wodesby grasped her daughter's fingers with a weak
squeeze. "The Empress, my dear . . . she has always repre-
sented you. That is why . . . the cards called me . . . tonight.
You are at hazard . . . my love . . . grave hazard and somehow . . . Lord Brand's fate is entwined . . . with yours."

Chapter 4

During the ride home, Lady Wodesby drifted in and out of consciousness. Adam had seen self-induced trances before. Fakirs that he had studied in India could slip between consciousness and the altered state as fast as a cutpurse in Coventry could life a wallet. However, this was well beyond the usual act. Even his friends in Drury Lane could not counterfeit her unhealthy pallor and the dimmed light in her eyes—like a spark on the verge of extinction.

Miss Wilton cradled her mother in her arms, whispering soothingly during the moments that the woman came to herself. Lady Wodesby seemed genuinely distraught, murmuring of the Empress, the Hermit, Cups, Wands, and Swords. Whatever dire portents she had imagined obviously seemed quite real to her. Even the cat appeared to be distressed, twitching his tail as he stalked across the length of the carriage. However, this time, when Adam attempted to pick the animal up, Thorpe hissed and bared his claws.

"Thorpe!" Lady Wodesby reprimanded feebly. "You, of all . . . should know that it is wholly unfair . . . to fault Lord Brand."

"I declare," Lawrence murmured in amazement as the cat bowed its head submissively and crept to the corner of the carriage. "The creature seems almost ashamed."

"'T'was merely the tone of his mistress's voice, nothing more," Adam said.

"Have you ever known a feline to give the least attention to the affairs of humans?" Lawrence asked dubiously.

Adam's reply was a disapproving frown, but before he could say anything, the carriage slowed and turned onto Portman Square. Thorpe leapt out through the open window, but the ladies did not seem the least bit perturbed. When the carriage halted before an elegant town house, there was a small army of servants waiting, with the cat at their forefront.

"Next you will be telling me that Thorpe went on to warn them," Adam commented, but to his irritation, his uncle merely looked thoughtful.

Gypsies, Adam noted as they alighted. Every single member of the Wodesby staff, from the coachman to the housekeeper, had the dusky cast of the Romany breed. Miranda and the footmen helped Lady Wodesby upstairs while another footman ushered the two men into the mahogany-paneled library. With silent grace, the butler brought a tray with biscuits, wine, and three glasses.

"Thank you," Adam said in perfect Rom.

The butler did not so much as bat an eyelash in surprise. "Do you wish me to pour?" he asked in the same language.

"No, we shall serve ourselves. Has there been any word of Lady Wodesby's state?"

"My grandmother and Miranda attend to her now," the butler informed him, shaking his head. "Never before have I seen it so, the Weakness. She took a great risk, the Lady."

"Risk?" Adam asked, instantly regretting the question. The butler's open expression rapidly shuttered, returning to its formerly rigid mien.

"Will that be all, sirs?" he asked in accented English. However, it was rather clear that it was they who were being dismissed.

Adam nodded and the man withdrew, not bothering to close the door behind him. With trembling hand, his uncle picked up the decanter, splashing the tray with Madeira. "Here, Uncle Lawrie, let me fill your glass before you break it. I swear, you are as nervous as a lamplighter near a powder keg."

"She looked so frail, Adam." The older man's voice shook. "So vibrant one moment and the next, fragile as glass."

"There is naught to worry about. She's merely driven herself into a *crise de nerf*, no more. Like as not, she will be back to herself tomorrow," Adam said, touching his uncle's shoulder reassuringly.

"I would vow that this is no simple case of hysterics," Lawrence maintained. "She was so young and lively at dinner. It was almost as if half my life had never been and I was a sprig of thirty again."

"Ah, that explains it," Adam said, taking the opportunity to turn the subject. "You were telling Lady Wodesby of this evening's adventures, I suspect, you talkative sprig, you. But why in the devil did you spill Guttmacher's real name? Part of our advantage lay in allowing Taylor to believe his past undiscovered. However, it is no great matter, so long as you did not reveal our disguise."

"I did no such thing! Nor did I mention anything about Taylor or Guttmacher or whatever his name is!" Lawrence asserted vehemently. "The subject of your bet to unmask him was mentioned, to be sure. How could it not be the talk of the Town, with you so bent on making a public spectacle of his humiliation? However, I did not even speak of the fact that he was too ill tonight to stage his healing tricks, for fear that it might upset your schemes."

"Then how did she know all that she did about my affairs? No, no, Uncle Lawrie, do not even say what seems to be on your tongue's tip. There are many ways that these mediums can discover information, as well you know. Why, there is even a list of prime pigeons in London, which can be had for a price. They call it 'The Blue Book' and it details seemingly everything about those who are ripe for plucking in their effort to communicate with the spirits. Names of departed dear ones, old scandals, circumstances of death, even their deceased servants, for pity's sake! All is documented and constantly brought up to date, anything that will help them to believe that their guide beyond the veil speaks truly is contained there," Adam said, his agitation growing as his uncle's expression grew more doubtful. "No doubt my life's detail is catalogued there as well."

"And how would Taylor's identity come to be in such a book?" Lawrence asked.

"I don't know how Lady Wodesby came upon that name,"

Adam admitted. "A lucky guess, perhaps. Or maybe she had me investigated. Everyone knew that I was to attend Lady Enderby's affair."

"You are implying, then, that Adrienne staged all this," Lawrence said, his words stilted by anger.

"That is exactly what his implications are, sir." Miranda's voice rang from the doorway. "Even though our arrival in London was delayed by traffic and we had barely time to dress for Lady Enderby's gathering, much less eat a bite after the journey. Even though Mama had neither made your nephew's acquaintance nor seen you for over a quarter of a century. Even though, had she any inkling that Lady Enderby would impose upon her to read the Tarot, my mother would never have accepted the invitation. Nonetheless, she had naught better to do but to research the almighty Lord Brand."

She entered the room, followed by the Gypsy butler. "Your nephew seems thoroughly convinced of his own importance, Mr. Timmons, and like most self-centered men, he believes that the world is vying for his attention. Unfortunately, he will deny the evidence of his senses, deny even logic, and seize upon any farfetched excuse to discount what his heart knows, rather than admit that he has encountered something that is beyond his simple understanding."

"You must have spoken with Adam at length during dinner," Lawrence said, ignoring his nephew's indignant expression, "for you have just described the boy to his very toes. Why, Adam, would you believe that Lady Wodesby would do such a thing?"

"I make no accusations," Adam said carefully. "But to confound me in public would naturally establish her credibility as a sorceress."

The Gypsy threw back his head and laughed, as Miranda's peals of mirth combined in chorus with Lawrence Timmon's chuckle.

"Oh, dear," Miranda said, clutching her side. "How very droll. That Mama should need *your* endorsement of her powers."

"I do not see what you find so amusing, Miss Wilton," Adam said in stiff indignation.

"Miss Wilton, I assure you, his pomposity of nature does not come from my side of the family," Lawrence said.

"He is very ignorant . . . this one," the butler said in gasps, "and very . . . arrogant. Your mother has set you a difficult task, little one."

"Ignorant and pugnacious," she said with a sigh. Lord Brand's stance was much like that of a boxer set for a fight. She would much prefer to postpone the match for the morning, when her mind was clear. However, there had been no arguing with her mother. As Lady Wodesby had been urged to her bed, she had commanded that Miranda speak with him this very night. "An impossible task, I fear."

"Enough of Adam's foolishness," Lawrence said, his smile fading as the careworn expression returned to the young woman's face. "How does Adrienne do?"

Miranda favored him with a weary smile. "Much more the thing, sir, now that we have coddled her and dosed her. She would like to see you, but I must ask that you please be brief. Mama extended herself too close to her limits tonight. I fear that she would prefer to believe that the second George is still king and herself a green girl."

"Ah, I know the feeling, young lady," he said, his eyes misting. "A terrible thief is time, but your Mama need not fear. She will always be to me as I first saw her."

"Your presence will cheer her, Mr. Timmons," Miranda said. "Dominick will show you upstairs."

The butler eyed Adam dubiously and Miranda answered his silent query with an exasperated look.

"Send Thorpe in, if that will put you at ease, Dominick," Miranda said. "Mama's instructions were quite specific and though I do not like it above half, I must have private words with Lord Brand."

"Meowrrr!" Thorpe padded into the room and settled himself before the fire.

"Well," Miranda said, "it would seem that Mama anticipated the problem. Dominick, please make certain that she does not exhaust herself once more."

"The Lady, she does what she will, Miranda," the Romany

said. "But I will remind her yet again of the great worry that we share. Come, please, Mr. Timmons."

"Rather familiar fellow, isn't he?" Adam asked as the door closed behind them. "Do all your servants call you by your given name?"

"Yes, actually, they do," Miranda asked, pouring herself a glass of wine. She stared at the ruby liquid, feeling the full measure of her fatigue. Food was what she wanted; a meal and sleep in that order. But both would have to wait. She limited herself to a single biscuit, forcing herself to nibble in slow bites between sips of wine instead of wolfing down the whole. At least in this she could appear somewhat the lady.

As she gnawed, she surreptitiously observed Lord Brand's reaction. Firelight flickered across his face, illuminating the stubborn set of his chin, the patronizing lift of his lips that bordered uncomfortably upon a sneer. What right had he to judge that which he did not understand? She wished that she could escort him to the door and slam it at his back, but her mother had decreed otherwise. "Dominick has known me since I was in swaddling clothes. In fact, the members of his tribe have been serving the Wodesbys for nigh above two hundred years now."

"I have never known Gypsies to serve anyone but themselves," Adam remarked.

"Perhaps 'serve' is the wrong word, milord," Miranda said, easing herself into a chair and trying to avert her eyes from the tempting contents of the tray. "'Tis more of a relationship of mutual benefit. Dominick's people spend winter and fall at our London residence, certainly more comfortable than camping in the open. Come spring, they wander the countryside according to their custom, but every autumn, they return to wear the Wodesby livery. Many generations ago, they swore their allegiance to the first Lord Wodesby." She nodded toward the portrait above the fire. "Their king had been accused of witchcraft and condemned to burn. Lord Wodesby used his considerable influence with the queen to save him from death."

Adam studied the portrait, obviously Elizabethan from the man's beruffed, doubleted garb. Those eyes, so like Miss

Wilton's, seem to follow him, shifting with the dance of flames. "He was part of the queen's circle then?"

"One of her most trusted advisers," Miranda said with pride. "He was her chief astrologer and her majesty credited him with no small part of the victory over the Spanish Armada. It was then Sir Wodesby was elevated to a baron."

"What a fortunate coincidence for your ancestor that England won," Adam said, turning away from Lord Wodesby's disconcerting scrutiny.

"There was no happenstance involved, milord," Miranda said, forcing herself to ignore the acid in his voice. "That portrait that you see was painted just before the attempted invasion. As you may note, his hair is much the shade of my own and his brow youthful. However, a second likeness in honor of his ascension to the title hangs at The Wode. Although it was completed barely a month later, it shows his appearance horribly altered. His face is lined, much as that of a man twice his forty years, and his hair transformed to a shock of white. The sorcery that he wove for Elizabeth was most powerful. A spell of such magnitude exacts a most heavy price."

Wine spilled over the lip of his glass as Adam set it down. At this late hour, he had endured more than his fill of the magical madness. With three swift strides, he stood before Miss Wilton's chair, intending to tell her just what he thought of the Wodesbys' outlandish claims. But before he could speak, a small body streaked from the hearth, swiftly interposing itself between Adam and the woman. Thorpe's fur rose like a battle flag, his warning hiss giving voice to his disapproval of Adam's menacing posture and proximity.

"Tell your feline chaperone that I mean no harm," Adam said, taken slightly aback.

"His judgement is usually most reliable," Miranda said, amused at the marquess's startled expression. "I recall, during my Season, when Lord Hatfill tried to corner me in the garden, Thorpe was similarly on the spot. His lordship claimed that it was the roses that had shredded his legs so. Trouble was, there was not a rosebush in the entire garden. However, I am no longer an inexperienced child, Thorpe, so you may sheath your claws and return to your place at the fire. The devil knows you deserve it after your efforts this evening. I can deal with Lord Brand."

His furry pelt grew smooth once more. However, Thorpe settled himself firmly at Miranda's feet.

"It would seem that Thorpe does not entirely trust your ability to 'deal with' me, Miss Wilton," Adam said, groaning inwardly as he realized the implications of his words. "Not that I actually believe that Thorpe has the capacity to—"

"I know, I know!" Miranda said, jumping to her feet in exasperation. "You believe in nothing, in nobody but yourself, sir. You alone have the keys to all truths and there are no things in heaven or earth that cannot be explained by your prosaic natural philosophy. Miracles could happen all around you, but you would not see them. Or worse still, you would make those wonders into commonplaces and ridicule us all for seeing rainbows instead of a chance result of lighting conditions. How empty your world must be, sir—a place without faith or magic, where man dwells entirely alone. I pity an existence so sterile."

Horrified by her loss of control, Miranda went to the hearth and leaned against the mantel, staring into heart of the flames. There was no explanation for her outburst but weariness, she decided. Times beyond count she had faced ridicule, considering it an irksome but inevitable consequence of the Wodesby name. Derision was infinitely preferable to the fear and persecution that resulted from ignorance, she had told herself. But before, pride had always proven an adequate defense, shielding her from the flogging of the Ton's scorn. Never had she felt this need to lash back. "I am sorry, milord," she said, subdued by the force of her own rudeness. "'Tis a poor excuse, but I am bone tired and much as I hate to admit it, more than a trifle overset. I had no right to say those things, especially since I have no real knowledge of you or your motivations."

"All the more remarkable, then, that you have come uncomfortably close to the mark, Miss Wilton," Adam said softly. Her head leaned against the marble of the mantel and he cursed himself for a boor. Only a blind man could have missed the obvious signs of exhaustion. She could barely keep her lids from drooping. From the longing looks that she had directed toward the biscuits, it was simple to deduce that she was famished as well as frazzled. He walked to the tray, picked up the plate, and went to her side, silently proffering the biscuits.

"A peace offering, milord?" Miranda asked.

"Call it a temporary truce. If you have not eaten since you set out for Town, you must be more than half starved," Adam ventured, encouraged by the hint of a smile lurking in the corner of her mouth. "I must confess that I found Lady Enderby's repast less than satisfying."

So, he *did* accept that they had just come to London. It was no apology, to be sure, but Miranda realized that it was as close as he would come to an expression of regret.

"I am ravenous, milord," she admitted, taking a biscuit, "and I fear that I am beyond nectar and ambrosia, in fact beyond biscuits. Shall we repair to the kitchen and see what we can find in the pantry?" Explanations were always easier on a full stomach, Miranda told herself. "But first, I had promised to locate a book for my mother." She picked up a branch of candles and walked to the shelves on the far wall.

Adam followed. Leather-bound books covered the walls from floor to ceiling. "*The Constitution of Honorius!*" Adam exclaimed as he unshelved a volume at random.

"You are acquainted with it?" she asked in surprise.

"One of the first grimoires ever printed," Adam said, opening the pages reverently, scarcely able to credit that so ancient a copy existed. "They are quite rare."

"And utterly useless as a guide to conjuring," Miranda remarked as she scanned the upper shelves for the book she sought. "Some of the suggestions for calling up spirits would be rather laughable were thy not so gruesome. Still, it is a curiosity. The *Seal of Solomon.*" She handed him a bound packet of parchment. "Now, here is a grimoire with some meat to it. Unfortunately, so much was garbled when the book was transcribed. In fact, that is a common problem with most printed grimoires, especially popular works such as *Le Veritable Dragon Rouge.* So much of our tradition is oral in nature, handed down from parent to child over generations. In a proper spell, every word, each intonation is vital; a muddled formula gets no results."

Adam did not even attempt to challenge her statement, so awed was he by the beauty of the illuminated manuscript, with its carefully drawn seals and pentagrams. "By Jove," he exhaled sharply. "Have you any idea how valuable this is, Miss Wilton? This must be at least three centuries old."

"Closer to four hundred years, actually, but there is an older, more accurate version of the Seal at The Wode," she said absently, as she peered at the shelves. "This collection is rather paltry, I fear, when compared to the one at home. When I began to catalogue our libraries, it became obvious that there were serious gaps among the references. Papa would take a grimoire to while away a journey, for instance, and forget to return the book to London. So as a consequence, we have three copies of *The Ars Magus* in the country and not a one here. I keep telling Mama that she really ought to supplement this library, but since she so rarely comes to London—"

"Supplement? I cannot see what you lack," Adam said enviously, running a loving finger across the vellum-bound spines. "There are titles here that I have only heard of in legend, books known only in reference, that were believed lost forever. You have nearly every recent work on magic that I know—Decremps, Guyot, Ozanam . . . and I have never even come across some of these arcane titles. *The Art of Potions*, *Philtres D' Amour*, and . . . Jane Austen?"

"Ah! Thank you, Lord Brand, just what I was seeking," Miranda said, slipping *Pride and Prejudice* from the shelf. "Mama finds Miss Austen most relaxing. However, I cannot think why she shelved it here; this section deals with potions and philters."

"Perhaps she thought that a good philter would saved Elizabeth a great deal of trouble," Adam remarked, shaking his head as he spoke. This could only be a wild dream, he told himself. No other explanation was possible for the library, the cat, and especially the woman who seemed to be giving serious consideration to his foolish words. Surrounded by an aureole of light, she was the incarnation of a conjurer's vision. Her hair had come half undone, caressing her bare shoulder in a shining mantle. The jewel at her throat seemed to shimmer with a thousand facets, drawing him into its cool green center. When she spoke at last, her voice seemed to come from somewhere within the heart of the night.

"A potion might have brought Darcy to the point sooner," Miranda agreed. "Certainly, he was inclined to like Elizabeth from the start. But love is not some hothouse flower to be forced at will, milord, and even a simple philter exacts a price. I suspect that she would have spent the rest of her life wondering whether he loved her for herself, or whether Darcy's regard came from a witch's brew."

"And an instantaneous proposal would have left scarce material for Miss Austen's book," Adam said, striving to return the conversation to a more sensible plane, telling himself that this was a type of sorcery that he could well understand. Night was creeping into morning and the unholy combination of a beautiful woman, too much wine, fatigue, and darkness was a potion almost guaranteed to muddle a man's mind. A few seconds more, and he would be tempted beyond reason to sample the pleasures that her full lips promised. Was she real or woven from the strands of his secret imaginings? Involuntarily, he took a step forward.

Thorpe gave a hiss that sounded suspiciously like a warning.

"Really, Thorpe, he would not!" Miranda said, starting for the door. "Thorpe views the world through a cat's eyes, you must understand," she apologized, "and for him there is scarce difference betwixt a gentleman and an alley tom."

A dream or madness, one or the other, or perhaps a bit of both. Adam cast a reluctant backward glance at the shadowed shelves, then followed behind Miss Wilton. The sensuous grace of her walk beneath the clinging folds of silk was glorious to behold. If he was experiencing some strange form of lunacy, then Bedlam might have something to recommend it, and if this was a dream, then he would wake all too soon.

"Lead on, Thorpe," Adam said, abandoning himself to the fantasy.

* * *

The sound of a violin wafted up the stairway, along with a scent that tantalized Adam's nostrils. "Paprikash," he whispered in wonder. A turn on the landing and he no longer doubted that he was in the midst of sleep. In the corner of the kitchen, bubbling on the Rumford stove, was a huge kettle, charred with the smoke of many an open fire. A boy in bright garb stood upon the table playing a violin, while an elderly woman brandishing a wicked knife chopped garlic in time to the music. The boy's bow halted in mid-note as he caught sight of them.

"Tante Reina?" Adam asked uncertainly. "You old bag of bones, is that you?"

The Gypsy woman quirked an amused brow. "Did I not say we would meet again, Englishman? You do not believe when I tell you that destiny does not part us for long." She whacked a clove for emphasis. "My grandson tells me the Gajo guest speaks like a Rom. Then I know."

"You are acquainted with Lord Brand, Tante?" Miranda asked, going to the stove and lifting the lid.

"Aye, child," the old woman said. "With my son Alexi's caravan he traveled, six summers ago. He has some skill with coins and cards, the English Gajo, but no real knowledge of magic. I read his palm."

Adam laughed. "I had almost forgotten about that."

"Still you mock, eh? Has not everything that I saw in your hand that day come to pass? You have come safely home. You have now great wealth—"

"And what of those other things that you promised, Tante?" Adam asked.

"I tell you then, Gajo," she said with a wave of the knife, "soon two roads are before you. Now, it is the parting time and you must choose—between trust and loneliness, between peace and restless spirit. From what the lady say to me, danger accompanies you upon either path."

Miranda set two steaming plates down upon the table and gestured toward a chair. "At present, Tante, starvation is the immediate danger. Lady Enderby's table left much to be desired."

Adam was content to avoid further discussion of the

Gypsy's predictions. Eagerly, he applied himself to the savory stew, with its tender bits of chicken floating in rich paprika gravy. Fresh bread, savory with saffron, sopped up the juices. After finishing a second plate, he sat back with a sigh of satisfaction. "'Pon my oath, Tante, I have tasted the cooking of the best chefs, but even Prinny's Careme could never hope to equal your paprikash."

"Beware, Miranda, a shameless flatterer is this one."

"He speaks no more than the truth," Miranda said, using the heel of her bread to wipe up the last bit of broth. "Damien says that any caravan that travels with you eats royal fare."

"Pah! Do not talk to me of that young cub! Your brother should be at home, tending to his people," the old woman said, attacking the vegetables with a vengeance. "Instead, he goes off to play at war and your poor mama is left to shoulder the burdens that should be his. At least she has summoned him—"

"Mama must not summon Damien!" Miranda rose from her chair in agitation. A summoning over vast distance required considerable effort, even with two minds as closely attuned as her mother's and Damien's. The exertion necessary to send a clear mental message might prove too much of a strain.

The elderly woman put a restraining hand on her shoulder. "Is already done, little one, and all is well. You do not know your mother's strength."

"Perhaps it is just as well that Lady Wodesby has sent for your brother," Adam said, secretly relieved. A firm masculine hand was just the ticket. Although the family had a decidedly odd reputation among the Ton, young Lord Wodesby was well known at Whitehall. An excellent soldier, an extraordinary tactician whose brilliance had already distinguished him on Wellington's staff, he would have no difficulty in marshaling this chaotic household into order. Unfortunately, even if a messenger had already been sent, it would be weeks, at the least, before any dispatches would reach Wodesby in the field.

"I suppose so," Miranda said. "For until Damien arrives, there is only Mama."

"You discount yourself, little one," Tante Reina said.

Miranda laughed bitterly. "I? What magic do I have beyond this?" Misdirecting their attention she palmed two eggs from the table, reached behind the boy's ear to make the first white orb appear from the ether. Deftly, she flipped it into the air, caught it, and made it vanish. "Check your pocket, Tante," she said. The woman plunged her hand into her pocket and pulled forth an egg.

"Not even did I feel you slip it there, Miranda. Since last I saw you, your skills have improved," she said with a toothy grin of approval.

"Fakery," Miranda said disparagingly, "no more than deceiving the eye. The type of magic that any child can do."

"It took me quite some time to perfect the skills that you deem childish, Miss Wilton," Adam interposed, impressed by her dexterity. "Years, in fact. I spent well over a month with Tante Reina's grandson, just learning how to work locks."

"Why?" Miranda asked. "Why would the son of a well-to-do English lord bother to acquire such a repertoire?"

"Why would an English lady need such knowledge?" Adam countered.

She knew that he was evading her question, but it was as good an opportunity to broach the subject as Miranda could have hoped for. "By the time I was five, Lord Brand, my brother had taught me how to make my dolls disappear. At nine, I could shuffle and force a deck of cards nearly as well as my mama. Before true magic, one must learn the illusion of magic—how to create an atmosphere conducive to sorcery."

She could see the dubious expression on his face and continued hurriedly. "Witchcraft works best if the desired results are in concert with nature. A cloud that is headed, shall we say east, can be hurried along to its destination with a minimal effort. However, to make that same cloud go west would require far more exertion. Similarly, it is simpler to work a spell *with* belief than against it. Basic illusions help to produce a certain amount of faith, which makes the work of a witch easier by far."

"Are you telling me then, Miss Wilton, that you are a witch?" Adam asked.

"No, milord." Her skin flamed in embarrassment and she

rose from her seat, turning her back so that he could not see her shame. "I am not a witch."

Adam breathed a sigh of relief. Perhaps matters were not as muddled as he feared.

" 'Tis Mama who is a sorceress," she said softly. "And she has placed the Wodesby seal of protection upon you. If Damien were here, there would be no need for concern. However, I fear that because of my mother's present condition, the responsibility for your protection must now fall upon me."

"*You* are going to protect *me*?" This last ounce of absurdity tipped the scale. Despite Tante Reina's frowns, his chuckle built to a laugh and the laugh grew into a side-splitting roar. By the time his Uncle Lawrie found him and hauled him out to the carriage, Adam was howling hard enough to do a banshee credit.

Chapter 5

"He laughed, Mama," Miranda said as she picked up her embroidery from its resting place on the table by the window seat. Against the combined advice of herself, Dominick, Tante Reina, and Thorpe, Lady Wodesby had insisted upon being moved from her bedchamber to the sunnier morning room in the front of the house. Ensconced in a pile of pillows, with a bright blue turban upon her head, her mother made an exotic, if somewhat wan, appearance. Thorpe was still making his displeasure apparent, stalking back and forth in a pelter, his fur ruffled. "When I told Lord Brand what it meant to be under Wodesby protection, he simply sat there and laughed until his sides were aching. Tante Reina was ready to wring his neck and by The Merlin, I was ready to let her do it."

Lady Wodesby eased back into the mountain of cushions and gave a gurgle of laughter. "What I would not have given to be a fly on the wall last night."

"Do not even think of a transformation at this time, Mama," Miranda said firmly, stabbing her needle into the cloth. "Not after what you did last night! To attempt a summoning hard upon the Weakness. When Damien hears of this!"

"Your brother will not hear of it from you, I presume," her mother said, leaning forward sternly. "Or you, Thorpe." She fixed the cat with an annoyed glare. "I find myself tiring of your hissing fits and when I think that I could have chosen a nice quiet toad for my companion, your tantrums become all the more wearisome. Now you may put your fur down, *both of you*. I did what I thought necessary and even Damien cannot gainsay me, for all that he is now Chief Mage of England."

"I will keep my silence, Mama," Miranda agreed, watching as Thorpe settled himself at her mother's feet. "And so will your familiar, but only because we know that you will have more than enough in your dish when Damien returns. He will be livid, I am sure, even if we succeed in keeping him ignorant of the risk that you took in getting him here. You were far too weak to expend the energy to contact him across the Void."

Thorpe meowed in agreement.

"To send for him when he is needed at Wellington's side is bad enough, but to place our seal upon a man like Lord Brand?" Miranda continued, ignoring her mother's frown. "I cannot fathom your purpose in putting him under Wodesby protection. Why would you wish to support a man who would like nothing better than to make you into a laughingstock? He mocks all you are, reviles all that we believe in."

"To the contrary, my love. He would unmask the charlatans who trade upon magic, who defame us by preying on the gullible," Lady Wodesby said. "Is that not a worthy goal?"

"If that is his goal," Miranda said, doubt in every syllable. "From what I see, he is bent on self-aggrandizement. While you slept this morning, I asked Dominick to see what he could discover about Lord Brand. What he has found is less than pleasing, you may be sure. Apparently, every servant in Town knows that Brand will pay for information. If milady or milord chooses to have a reading or a séance, it is worth the footman or maid's while to make sure that Brand hears of it. Naturally, his lordship somehow wheedles his way into the ritual."

"A difficulty, to be sure, to read with a disbeliever present. But if one is truly Gifted, I see no harm to it," Lady Wodesby allowed.

"No harm?" Miranda fumed. "All the mediums and card readers in London are looking over their shoulders these days for fear that the marquess will defame them, not to mention anyone who professes to have talents in finding, or dowsing, or reading the portents of the stars. Brand's wager to expose

Professor Guttmacher as a charlatan healer is the talk of London. I thought initially that the marquess was beyond the common run, but he is no different from Lord Petersham and his snuff boxes for each day, or the Green Man, who dresses entirely in green clothing. It would seem that magic is Lord Brand's means of calling attention to himself."

"You seem rather disappointed," Lady Wodesby said, watching her daughter's expression carefully.

"Disappointed? Why should I be disappointed, Mama? I have long ago learned to expect nothing from those people who style themselves the cream of society. It is the results of Lord Brand's public affectations that disturb me," Miranda said, trying to convince herself that her feelings were no more than just outrage. Her stitches went crooked as she attempted to keep her voice calm. "With every false mage that he reveals, are there not fewer people who will put faith in magic at all? How many wise women are losing their custom to physicians, men who often kill more than they cure and then charge dearly for the privilege? Due to people like Brand and their mockery, May Day becomes nothing more than a chance for bawdy frolic. The old ways disappear, becoming no more than hollow ceremony."

"And you blame Lord Brand for all that? My, what a busy man he must be! To hear you speak, he has singlehandedly destroyed the old worship," her mother chuckled.

"How can you make light of this, Mama?" Miranda asked, her needlework slipping to the floor. "After all that has been lost since King James began his witch-hunt after the death of Elizabeth."

Fire ignited in the core of Lady Wodesby's jade eyes. "Do you dare think that I would be flippant about such matters? Your Great-grandmother Le Fey very nearly went to the block and, were it not for a hefty bribe, would have been beheaded. But much as you might desire, you cannot turn back time to those days before the Great Persecution. It was not the halcyon era that you young ones wish to believe, though it might seem so. 'Twas not all virgins dancing round a maypole."

"I know that," Miranda said. "It is just that things seemed so much simpler."

"*Seemed* is the key word, my dear," Lady Wodesby said, her tones softening. "King James might have lit the fire, but do not forget that it was we who built our own pyre. Many abused their Gifts, some who sought power and wealth through the dark side of our art. *The Black Grimoire*, with its instructions for human sacrifice and its violations of Nature's covenants, is not the invention of a twisted fancy, but the receipt for evil."

"But so few have ever—" Miranda protested.

"A few were all that were needed, a few whose selfish actions sufficed to give the odor of truth to the calumnies that our enemies brought against us. Witchkind stood back and did not intervene to stop the corruption in our midst, as was our obligation. For that arrogance, we have paid dearly and many innocents perished with us. Remember that, child. Remember that for the few who prostituted the Gift, others paid the price, some were men, but mostly it was women who suffered."

"And their only crime was to be odd, or old and without protection," Miranda said softly, reaching down to pick up her fallen stitchery. "I know."

"Aye, child, I am well aware of the extent of your knowledge," Lady Wodesby said with pride. "But do not be so quick to condemn a man who sees deceit and thinks to right it."

"Lord Brand is wrongheaded and arrogant," Miranda asserted, her needle flashing as it pierced the linen.

"I have yet to meet a man worth knowing who does not sometimes exhibit those traits," Lady Wodesby said.

"Martin is never arrogant and I have never known him to be the least bit stubborn," Miranda said.

"You prove my point, my love," Lady Wodesby said with a gentle laugh. "But let us not speak of Martin when there are more important matters to discuss. Will he or nil he, Lord Brand is under the shield of Wodesby protection. However, in my present condition, my capabilities are limited. Until Damien arrives, we must contrive some means of keeping Lawrie's nephew under safeguard. Perhaps a warding spell—"

"No!" Miranda said firmly. "You will not even charm so much as a wart, Mama. I have taken the liberty of putting your Tarot away for safekeeping and after last night, I sincerely doubt that you could even begin to try a cardless reading again. So we are safe on that score."

Lady Wodesby nearly exploded in fury. "How did you dare do such a deed? You will return my cards, young lady, at once! There are portents that must be probed immediately."

"So, Thorpe was correct in his assessment," Miranda said, catching an "I told you so" look in the cat's eye. "This morning he was entirely certain that you would seek to scry the signs and be entirely heedless of your well-being. How could you be so foolish?"

Lady Wodesby's eyes narrowed as she regarded Thorpe with a look of disgust. " 'Choose a toad,' my Mama told me. 'They are mild, compliant, unobtrusive creatures who cause no trouble. Cats are the most capricious and devious of familiars.' But did I listen, fool that I was?" her mother muttered between clenched teeth. "I elected to befriend a furry turncoat."

The cat quietly padded to the fireplace, his look of feline amusement doing little to calm his mistress's temper.

"I assure you that my thoughts were galloping along the same road as Thorpe's," Miranda said, taking a deep breath; better for the bombs to burst all at once. Her mother might as well know the full measure of her family's perfidy. "However, I removed your herbs and talismans for safekeeping before the Tarot occurred to me."

"What is more woesome to a mother's heart than a disobedient child?" A single tear trickled down Lady Wodesby's cheek. "It was a sore trial to raise you children without your papa's firm guidance. I am certain that your father, if he is watching from beyond the veil, is quite incensed."

"If he is still same as the Peter who walked this earth, your man applauds your daughter for cleverness, Adrienne," Tante Reina said, entering with a luncheon tray and setting it down on the table. "Drury Lane tears, child, pay them no heed. Even as a little one, always just like this she was. When she could not get her way through tantrums, always weeping was her next."

Thorpe meowed in concurrence.

"Everyone is against me," Lady Wodesby sniffed. "There is danger afoot, I tell you, and you all deny me the tools I need to find its source."

"Pah," the Gypsy woman exclaimed. "You think you do your daughter service if, in your Weakness, you lose yourself in the Great Void? You violate the Second Rule: The Force of the Mind must be greater than the Nil of the Void. Thorpe he says, he could barely keep you from slipping from the Nil to the Realm of Darkness last night."

Miranda gasped. There was no return from the Dark Realm, the connection between body and mind was permanently severed, leaving no more than a breathing husk behind.

"As usual, Thorpe says entirely too much," she snapped.

"You rest, Lady," Tante Reina said, her tones soothing. "Soon, soon, your strength returns and then we will give you back your things."

"I am not a child," Lady Wodesby said petulantly.

"Then stop acting like one," the Gypsy replied, picking up the bowl and handing a spoon to Miranda's mother. "Eat your broth."

"And what are you smirking at?" Lady Wodesby eyed her daughter.

Miranda sucked in her cheeks and gazed intently at the crooked line of her stitchery. "Smirking? I?" she said, trying to contain a gurgle of laughter.

"There is no place for levity. If I can neither determine the source of the threat nor place a spell of protection, then we are hamstrung until Damien comes home. This is a most serious situation, Miranda Ariel."

The use of Miranda's middle name was sobering. "What do you suggest, Mama?" she asked.

"Vigilance is the key. We must somehow keep a constant watch on Lord Brand."

Thorpe rumbled deep in his throat.

"I suppose you could follow his lordship," Lady Wodesby said. " 'Tis true that you are quite adept at getting about unremarked."

The tom purred.

"Yes, I admit that is so," Lady Wodesby concurred. "A cat

may go where no toad could. But a feline would not be welcome in a ballroom or a drawing room. I suppose, Miranda, that I must leave you in full charge of Lord Brand's safekeeping until I am more myself."

"But Mama," Miranda protested, "I told him that the task would fall to me, and he thought the very idea ridiculous. And now that I think upon it, I suppose that I cannot truly blame him. After all, I am no mage."

"Perhaps not, but you are clever and an excellent hand with a pistol," Lady Wodesby pointed out. "All the enchantment in the world is not proof against a keen mind or an iron bullet. As any witchling knows, magic is useless against iron."

"Cold iron?" Miranda stood, aghast. "You would actually wish me to use iron against another witch?"

"If it is magic that presents the hazard, then we face a rogue among us, one who might bring persecution upon us all. If the jeopardy is posed by an ordinary mortal"—she shrugged—"iron works as well as lead. However, if I could just peek at my Tarot, just the Minor Arcana, I could find out."

"No!" Miranda and Tante Reina chorused.

Lady Wodesby made a moue of irritation, but said nothing as Tante Reina pressed food upon her. Though her mother could feed herself, Miranda noticed a decided tremor to her hand and knew that the lady was far more frail than she would have them believe. Miranda was about to insist that the older woman retire when Dominick entered the room.

"Lady, there is a visitor," Dominick said, presenting a salver with a card. "Shall I tell her you are too ill to receive?"

Lady Wodesby looked at the piece of pasteboard thoughtfully. "Hester, hoping, no doubt, to find me on my deathbed as a dramatic finale to last night's debacle. Tell her that I will see her, Dominick."

Miranda made an exasperated noise and moved to bar the door. "Why in the world would you wish to see her, Mama? 'Tis she who is the cause of all this. Unless . . ." Her eyes narrowed in speculation. "Unless you intend to place a curse on her."

Lady Wodesby waved her hand dismissively. "Nonsense. Hester was nothing more than a pawn of fate. There is no cause for a curse. Besides, you did taste the food last night, did you not?"

"It was horrible, except for the sweets," Miranda said, "but what has that to do with the matter?"

"'Tis quite obvious that Hester is already under a malediction of the most devious kind, denying her real nourishment, yet causing her to grow as corpulent as a crock. Any bane that I might lay would merely be gilt to the lily," Lady Wodesby said. "But I must see Hester, my dear. If I refuse to receive her, she will noise it about that I am at death's door. If there are magical enemies abroad, they must not become aware of my present condition of weakness."

Reluctantly, Miranda stepped out of Dominick's way. Tante Reina gave a disapproving shake of her head, but made no comment as she whisked the tray away. Miranda returned to her seat in the corner window.

"Adrienne, you poor dear!" Lady Enderby bustled in, her stentorian greeting echoing in the room as she squeezed her bulk into a delicate Chippendale chair near Lady Wodesby. "I am absolutely riddled with remorse. To see you laid low and it is all my fault."

"Nonsense, Hester," Lady Wodesby said. "The onus is entirely mine. I should never have attended a gathering so close upon a long carriage ride. At our age, travel becomes terribly fatiguing. That is why I usually prefer to stay close to home."

"Lord Brand and Mr. Timmons, Lady," Dominick intoned, presenting their cards.

"Show them in, if you please," Lady Wodesby said, disregarding her daughter's frown.

To Miranda's irritation, the marquess ignored the chairs at the opposite end of the room near Lady Enderby and took himself to a seat near Miranda's window, picking up her fallen needlework and examining it critically.

"Not dead yet, but mortally wounded," Adam said in an undertone. "Unusual that a woman so deft with an egg would be so clumsy with a needle."

"How kind of you to say so, Lord Brand," Miranda remarked, pulling the frame none too gently from his hand.

"Unfortunately, 'tis far easier to make eggs and guineas disappear than people."

"I take it that you are requesting that I vanish, Miss Wilton," Adam said.

"Take it as you choose, milord," Miranda replied, pasting a smile on her face for the sake of appearances. "After last night, I am surprised that you have the audacity to show your face here."

"I owe you thirty guineas; a gentleman always pays his debts of honor." Adam said, pulling a small pouch from his pocket. "You wagered thirty guineas that you knew Barone's methods. You won."

"I do not want your money, Lord Brand," she whispered. "Thirty pieces of gold or silver, for that matter. You know full well I would never have revealed the conjurer's secret to you had I known what you were about."

The bustle and scraping of chairs ceased, making further private conversation impossible.

"I must confess to being astounded, Adrienne," Lawrence said, his brow furrowed in concern as he seated himself beside her. "Are you certain that is it wise to be about so soon?"

"Adrienne claims that it is merely the ill effects of her journey," Lady Enderby said in obvious disappointment. "But I am still inclined to believe that it is the result of the magical forces that she confronted. Do you not think so, Lord Brand?"

Adam refused to rise to the bait. "I would not presume to doubt Lady Wodesby. The roads to London can be rather hellish."

"Just so," Lady Wodesby agreed with an approving nod. "In a few days, I am certain that I will be back to myself, but until then, I am faced with a dilemma. There are any number of invitations that I have accepted on behalf of Miranda and myself, but now, I fear, that I must send my regrets. It is a pity that she must miss it all."

"I would be pleased to take her under my wing until you are on your feet," Lady Enderby volunteered swiftly.

"Were I you, I would prefer Thorpe's paw to her wing," Adam remarked sotto voce. "If not for the fact that he were a tom, he would do well among the rest of the cats."

"No, Lady Enderby, you are too thoughtful," Miranda said, rushing to save herself. "But I would be stricken in conscience if I left Mama on her own."

"How foolish, child! Although you are eight and twenty and well on the shelf, you may still sample the joys of Town," Lady Enderby stated in a sonorous pronouncement. "I am sure that people have long forgotten the disaster of your Season. Lord Hatfill walks with only the smallest of limps these days and Lady Simms's daughter married at last, so she can scarcely claim that you placed a curse to chase away her beaux, can she?"

"Are you speaking of the girl Brummel anointed 'Sour-face Simms'?" Adam asked, his eyes narrowing in annoyance at Lady Enderby's unfair attack. It would appear that Miss Wilton was being held for every catastrophe that had marked her debut.

"There were some rudesbys who used that sobriquet, Lord Brand," Lady Enderby said in tight-lipped disapproval.

"I agree it was rude, though wickedly appropriate. That young woman perpetually appeared as if she was sucking upon lemons and her disposition, I am told, was as sour as her phiz," Adam remarked. "Did they blame Miss Wilton as well for the South Sea Bubble and the beheading of King Louis, Lady Enderby?"

Lady Enderby's lips pursed as she cogitated. "No," she said at last, "I had never heard any mention of Miranda being associated with either of those incidents. Though you can never tell about what people will say, especially when there is magic involved."

Adam could not entirely contain his expression of disbelief.

"There are some of us, milord, who do place credence in such things," Lady Enderby said, her chins wagging in indignation. "Lady Pelton, for example. The unfortunate woman was almost in tears last night when Monsieur Barone said he had to cancel the séance he was to perform for her. He said that the spirits were not receptive due to the evil influence of Beelzebub, so the time would not have been propitious."

"How disappointing," Adam murmured.

His expression was bland, but Miranda could see a look

that seemed suspiciously like satisfaction lurking in the corner of his eye. It was obvious that he had something to do with Barone's sudden refusal to contact the spirits, especially as she recalled his remark the previous evening, before her mother's interruption.

"Why did Lady Pelton wish to have a séance?" Miranda asked, her curiosity piqued. "Was there any reason that she felt a need to disturb the dead?"

"It is so terribly romantic," Lady Enderby said, her voice flowing heavy as syrup, but her face devoid of emotion. "A love match it was, between Pelton and his wife and when he died ten years ago—"

"She proceeded to spend every last farthing that she had to contact his spirit," Adam broke in, trying to keep her in rein. "I see naught that is romantic about it, Lady Enderby. Poor Pelton is doubtless revolving in his grave over his widgeon of a widow. She has a handsome jointure, but she is barely one step before the bailiff due to this madness of hers. At least Barone has saved her a few guineas by bowing out."

"Oh, but he has not, Lord Brand," Lady Enderby said, then put a horrified hand over her mouth. "Oh, my, I should not have spoken of it," she murmured.

"But you have," Lord Brand said smoothly. "I assure you, Lady Enderby, anything that you say will not go beyond this room."

"Lady Pelton told me very expressly not to noise it about too broadly," Lady Enderby said in a whisper that could be heard to the farthest corner of the room. "Monsieur Barone does not wish to anger Beelzebub again. That is why he told her to make absolutely certain that no one outside the circle will hear of the séance two nights hence."

"So that Beelzebub will remain in the dark?" Lawrence asked, looking significantly at Adam.

"Precisely, Lawrence," Lady Enderby said with a nod of endorsement.

"I presume you will be part of the circle, Lady Enderby?" Adam asked.

"Of course," Lady Enderby said. "Although twenty-five guineas is a steep price, I consider it a rare bargain."

"There is a charge?" Lawrence asked.

"All of us are helping Lady Pelton to defray the burden," Lady Enderby sniffed.

"Would you like to divide the burden even further?" Adam asked. "Or mayhaps, even whittle it down to nothing?"

"What do you propose?" Lady Enderby asked, her interest whetted.

"I wish to observe Monsieur Barone at work," Adam said. "For that privilege, I am prepared to pay your fare and Lady Pelton's."

"I am not sure," Lady Enderby said. "Beelzebub—"

"Is due to be spending the week's end in Brighton, I'm told," the marquess declared. "Perhaps that is why Barone feels that he may ply his trade with assurance. I was planning to be with Prinny by the Steine myself at his pavilion, but if I have the opportunity to share so special an evening with you, Lady Enderby . . ."

Miranda rolled her eyes as the woman tittered, swallowing his flattery like treacle.

"I do not know . . ." Lady Enderby said.

"Come, milady, if you still fear the demon's wrath, I shall go in disguise," Adam offered. "It will be our little secret."

"Miranda, perhaps you would join us," Lady Enderby said, torn between foreboding and frugality. "Surely Beelzebub would suspect nothing with a Wodesby in the party."

"Since we are on such friendly terms with demonkind," Miranda said, her tone even, but with a look that could scald ice. "Lady Enderby, as far as I am concerned—"

"She would be absolutely delighted to join you, Hester," Lady Wodesby concluded, throwing her daughter a warning glance as she and Lady Enderby proceeded to discuss the particulars, the latter's voice booming sufficiently to rouse the dead.

"*Were* you about to express your delight, Miss Wilton?" Adam asked quietly, under cover of Lady Enderby's din, his amusement patent.

"I was preparing to inform you and Lady Enderby that you may both join Beelzebub," Miranda told him, a furious gleam midst the sapphire of her eyes. " 'Beelzebub would suspect nothing,' indeed!' "

"Your attitude is most curious," he said. "On the one hand, you seem to take great pride in this supposed sorcerous heritage of yours. On the other, you become infuriated with those who take you at your word and presume you have magical connections. Something of a contradiction, wouldn't you say?"

"None at all," Miranda said, gathering the shards of her composure. "I merely dislike people who use others for their own ends, Lord Brand; no matter whether is it Lady Enderby or yourself. I can understand her motives, for they are very simple." Miranda nodded toward the woman. "For her, we of the Wodesby family are little more than curiosities, odd exotica who might catch the jaded interests of the Ton and thus give her cachet for as long as that fascination lasts. But you, milord? You used my knowledge to nearly destroy Barone's performance; I will not easily forget that and I have yet to find reason to forgive. And though you propose to save Lady Pelton from herself, I do not concede that you have the right to do so."

She cocked her head, as if trying to gain a different perspective. Once more, Adam had the extraordinary sensation that she was stripping him down to his soul. But there was puzzlement in her eyes when she spoke again.

"You, sir, are a man whose purposes I have yet to unravel. Is this a game to you? Some men bet upon the progress of raindrops down a pane, but you wager with reputations as stakes. Do you do this for the sake of innocent fools like Lady Pelton, or to make others, innocent or not, appear foolish?"

Adam shifted uncomfortably in his chair, reminding himself that his aims were of the purest. He had done nothing wrong in his quest to save the credulous from the clutches of charlatans. There was absolutely no reason to explain himself, especially to a woman whose sympathies were more likely to lie with the devil than with Adam himself. Still, he had to admit that she was honest and straightforward, an entirely sensible women—with one major exception. "I have my reasons for seeking justice, but if you wonder so much about my motives, why not ask your mama to take out her cards?"

"I wish that she could," Miranda said guiltily. "But after last night, she is almost too weak to read Jane Austen, much less the Arcana. I know that you mock my mother and myself, Lord Brand. Nonetheless, the Tarot has decreed that your affairs have somehow become entangled in mine. Until Providence sorts our destinies, I will endure and perhaps, milord, I may even come to understand you a little."

Lady Enderby extracted herself from her chair, her conversation with Lady Wodesby concluded. "Excellent! Then Miranda and I will both go directly from Lady Millford's ball, to Lady Pelton's."

"I shall, naturally, send my regrets," Lady Wodesby said, "but it is most generous of you to play duenna, Hester."

"'Twill be my pleasure," Lady Enderby said, regarding Miranda with a calculating smile before turning her attention to the marquess. "And do you go to Lady Millford's ball, Lord Brand?"

Adam nodded. "I will be there. My disguise will be in my carriage, so I will be able to accompany you directly to Lady Pelton's."

Lawrence groaned. "You will have to manage yourself this time, Adam. I swore last night that my career as your abigail is at an end."

Lady Enderby stared at Lawrence curiously, waiting for him to elaborate, but when he did not, she plodded to the door. "All is satisfactorily arranged," she pronounced. "Until Friday, then."

"We ought to be leaving as well," Adam said, getting to his feet. "We would not wish to overly tax you, Lady Wodesby, after last night's ordeal."

Lady Wodesby acknowledged the sentiment with a graceful tilt of her head. "Dominick will show you out." Thorpe rose from his place by the hearth and slipped out of the room.

"Until Friday, Miss Wilton," Adam said with a short bow.

It seemed more a threat than a farewell, but Miranda kept her tongue between her teeth until the door closed behind them.

"Why?"

The single word contained more than one question, which her mother easily discerned. "Why did I consign you to the care of a harpy? Because though you are a third her size you will not be intimidated by her. Why did I allow you to become involved with the séance at Lady Pelton's? Because Thorpe cannot possibly be there, nor did he receive an invitation to dance at Lady Millford's. We must watch his lordship as best we can. Why did I stop you from insulting Lady Enderby? Because she would be a powerful enemy and so long as Lord Brand is under our protection, we need her as our ally. Moreover, Miranda Ariel, I find myself surprised that you would allow yourself to be bothered by the blather of a foolish woman."

" 'We would not wish to overtax you, Lady Wodesby,' " Miranda mimicked, exaggerating Lord Brand's mannerisms. "I vow, you could have cut the sarcasm with an axe."

"And give worth to the statements of a man that you have labeled heretofore as shallow," Lady Wodesby added, trying to hide a smile as her daughter gathered up her needlework.

"I am going out, Mama. Suddenly, I am in dire need of fresh air. And if I must endure Lady Millford's ball, I think that I deserve a new gown to see me through it," Miranda said, going to the door.

"Do you think Madame Felice a mage?" Lady Wodesby asked. "Two days is precious little time for her to bring a gown to completion."

"I think that a few extra pounds might render her capable of working wonders," Miranda said thoughtfully. "Is there anything that you will require from Bond Street?"

Lady Wodesby shook her head. "Wonders indeed," she said to herself, as he daughter's retreating footsteps echoed. "The first time in years that the girl has shown the least interest in her appearance, Martin Allworth notwithstanding. Intriguing portents, most unusual, and me without my Decks. Where in Hades could they have hidden my cards?"

Chapter 6

Friday's shadows were stretching into dusk as Lord Brand casually produced a coin from behind the ear of the doorman at White's and placed it into the man's hand, evoking a smile from the normally stodgy old servant.

"Keep it under guard, Charlie" Adam admonished as he took up his hat and gloves. "One can never tell about those vanishing coins."

"Aye, Lord Brand, I shall," the man promised, tightening his grip.

Lawrence chuckled as they walked down the steps and turned down St. James's Street. "I suspect he will not let loose his hold on that bit of gold all evening."

But Adam did not reply. As soon as he had set foot on the walk, the feeling that had been plaguing him for the past few days returned, that odd prickling at the back of his neck. "Do not look back, Uncle Lawrie," he said in hushed tones. "I believe I am being followed."

"Guttmacher's minions?" the older man asked.

Adam shook his head. "I think not; my shadow has been far too subtle, the touch of a breeze almost. No matter how quickly I look about, I see nothing. Taylor's crew is comprised mostly of the denizens of the ring and they tend to be as recognizable as a brawler in a corps de ballet. A quick confrontation in a dark alleyway is more in accord with Taylor's tastes."

"Unfortunately, you have no shortage of enemies these days," his uncle sighed. "It has been less than a fortnight since Madame Fortuna publicly threatened you. When you published a list of her ludicrous predictions over the past ten years and documented that none of them had come true, I am told that she was livid."

"I believe she declared that I would be struck dead by lightning," Adam said, looking up at the fading afterglow of the sun. "However, as there is not a cloud in the sky, I am presently unworried on that score."

"Madame Fortuna is by no means the only dabbler in the occult who would like to see you laid low," Lawrence said with a frown, skirting past a pile of lumber being used in the refurbishing of one of the shops. "Moreover, your covert activities while you were traveling on the Continent gained you some highly placed enemies."

"I doubt that Fouché would strike just now. Napoleon's chief of secret police presently has enough on his hands without seeking for petty revenge," Adam said, pretending to look in the chemist's window at number 29. While the display at D. R. Harris and Co. was of limited interest, he used the mirror effect of the glass to surreptitiously scan the street behind them, but there was nothing suspicious to be seen.

"There are others who would enjoy seeing you harmed," Lawrence said, "but with Adrienne's prediction, I would still consider Guttmacher né Taylor the most likely menace to your safety."

Adam groaned. "Not you, Uncle Lawrie. You have seen far too much of the charlatan's lay to be taken in by Lady Wodesby's histrionics."

"Do not be so quick to dismiss her, Adam," Lawrence said, his lips tightening in annoyance as they moved on past Boodle's. "She is not to be compared to Madame Fortuna. Lay Adrienne's predictions against actual fate and you will find her accuracy remarkable. But then, she is a Le Fey."

"Generalities of the Nostradamus type, I suppose," Adam said with dismissive disdain. "Unexceptional prophecies that can be twisted to suit specific events."

"Highly specific, highly detailed," Lawrence disputed. "She did a reading for me nigh onto thirty years ago and most of it has come to pass."

"Most?" Adam asked, pausing to pull on his gloves.

"I am not done with my turn on this earth yet, greenling,"

Lawrence said in a huff. "But do not spurn Lady Wodesby's advice out of hand, is what I say. The Wodesbys and Le Feys have been advisers to kings and queens for over half a millennium, to my knowledge. If Charles had taken Le Fey's advice, there would never have been a Cromwell. And if our own George had listened to the previous Lord Wodesby, the Colonies would still be under England's wing."

"There were many who said that the Colonies might attempt to fly the coop," Adam said skeptically.

"Twenty years before the fact?" Lawrence asked with a snort. "Peter predicted when and where the opening shots would be fired, dates down to the hour. Sadly, Farmer George's attitude mirrored your own. He rejected Lord Wodesby's advice and you may see where it has got him."

"How is it you come to know so much of the Wodesbys?" Adam asked.

"I have made something of a hobby of the histories of the Wodesbys and Le Feys. The study of their past and those of the families intertwined with theirs has been more than intriguing," Lawrence said, his expression growing distant. "The Wodesbys, the Le Feys, the Gwynns, the Morgans, the Macfies, the Peregrines, and the Donallys. Almost from the first written chronicles, those names have been inexorably tied with the use of witchcraft and arcane power."

"A useful reputation to possess, if only in rumor, to give one's enemies pause," Adam commented drily, resisting the impulse to whirl round and look back. He could feel the eyes upon him how, the steady watching that seemed to bore into his back. "Might I ask the reason for your unusual interest, Uncle?"

"You have only to look at Miss Wilton to see why," Lawrence said with a bittersweet smile. "I vow, the girl is almost the mirror of Adrienne in her earlier days. Though it is doubtless difficult to believe, her mama was even lovelier, a vivid creature with a fey charm. All of us were mad about her, pressing our suits, even though we knew that Adrienne Le Fey had been promised from the cradle to Peter Wilton. The Le Feys and Wodesbys have long had connections, along with those other families that I mentioned. It was well known that

their women came to their Season already promised." He
sighed in memory. "Adrienne never encouraged us, yet can a
moth contain its longing to kiss the flame?"

"You were in love with her?" Adam asked in surprise as
they stopped to wait for a crossing cart. But though he
glanced back, there was no one who followed.

" 'Were' has the connotation of the past," Lawrence said
quietly. "All of my life, I have measured every woman against
Adrienne, but there has yet been none to match her. That is
one of the few predictions that has not yet come to fruition.
She promised that in time I would find the companion of my
heart."

Adam was silent. It was obvious now why his uncle could
not be relied upon to be sensible when it came to the matter of
the Wodesby women. Uncle Lawrie's judgement was clouded
by emotion. Yet the marquess could not help but ask, "If the
Wodesby custom is one of childhood betrothal, why is Miss
Wilton not married?"

"I cannot say. I made it my business to be out of Town
when I found that Lady Wodesby was to present her daughter.
The thought of seeing Adrienne on Peter's arm was too
painful." Lawrence scratched his head in puzzlement, and
started down the street toward his apartments. "I do know that
Miss Wilton's Le Fey cousins made their curtsies in London
already affianced. However, strangely enough, the girl did not
seem to be spoken for. As you may have gathered from Hester
the other day, Miranda's Season was an unmitigated disaster.
Every mishap that occurred among those on the hunt for a
husband were attributed to the supernatural influences of the
Wodesby girl or her mama."

No wonder that Miss Wilton sometimes seemed as skittish
as a badly broken filly, Adam thought. Society could be cruel
without benefit of excuse; however, a miss with purported
magical powers would be an all-too-convenient target for
blame. "I suspect that she may encounter the same difficulties
again," Adam said. "Especially since her mama has made a
public spectacle of herself. Now do not bristle at me, Uncle
Lawrie, for you know it to be the truth. Miss Wilton has once
again become the subject of speculation. At Mrs. Hogg-

smyth's yesterday, she received more than her share of stares and whispers."

"She is a striking young lady," his uncle said defensively.

"Yes, she is," Adam admitted. "Nonetheless, even her looks cannot fully account for the way that the cats were sharpening their claws upon her. It is rather unbelievable the credit that people place in superstitious nonsense in this day and age."

"The poor child." Lawrence scowled. "I would not like to see Adrienne's daughter hurt, Adam. She is a sweet girl."

"Not a girl," Adam disagreed. "Miss Wilton is no school-room miss, to allow herself to be intimidated. Although I think her beliefs misguided, I have never seen such a display of sang froid in the face of sarcasm. Every query about her mama's health, including the snide, was answered with amazing aplomb. Even Brummel did not shake her assurance, though for some reason George was at his nastiest."

"I think that I can explain that," Lawrence said with a shake of his head. "Brummel insulted Adrienne's sister, Titania Peregrine, just last season. Madame Peregrine served the Beau a rather shocking prediction. Knowing Brummel's nasty nature, it would not surprise me if he were holding Titania's words against Miranda."

"And what did this 'prophetess' proclaim?" Adam asked in amusement.

"She predicted that the Beau would perish a pauper, alone and away from his native land," Lawrence told him.

"How absurd! The man has never been higher in Prinny's favor. George has become a virtual power unto himself," Adam laughed. "Yet by the end of Mrs. Hoggsmyth's affair, even Brummel seemed impressed with Miss Wilton's dignity. He even deigned to ask her if she intended to be at Millfords' tonight."

"If she succeeded in soothing an angry Brummel, then she may well be a witch," Lawrence said.

"Oh no," Adam said with a chortle, "she emphatically denies any skill in that sphere."

"Perhaps that is why—" Lawrence began thoughtfully.

Adam's astonished oath cut his uncle's speculation short,

his face reddening as he stared into the window of Number 24 St. James's. The usual assortments of prints and travesties adorned the front window of Mrs. Humphrey's print shop. Prinny and various prominent personages were portrayed in their various frailties and foibles. However, prominently displayed was a wicked caricature by Gillray. Lady Wodesby had been made into a fleshy crone and a wart adorned a voluptuous Miranda's pert nose as the two of them, naked as Eve in Eden, stirred a cauldron labeled "Society." But that was just the half of it. A bewigged magistrate wearing Adam's face leered at them from the bench as Brummel raised his quizzing glass and uttered "Thou shalt not suffer a witch." Apparently, Brummel's feud with Miss Wilton's family was known to the caricaturist.

Lawrence stared aghast. "How dare they!" he said, pulling his purse from his pocket.

"What are you going to do, Uncle Lawrie," Adam asked, catching him by the arm.

"Buy every one of those prints and then give that Gillray fellow a piece of my mind!" Lawrence sputtered.

"They will only print more," Adam warned him. "And then put out word of your actions, which will only cause more prints to be sold."

"I'll pay them *not* to print any more," Lawrence declared.

"Even if you could buy off Gillray, which I doubt, what of Thomas Rowlandson or any of the others who dine on ridicule?" Adam asked softly, dropping his restraining hand as understanding dawned on his uncle's face. "You cannot still all of their pens."

"Poor Adrienne," Lawrence said.

"Lady Wodesby brought this upon herself," Adam said harshly. "'Tis not her so much as her daughter who will truly suffer once this gets abroad." He turned away and walked quickly onward. His uncle followed reluctantly.

"I would not be so quick to place blame on anyone other than Gillray. This is tragic," Lawrence said, shaking his head as he drew abreast with his nephew. "If Adrienne hoped to see her daughter married, this could well ruin her chances."

"I thought that the Wodesbys only married within their own weird sphere," Adam said.

"You will doubtless sneer if I present my speculations," Lawrence replied, his lips pursing.

Adam raised a hand solemnly. "No sneers, my pledge upon it."

"You mentioned that she denies any magical gifts," Lawrence began with a frown. "And we have just witnessed why her chances on the marriage mart are none to nil. What if no one among the usual families wishes to wed her, Adam, precisely because she is not a witch? And what if society disdains her because they believe that she is."

"That is ludicrous," Adam declared. The smell of oaken casks, wine, and spirits assaulted them as they strolled past the shop of Berry Brothers and Rudd. "She is lovely, charming, witty, and—from what Lady Enderby is declaring to all and sundry—well-dowered to boot."

"But *not* a witch," Lawrence said. "Adrienne made me no answer when I asked if her daughter shared her talent. She seemed rather sad, so I guided the conversation elsewhere."

I am not a witch. All at once Adam recalled Miss Wilton's assertion, whispered as if in shame. She had turned away. Could she truly be lambasting herself for not having powers that existed only in the imagination? "That is absolutely ridiculous," Adam said. The hairs on his neck began to niggle at him. "Uncle Lawrie, a quick about-face, now."

Obediently, the older man whirled on his heels. "Not a soul behind us," he said. "Only a cat."

"What color cat?" Adam asked.

"What does it matter?" Lawrence asked in puzzlement. "Black, I think."

"Twice yesterday, I saw a marmalade cat, much the color of Lady Wodesby's tom," Adam said.

"And you bandy about the words 'ridiculous' and 'absurd.'" Lawrence gave a derisive snort. "The animal seemed to be fond of you, but do you honestly think that Adrienne's cat is trailing you about Mayfair?"

"All this talk about witches, familiars, and spells, I suppose," Adam said with a sheepish shrug of his shoulders.

"Will I see you at Millfords' tonight?" he asked, as they stopped at the entrance to Lawrence's apartments.

"I am dining with a friend this evening," Lawrence replied.

"Ah, I envy you," Adam said, not noticing the slight flush above his uncle's necklinen. "I'd much rather enjoy a tête-a-tête with intelligent company than endure the crush at Millfords' tonight."

"Then why attend at all?" Lawrence asked, as he rapped the knocker.

"It may seem somewhat quixotic, but I think that Miss Wilton may need me. She may have endured the slings and arrows of her mama's fortune-telling tendencies thus far, but yesterday's will be a mere skirmish in comparison to the onslaught that she will meet in Lady Millford's ballroom."

The Millford Ball was usually among the earliest entertainments of the Season. Nonetheless, despite its premature place upon the Ton's calendar, the huge ballroom in the house on Grosvenor Square was tightly packed. Many a match had been made between the dance floor and the supper room and the fate of the nation was oft decided over cigars and port in Lord Millford's library. Therefore, it was not surprising that the annual crush attracted everyone with any claim to breeding or anyone with ambitions.

From their roost among the matrons, the Princess de Lieven and Lady Drummond-Burrel surveyed the newest crop of debutantes, sentencing them to exile from the sacred halls of Almack's by dint of a curtsy too shallow or a smile too forward. In the corner opposite the entry, George Brummel had set up a figurative bow window. The usual crowd of acolytes surrounded him, waiting avidly for his acid comments on the crowd. To their delight, this evening promised to be more entertaining than most. Due to Gillray's wicked caricature, Brummel was at his most biting and the Marquess of Brand had been unlucky enough to wander into the Beau's orbit.

"It was weird beyond words," Brummel commented smoothly, pausing for a sip of champagne. "Alvanley and I had just paused in front of Mrs. Humphrey's shop to inspect Gillray's newest print. Have you seen it?"

Adam kept his face expressionless, knowing well enough that George was out to ruffle his feathers. "I have. Unfortunately, the man has passed the boundaries of satire. One can well believe the rumors that Gillray is going insane. No one who pretends to taste could abide so nasty a portrayal of two helpless women who have done no harm."

"No harm?" Brummel jibed. "Have you not told me numerous times that all fortune-tellers are a blot upon society?"

"Miss Wilton makes no pretense of such powers," Adam said stiffly, refusing to be baited. "As a gentleman, George, you know that one must be fair."

"True enough," agreed Brummel, softening slightly at the appeal to good breeding. "The child will have a rough go of it."

"Hesitate to characterize the Wodesbys as helpless, I would?" Lord Alvanley chimed in. "Not after what happened to poor Gillray."

"Precisely what did occur?" Adam, asked, trying to feign nonchalance as he sipped at his flute of champagne.

"As I said, the two of us were looking at that odious print, when Gillray himself walked out of the shop. I was about to tell him what I thought of his sophomoric scratchings, when all of a sudden, he was set upon by this spitting, screeching fury of a feline," Brummel began.

"Lucky man, Gillray," Adam commented, sipping his champagne. "Far better to be attacked by a cat than an angry Brummel."

"Never seen the like of it," Alvanley asserted. "The creature must have been mad, for it sprang upon Gillray and set him to staggering. Luckily, he did not fall, else I shudder to think what might have happened to his face. As it was, the beast proceeded to claw the man to shreds. 'Pon my soul, I was so stunned I did not act immediately, but when I attempted to help Gillray, I got this for my pains." He held up a bandaged hand. "Scratched me, it did, the filthy creature."

"Every inch of that feline was full of soot." Brummel sniffed. "As if it had rolled itself in a coal bin. Luckily, I did not handle it. Alvanley and Gillray looked like a pair of chimney sweeps by the time it was over."

"Odd, because cats are usually the most fastidious of animals," Alvanley observed. "Think that this one was a marmalade tom beneath the dust. But in any case, by the time I managed to pull the cat away, Gillray's legs had been pretty well mangled, not a square inch of his trousers were left whole."

Thorpe deserves nothing less than a salmon, Adam thought, then shook himself mentally for the preposterous direction of his reflections. Cats did not disguise themselves. Cats could not conceptualize drawings, much less identify their creators. Cats were incapable of fidelity or vengeance.

"Same as happened to 'Hobbling' Hatfill," Alvanley said solemnly. "Told us all it was a tussle with a rosebush, but we knew different. Wonder if *that* cat was a marmalade, too? Ought to ask him."

"Or the Wilton Witch!" Another Brummel disciple commented.

"Really, Alvanley," Adam said with a laugh and a scornful look that made the other offender flush. "That occurred years ago. If a man were to make such inquiries of me, I would have serious doubts as to his intelligence."

Alvanley frowned. "Hadn't thought of that. Hatfill's cat would be a toothless old tom by now, wouldn't it? Have to fly, promised for a dance, y'know."

The two men watched as Alvanley crossed the room to make his bows to his partner. As if he were seated in the famous window of White's, Brummel banished his other sycophants with a raised brow signifying dismissal. Once the last of them had reluctantly left, Brummel indicated a vacated chair beside him. "Well, you may have nullified Alvanley, Adam," Brummel began. "But I suspect that he will not be the only one to draw a parallel between Gillray and Hatfill, once the story gets round."

"There is no shortage of fools," Adam said.

"Especially in Mayfair," Brummel agreed, slowly twirling the stem of his empty glass between his fingers. "I put no more credence in the tales about the Wodesby witches than the stories that my old nanny spun by the fireside. But there are many here who are less than sanguine on the subject. Pity that the chit will be the one to suffer for her peculiar family."

"Unless you put a good face on it," Adam began.

"Why should I?" Brummel asked like a petulant child. "Neither the Wodesbys nor their kin have been particularly friendly to me."

"That does not signify, George," Adam said, with an air of nonchalance. "However, if you condemn her, you will do naught but promote Gillray's sales. It would seem to me that you would be wise to back Miss Wilton, if only for your own sake. To do otherwise would cause you to appear mean-spirited. Moreover, a cut might imply that you place some credit in witchery and its prognostications."

Brummel gave him a shrewd look. "Yes, it would, wouldn't it? Very well, I shall shower my praises upon her, because I rather like her and because you request it, Adam. But 'tis doubtful that even *my* consequence can pull her from this pit."

There was an audible stir as Lady Enderby and Miss Wilton were announced. Once more, Lady Wodesby's daughter was attired in green, the color of a newly unfurled leaf. To Adam, she seemed the embodiment of spring. Her hair was piled high upon her head, the wheaten tresses held in place by glittering emerald combs. Matching emeralds hung from her ears and the emerald pendant was once again suspended in the hollow of her throat.

What in the world could her mother have been thinking of? Adam wondered. To allow her daughter to appear thus in public! Every male eye in the room was fixed upon Miss Wilton.

"Madame Felice has outdone herself," Brummel said.

"Outrageous," Adam murmured, abandoning any hope that Miss Wilton might somehow pass unnoticed.

"The décolletage is demure enough for a miss fresh from the schoolroom," Brummel noted. "The fabric is not damped and not the least bit transparent."

"Yet that gown appears as if it is defying the laws of gravity," Adam said.

"And it seems about to succumb to the earth's pull at the slightest movement," Brummel agreed, observing Lord Brand's staggered expression with growing amusement. "Ingenious, really; I must send the modiste my compliments. Shall we take a closer look, dear boy?"

Miranda's eyes swept the room, meeting their stares defiantly. Great-grandmama Wodesby had gone to the stake with her spine stiff and her head held high and though the circumstances differed, her descendant vowed to endure with dignity. These men and women could do Miranda no physical harm, but they had caused her great pain in the past. But she was older now, and mayhap a bit wiser. By The Merlin, they would not have the satisfaction of seeing her cringe this time.

As she and Lady Enderby made their greetings, Miranda felt a presence behind her. Suddenly, the room grew warmer, the candles seemed to shine with a brighter glow. There was no need to turn to know that Lord Brand had arrived. She turned to find him looking at her and, unbelievable as it might seem, a smiling Brummel was with him.

"I hope that you will recall the dance that I was promised," Brummel reminded her as he gave his greeting.

"Of course, Mr. Brummel," Miranda said, deeply touched. It was too much to hope that he had not yet seen that scurrilous caricature of himself in Humphrey's window. The Beau was perverse enough to put the blame on a fellow victim, and coupled with his antipathy toward her family, his magnanimity was wholly unexpected.

"Brazen it out, my girl," Brummel whispered as he made his bow. " 'Tis the only course."

Adam bowed and forced himself to smile, aware that every eye in the room was upon them. "Good evening, Miss Wilton," he said, a shade too loudly.

His brown eyes were as hard as the earth in winter and Miranda felt a sinking feeling in the pit of her stomach. Lord Brand had seen the drawing and resented being drawn in to the sphere of ridicule. "Well met, milord." Miranda modulated her next words carefully so that they were inaudible beneath the strains of music. "I am sorry, milord. My mother is quite distressed that you have met with such malice due to your association with our family."

"I take it that you have heard," Adam said, wondering how she had gotten word of the drawing so quickly.

"And seen. We sent Dominick to purchase a copy as soon as we were informed." Miranda inclined her head graciously and smiled as if she had been told something particularly pleasant. "I think that your friend Brummel gives good advice, milord. There is no choice but to put the best face on things."

"Perhaps you ought to curtail your social activities until your mama is on her feet once again, or until your brother returns?" Adam asked, regarding Lady Enderby, who had gone off to titter in a corner with one of her cronies. The woman was worse than no support at all.

"I will not run and hide as I did when I was an unfledged girl, Lord Brand," Miranda said, taking the arm that he offered, her chin lifting as the hum swelled beneath the music. "After all, I am told that it is no longer fashionable to burn witches, so what do I have to fear?"

"But you are not a witch, Miss Wilton," Adam said, observing her reaction carefully. There was a glitter in the corner of her eye that was suspiciously like a tear and when she spoke there was a definite catch in her throat.

"Do you often go about reminding people of their infirmities?" she said with forced brightness.

Uncle Lawrie had obviously been close to the mark. "I am sorry if I have pained you in any way," Adam said honestly. "But as far as I can see, you lack nothing other than common sense. There are no witches, any more than there are elves or fairies or demons." He felt her stiffen. "Remember, Miss Wilton, we tread the boards tonight. Act as if you are enjoying yourself and I shall pretend that I am utterly enchanted."

" 'Enchanted' is a dangerous term, under the circumstances," Miranda said, molding her lips into an expression of pleasure as he walked her onto the floor. It took no special magical sense to realize that every gaze was fixed upon them. "Do I still have some coal dust upon me, milord?" she asked. "I had thought that I removed all the traces and I asked Lady Enderby, but I would not put it past her to deny seeing anything only to laugh about it behind my back."

"Coal dust?" Adam held his breath.

"For some reason, Thorpe took it in his head to roll in the ash bin. He was in quite a pother this evening, put dirty paw prints all over the Aubusson rug. It was wholly unlike him, but then he was rather upset." Miranda said. "I nearly did not recognize him. Why he would do such a thing, I cannot fathom."

"Perhaps he needed a disguise?" Adam bit his tongue, but not before the words had slipped out.

"A cat? In disguise? How droll, milord," Miranda could not resist the opportunity to tweak him. "Why not a little false beard? Or mayhap a wig?"

She was smiling naturally now and the stiff feeling between them ebbed away. "A tricorne," Adam suggested, "instead of the fur hat that he usually wears? And if Thorpe goes to Almack's, I would suggest he might try breeches."

"Or else the patronesses might bar his entry, as they did Wellington's," Miranda agreed solemnly, her eyes twinkling. "So did Thorpe mark me, milord?" His gaze made her shiver as it swept her from her slippers to the pins upon her head.

"You are perfect, Miss Wilton," he whispered. "Entirely perfect."

The band struck up the opening air, a waltz.

"I know the steps, in theory, but I've never waltzed before," she whispered. "The dance had not yet become popular during my Season."

"Then let us put theory into practice, Miss Wilton. Follow where I lead." Adam took her into his arms, holding her as close as the bounds of propriety allowed.

She stared up into his eyes, trying to read his intent, following the gentle pressure of his hands as he guided her steps. But this was not a recalcitrant Damien, forced to drag his sister about at a dancing master's command. The marquess led with authority, surprising her with his agility and grace. Within a minute or two, she had picked up the steps.

"You have it now," he said encouragingly. "Keep your mind off your feet and look at me. Pretend that I am someone else, the man of your dreams. Imagine that my arms are his and I shall whisper adoring words in your ears, as he would no doubt do if he had this opportunity."

Obediently, Miranda tried to conjure up Martin's face, but somehow, that was impossible. Try as she might, she could not imagine Allworth whirling her about the room or holding her so close. The tip of her ear tickled as Lord Brand whispered nonsensical nothings, tidbits of gossip about the arbiters of society, making them appear foolish and capricious, causing her to stifle her laughter more than once. Never could she picture Allworth making light of those who ate and spat out reputations for their supper.

Only when he touched her could Adam feel the full extent of her nervousness. Outwardly, she did not betray herself by so much as a hair, but Adam could detect her apprehension in the stiffness of her carriage. He too was aware of the watchers, waiting for them to stumble, to make a mistake so that they could pounce upon her. With enormous effort, he kept himself from pulling her closer, from letting his hand stray to the fine spider web of filmy filigree that held the green silk gown tantalizingly suspended. Instead, he concentrated upon putting her at ease. "Dream, Miss Wilton; imagine this is all a vision of your own creation."

"A dream . . ." Miranda echoed softly, trying once more to conjure the dim shade of Martin, but he faded into the recesses of her mind. Although she had known him for most of her life, she could not recall if he had once walked into her sleeping hours. But she had dreamed, only last night . . . Miranda nearly missed a step as she recalled disturbing visions lost in the waking and realized that the man of her dreams wore Lord Brand's face, even though she had known him for less than a week.

But that was entirely natural, she told herself. Once Mama's prophecy came to pass, things would sort themselves out and she would be free of Lord Brand, free to return to her life at The Wode, to marry Martin, to work in the library. Suddenly, the emptiness of that vision stretched ahead of her like a long, endless tunnel.

With all the force of her imagination, she concentrated on Lord Brand's face, pretending, for this instant, that she was his dream as he was hers. Weaving a false spell, she substituted affection for the emotion in his eyes that was certainly pity; turned doubt and cynicism into respect; and allowed his light formal touch to be transformed into the genuine tenderness of a lover's hand. Although she knew that no spell of hers would ever work upon another, mortal or mage, Miranda succeeded in bewitching herself.

Slowly, the tension seeped away until she was supple in his arms. Every smile became a victory and each butterfly flutter of her fingers set his heart to pounding. Within the space of seconds, Adam came to regret his rash proposal, growing jealous of the unknown phantom that he himself had asked her to conjure. He wanted the look in those sapphire depths to be for him, the throaty chuckles that tickled softly at his ear to be his by right.

They whirled in each other's arms, each unaware of the spells that they were weaving for themselves, the magic no less powerful for being available to ordinary mortals. From his place behind the doors to the terrace, Thorpe absently licked the last bit of coal dust from his paws, wondering what the lady would think of this turn of events.

The music stopped, shattering the enchantment, but Adam's thoughts were still awhirl. While Brummel claimed Miss Wilton's hand for a country dance, Adam went to the refreshment table, eager to find something wet to ease the sudden tightness in his throat. He eyed her as he sipped, watching as she gracefully wove her way through the complex patterns, till the end of the set.

"Pretty armful, ain't she?" declared the slurred voice of Lord Hatfill, as the dancers were making their final bows. "Y'know, I had a bit of a sabbat with the young Wodesby witch myself."

Thoughts of pistols, rapiers, and bare knuckles raced through Adam's mind, but since any choice of weapon would mean certain scandal, he dismissed the possibility of a duel. Still, Lord Hatfill's foul mouth would have to be silenced by some method. The only acceptable challenge was a contest of wits. An unfair bout, Adam knew, since the drunken lecher was an unarmed opponent.

"I'd be wary of getting on the wrong side of the Wodesby clan," Adam said, lowering his voice confidentially. "Gillray, the cartoonist, did this very afternoon. They say it was a cat that ripped him to pieces."

Hatfill's red proboscis turned stark white. "Never tell me so," he whispered. "Not a marmalade, was it?"

Thorpe, you busy devil. "Aye," Adam told him. "So I would take care what I say about the Wodesbys. You can never tell who or what might be listening." As that thought sank into the man's sodden brain, Adam dropped the gold piece that he had palmed to send it rolling beneath the table. "I say, Hatfill, you had best see to your guinea. Your purse must have come undone." Under pretext of bending for a better view, the marquess firmly hooked the lacy edge of the cloth to one of Hatfill's buttons. "I think it went over there," he said, pointing to the far end of the table.

As the cloth and its contents started to shift slowly towards the edge, Adam picked up his glass and strolled casually toward Miss Wilton. 'Twas worth a marigold to convince Hatfill that it was not worth his while to malign her. Well, mayhaps a bit more than the coin. The first bits of glass began to crash upon the floor and Adam promised himself that he would find some way to make good the damage to Lady Millford. The orgeat, however, was no loss, Adam thought as he placed the remnants on the tray of an open-mouthed footman. The stuff was nearly as insipid as the bath water that they served at Almack's. In exchange for the orgeat he plucked up two glasses of champagne.

Miss Wilton's laughter served to banish the last of Adam's regrets. He no longer cared that he had just used superstition as a tool to manipulate a man. Lady Millford's shattered glass was a small sacrifice and even the eminently edible lobster patties that slid into the shards of oblivion were accounted well lost for the sight of Miss Wilton's face. It was like seeing her once again for the very first time, but as she truly ought to be. Gone was the wariness, the air of constant worry that had hung about her like a cloud ever since their initial encounter in Lady Enderby's drawing room. Tears of mirth slid down her face as Hatfill emerged triumphant from beneath the table, clutching the guinea like a child who has captured the coin in the Christmas pudding.

Chapter 7

With both glasses balanced carefully in one hand, Adam touched Miranda's shoulder with the other, urging her silently toward the terrace. All eyes were focused on Lord Hatfill, so it was highly unlikely that anyone would notice them slipping outside. She hesitated for a second, then nodded as the mocking crowd moved in for the kill.

"Like vultures, aren't they?" Adam commented as they stepped into the evening. "Give them a piece of fresh carrion and they will quickly abandon the old corpse for the new."

"How very mean of spirit I must be," Miranda said, leaning against the balustrade as she held her aching side. "I was laughing along with the rest of them at the poor man."

"I would reserve my pity for someone more deserving than Lord Hatfill, Miss Wilton," Adam said, producing the glasses with a flourish. "He would not have hesitated to sully your name if he could."

She shuddered at the memory, the last wisps of laughter fading like smoke as she recalled those moments of terror before Thorpe's timely intervention years before. "More than that," she said softly, her hand trembling as she took the glass.

More than a decade had passed, yet the fear was obviously still strong. No wonder she was so guarded and apprehensive. "Should have offered Hatfill a ten-paced walk at dawn," Adam murmured, running an angry hand through his hair.

Miranda's eyes widened in astonishment. "You did it," she guessed. "You primed him for the spill. But why, milord?"

Adam lifted his shoulders in a chagrined gesture. "A desire for justice, I suppose, if only in a small measure. Let him recall what it feels like to be the butt of scorn and mockery. Perhaps it will teach him to keep his foul mouth shut."

"He was talking about me, I take it."

Miss Wilton spoke quietly, but there was a distinct tremor in her voice. Adam cursed himself for a fool. "Not you," he lied, setting his glass aside, "but the Wodesbys, witches. It was more a general sort of slur, but he has been taught a lesson."

Miranda took a sip of champagne. "No need to whitewash it, milord. I thank you for playing the role of Chaucer's 'parfit gentil' knight. But if you mean to avenge every slur against me or mine thusly, there will not be a whole piece of glass left in all of London before long," she said, attempting a smile. "It has never been easy to be what we are. A hundred years ago, I could have lost my life because of Hatfill's smears. Too many of my forebears did. I account myself lucky that mere words are all that I must stomach."

"Words have a power all their own," Adam said, moved by her forlorn effort at gallantry. Plainly, from the pain in her eyes, her declaration was little more than a whistle in the dark. "I would not like to see you hurt any further, Miss Wilton."

"Miranda," she said, vouchsafing her name. He had earned that right and she wanted to hear him say it in the dark warmth of the night.

"Miranda," he agreed, testing the syllables on his tongue. Her name had a texture, a flavor that felt eminently right.

Yes, she agreed silently. *Words had their own power, especially names. A name, freely gifted, was indeed a force to conjure with.* Pronounced by him, "Miranda" became almost like a piece of Mozart, a mixture of loneliness and recognition, the grandeur of the heights and a view of the abyss. As the music of her name faded into the shadow, she felt a depthless void within her and knew that she had been caught within a spell of her own making.

The marquess reached covertly behind him and plucked a hothouse flower from the pot by the door. Misdirecting her attention with a wave of his left hand, he made the blossom appear in his right, as if from the ether itself. "Call me Adam," he requested, presenting the delicate bloom with a flourish.

"As you wish . . . Adam," she whispered, pleased with the gift, even though she knew that the offer of his name was of no real significance to him, nothing more than social reciprocity. She put her glass on the balustrade. "You have learned the art of illusion well," she remarked, stroking the petals gently, releasing their sweet scent into the darkness. "Had I not known your methods, I would have sworn that you pulled this from the fabric of the night."

"Ah, but you of all people should know that the night has its own magic," he said. Although lightly spoken, the words acquired a peculiar ring of truth. As her long fingers moved with supple tenderness, caressing the blossom, Adam felt touched by sudden heat. Sensual and fluid, the flowing line of motion led his gaze up the moonlit curve of her arm. In the shadow, Madame Felice's cunning web of netting had all but disappeared. Her shoulders seemed entirely bare except for the emerald that caught the moon in its heart of green fire.

Despite the aura of stylishness, there was something elemental and wild about her, the ingenuous charm of a doe poised on the edge of flight. He picked up his champagne, hoping to somehow temper this sudden powerful longing, but found the glass empty and absently put it aside. Much as he tried to resist, he moved toward her, tempted beyond reason. Moonlight silvered her skin and cast a shimmering glow on the silk of her hair. He wanted to pull away those jeweled combs and let the strands cascade like threaded gold through his fingers. His hand seemed to acquire its own will, moving without conscious volition to brush gently against her cheek.

The flower slipped from Miranda's hands, fluttering to the stone. A faint whiff of shaving soap blended with the fragrance of freshly starched linen and the warm champagne touch of his breath. A sharp stab of desire cut away her last tenuous hold on reason. Hesitantly, she put her hand on his shoulder, ignoring the fading echo of the voice within her that was crying "Fool, fool."

Her fingers held the sweet scent of flowers. Cradling her chin, he looked into the dark blue depths of her eyes, saw the questions and a single unspoken answer. He gathered her into his arms and she closed her eyes, tilting her head in a gesture that was implicit consent. Just as a kiss seemed to be as certain as sunrise, a cat yowled beneath the shrubbery. Miranda jumped back and he caught her hand to keep her from tumbling over the rail.

"I'm sorry," he said, shaking his head like a swimmer just come to the surface. "I do not have the foggiest notion as to what came over me."

As if she were some form of madness or malady. Miranda turned to face the darkness before he could see the hurt in her eyes. "There is no need to apologize," she said in deliberately wry tones. "What nearly happened is as much my fault as your own. One would think that I would have learned my lesson ten years ago."

The unspoken comparison was like a slap in the face. "I am not Hatfill, Miranda."

"I know," she said. "You made no attempt to force yourself upon me, as he did. I came into your arms willingly. Perhaps I was still pretending that you were the man of my dreams, so I was no less responsible than yourself." Gathering the remnants of her pride, she faced him. "I did not run, nor did I protest when you touched me. I could have done either, had I chosen. As you say, the night has a magic all its own and the combination with moonlight can be dangerous indeed."

He should have been thankful that she was willing to absolve him from blame. However, gratitude was definitely not the emotion that he was feeling. "And you would have let him kiss you, this phantom of yours?"

"The man of my dreams? Indeed and I would have returned his gesture of affection with equal fervor. That is part and parcel of loving someone," she said, recalling the times she had come upon her parents holding each other close, kissing and laughing like moonlings. Her heart contracted. That had always been her dream, to share the intimacy of a lifetime of loving. But even that hope had been compromised. Now that sharing of hearts seemed as much beyond her grasp as magic itself.

"You speak with an air of authority, Miranda," Adam asked. "Are you in love, then?"

"I have hopes," she whispered, trying to think of Martin,

but she could not even visualize his face. She could come to love him, she told herself. He was fond of her, at least. Many a marriage had succeeded with far less.

"And does he return your affection?" Adam queried.

"I think so," she answered wondering how he had managed to tap into the doubts in her mind.

"But you are not certain?" Adam asked, knowing that he had no right to question her so closely.

"I should never have come out here," Miranda said, closing the matter before he could dig more deeply. "But the temptation to get away from the Ton's eternal surveillance was beyond resisting. Now I must go back before my absence is remarked."

"They are far too busy with Hatfill," Adam said.

"And when they are done picking his bones, they will move back to the main course with additional relish, sauced now with the spice of speculation. There are many who think that Hatfill has been cursed, even though he chose his own bane by making Ruby Simms his lady. Now they will wonder if this incident is part of Wodesby's revenge as well."

"I had not thought of that," Adam murmured guiltily.

Miranda softened. "As you said, it was no more than the cad deserved and I must confess, in my accounts, the spectacle was well worth what it may cost me during this short stay in Town. 'Tis time beyond memory since I have enjoyed so hearty a laugh. Still, there will be more than enough on my plate tonight without the question of virtue being added to my portion."

" 'Short stay?' You and your mother are planning to leave London?" he asked.

"We were only planning a brief visit, until Mother made the promise of Wodesby protection," Miranda told him. "However, once Damien returns and we can leave your safety in his hands, I see no reason to remain."

"And you can return to the man of your dreams? A fellow who *might* view you with affection?" Adam asked, wondering at the angry edge to his voice.

"I fail to see what affair it is of yours, milord," she

snapped. "'Tis fortunate indeed that Thorpe stopped us before matters progressed from shame to blame."

"You wish to claim that the cat we heard was Thorpe?" Adam asked.

"He is mostly here for your sake, to be where I cannot," Miranda said with a shrug. "However, it would not be the first time that he has kept me from making a fool of myself."

"I do not need your protection, Miss Wilton, nor that of your mother, your brother, or any of your daft kinsmen," Adam said, his lips tightening to an angry line. "And you can call off the damned cat too!"

"Ah, milord, you do not mean to tell me that you actually credit that you are being followed by a feline," Miranda shot back, a sparkle of challenge in her eye. "To acknowledge such unusual abilities in a cat would almost require that you believe in the supernatural."

"I believe in nothing!" Adam protested.

"Ah, yes, a pity that. But you go well beyond lack of faith," Miranda mused. "You go about like a Grand Inquisitor, seeking out the heretics who deny your antimetaphysical creed. Is that your aim tonight? Is Barone the victim chosen to be burned on your stake of Reason?"

"You confuse the matter. Lady Pelton is the victim in this case," Adam said. "Having seen Barone, would you dare deny that the man is a fraud? Or would you claim that he has this nebulous talent that you define as magic?"

Miranda shifted uncomfortably. "No, there is no reason to believe that he is a mage. But what harm does he do? I have met Lady Pelton and she strikes me as a woman to be pitied. Why should she be denied comfort? She loved her husband dearly."

"Then let him lay buried!" Adam said vehemently. "Let her cry and mourn so that she may go on living. But as long as men like Barone feed upon the corpse of her love, she will be forever half in the grave with Pelton. And penniless as well, if Barone has his way. The mediums have well-nigh bankrupted her. Just as my—" He stopped himself. "You go in first and I will follow later," Adam suggested smoothly. "We had best not be seen returning together."

Never before had Miranda witnessed such remarkable control. It was as if he had suddenly donned a mask of ceremony. Raw emotion was buried beneath a civilized veneer in a cat's wink. Whatever lay hidden beyond the verge of revelation must have been painful indeed. She wished that there was some comfort that she could offer him, something that she could say to mend fences between them. But his stony expression precluded any further conversation. There was nothing she could do but leave him staring out into the shadowed garden.

No more than the length of a quadrille and a country set were required for Miranda's prediction to come to pass. Rumor did a rapid dance round the room. Lady Jersey swore that she had seen a cat run under the refreshment table just prior to Hatfill's escapade. Reports were rife that Hatfill had been seeking revenge on his old feline nemesis. No matter that Adam told them that Hatfill had merely been chasing after a lost coin. Stories of sorcery were far more to the taste of the Ton than arid actuality. Even Hatfill himself began to subscribe to the fabrication. Better to be thought a stalwart champion, confronting an uncanny foe, than a clumsy fool, seeking a lost sovereign.

With every whisper and stare, Miranda's chin rose marginally. Each speculative glance was squarely met and it was usually the furtively seeking eyes that fell first. She had a backbone of steel, Adam thought in admiration. But by the time he claimed his second dance, it was obvious to him that the talk was taking its toll upon her. "I fear that I have done you a terrible wrong, Miranda," he said as they came together in the pattern. "I fully intend to make a complete public admission."

Miranda smiled wearily as they clasped hands and paced the floor in stately measures. "They will not believe you or will claim that I have put some spell on you to cause you to take the blame. And even if they did place credence in your confession, it would be no less of a scandal for you to have contrived to humiliate Hatfill for my sake. I want no duels conducted in my name. Besides, it is just as well if people believe that I have magical powers at present. With Mama incapacitated and Damien in transit, it may be only the Wodesby mystique that stands between you and disaster."

"Miranda . . ."

She sighed, turning to face him as he bowed. "Yes, yes, I am well aware; you place no faith in witchery. Nonetheless, there is naught that you can do to untwine this tangle, Adam. So leave it be." She curtsied, rubbing the side of her neck unconsciously as they parted in the figure, changing partners momentarily.

Adam paid only cursory attention to the new lady at his side. His eyes were fixed upon Miranda as she went through the motions of the dance. Clearly, her partner had said something, for her eyes flashed anger and flags of color flushed her cheeks.

"What did he say?" Adam asked when she returned to his side at the end of the set. "If he dared to give you insult . . ." To his surprise, her lower lip began to tremble.

"You are a kind man, Adam Chapbrook," she said, trying to blink back an incipient tear. "And I thank you for the gift of your indignation, but my battles must be my own."

"Kindness has naught to do with it," Adam said, touched by her gallant effort, but even the armor of her pride appeared to have its chinks. "Who will protect my protector but me? Why not excuse yourself from Lady Pelton's spirit soirée and go home?"

Miranda looked at him in surprise. "Do you forget that it is only my nodding acquaintance with demonic company that gains you entry? If I do not accompany you, I sincerely doubt that Lady Enderby will consent to have you along."

"Beelzebub and I will contrive, somehow," Adam said with an impish look that quickly faded. "However, I am more concerned about you. Participating in this nonsense will only add fuel to the blaze of hellfire about you."

He was willing to give up access to Lady Pelton's séance for her sake. The notion left her feeling oddly buoyant and suddenly, the murmurs and the mockery did not seem to matter nearly as much. "There is scarcely anything left to be said. I am not ashamed of my family, Adam, nor do I deny what they are. My only regret is that I lack their gifts. Besides, I really must go with you and Lady Enderby if only to make sure that you are well—"

"Do not dare say 'protected,' Miranda," Adam warned with half a grin. "I do not wish to hear any more of that foolishness. The time is already late and by the time we arrive at Lady Pelton's it will be bare hours before the cock crows."

"I have long left the nursery set," Miranda said with a laugh, "so you need not fear that I will nod off before the spirits come calling. The darkness before dawn is the best part of the night, and actually the most propitious time for delving beyond the veil."

"Barone wants the participants to be weary, I suspect," Adam said as he took her arm and led her toward the newly laid refreshment table. "The better to perpetrate his frauds. That is the usual way of it. Anything that will make the victim more readily gullible."

"I take it, then, that you have been to a number of these?" Miranda asked.

"Dozens," Adam replied bitterly. "My first meeting with the mystics occurred at the age of eight, directly after my mother's death. That was the beginning of what was to become a regular parade of charlatans. My mother, you see, had made a pact with my father. If either one of them were to pass on first, an attempt would be made to contact the soul of the living survivor. Between them, they chose a phrase and if either received those words from beyond the grave, it would provide absolute proof that the afterlife existed. But the pretenders never guessed the message. That did not stop Papa, though—it was always going to be the next oracle of the netherworld or when she failed, the one after that."

As they made their way through the throng, Miranda mulled over what she had heard. Now she began to understand his antagonism to things magical. In Adam's wistful voice she had caught a glimpse of a disillusioned little boy, missing his mother, longing for that gentle touch from the beyond. She imagined what her life would have been if her mother had become so dangerously obsessed with the here-

after when her father had died so tragically. It was clear that
the late Lord Brand had ignored the here-and-now when his
young son had needed him desperately.

"I soon found that they were all frauds," Adam said, handing her a filled glass. With a glacial glare that made Brummel's frosty stare appear warm, the marquess routed two
young sprigs from a quiet nook. "Watching for their tricks became something of a game and I became rather adept at
botching up their works. Word must have spread, because I
found myself barred from the charlatans' shows as a 'disturbing influence.' Seems the spirits couldn't disport themselves
in my presence. Then Father sent me off to Eton and I found
that some of the fakery that I had learned from those frauds
was quite useful. More than one bully was foiled without the
need to resort to fists."

"Sometimes the very illusion of power can be as frightening as the reality," Miranda ventured. "I take it that you used
their credulity as a weapon?"

Adam nodded.

"Then how did you differ from those cheats that you so dis-
dained?" Miranda asked. "Were you not gulling your enemies
by playing to their fears?"

"Surely, the difference is obvious," Adam said, his brows
knitting. "The ends—"

Miranda broke in. "In this case, your physical safety, your
status in the school, justified the means—the chicanery you so
deplore," she concluded, a smile lurking. "As long as you feel
that the goals are laudable, it seems, you will not eschew
methods you might deem questionable when employed by
others."

Her barely suppressed humor irked him. "Do you call me a
hypocrite, Miranda?"

"I would not dare," Miranda said. " 'Tis merely a matter of
interest. I must confess that witches regularly must resort to
such stratagems. Oftentimes, people's problems can be solved
without the use of power. A pinch of powder, a puff or two of
smoke for effect, and a little common sense will solve nine
troubles out of ten."

"And what would one of your proper witches do with a

question such as 'Uncle Ned, where did you put the teapot, before you stuck your spoon in the wall?'" Adam asked.

"Arrange to raise Uncle Ned's spirit of course," Miranda replied in an undertone, her eyes twinkling with mischief. "There are ways of projecting the voice to make it appear as if the sound is coming from elsewhere. And Uncle Ned, crusty old badger that he was, would reply 'Leave me be, ye blatherin' ninny. Got better things t'be about than lookin' fer yer damned teapot. Look to it yerself, daft fool, iffen yer want ter find it.'"

"And what if it was a truly important matter?" Adam asked, hard put to keep from grinning at her masterful recreation of a disembodied old codger.

Miranda's expression grew serious. "Once, only once, can I recall a matter important enough to truly seek in the beyond," she said, a frisson of remembrance fluttering down her spine. "To disturb a soul's rest once must call on the deepest of magic. 'Tis not a task to be heedlessly undertaken, I assure you. No witch in my acquaintance would pierce the veil for mere lucre, not with the risk so high."

"Risk?" Adam asked. Her hand had grown cold, trembling in his palm. And though her countenance was outwardly calm, there was ominous memory swimming in those azure depth, like a soldier recalling a battlefield.

"The valley where the shadows of death dwell is anathema to the living. Few souls wish to be disturbed over something as trivial as Uncle Ned's teapot or someone wondering if Auntie Maude really did end up in hell. An angry spirit can be a powerful threat to the living who seek it," Miranda said, wondering why she was bothering to explain when he would only mock. "Moreover, from what the journals tell me, the Elysian fields are almost indescribable in their beauty. They say that there is a matchless sense of peace and beyond the horizon, a beckoning light. The temptation to dwell there forever or go explore that light is almost impossible to resist."

"Heaven?" Adam asked.

"Not quite," Miranda said. "As far as I can determine, the fields of shadow constitute something of a borderland, a place of dreams where two entirely different realities overlap.

Sometimes, souls with unfinished business will wait at the very edge of the veil, in instances even crossing briefly to our plane of being. They are the incorporeals, what you might call ghosts. As for what is within the light, I cannot say."

"And what happens to those who cannot deny the lure of the Fields, or follow that light of which you speak?" Adam inquired.

"The single séance that I attended was conducted by a woman named Gabriella, one of the Elders, close upon a century in age. She was born in the final years of the Great Persecutions; her mother hanged as a sorceress. A talisman of tremendous power was missing, its location known only to my late father. Gabriella attempted to raise his shade. But I suppose with her life so near the end of its course, the attraction of that ultimate harmony was beyond her ability to resist. Her soul left us."

Questions crowded Adam's mind, but the bleak look in Miranda's eyes forestalled them. She spoke errant nonsense, naturally. Doubtless there was some other reason for old Gabriella's death, but despite every logical explanation that he could produce, he could not keep himself from imagining his mother and father, dwelling together at last in that tranquil light.

The orchestra was about to begin the next dance and Adam reluctantly returned Miranda to Lady Enderby's side.

"The hour grows late, milord," Lady Enderby said pointedly. "Miss Wilton and I shall soon be leaving."

Adam checked his watch and was surprised to find that the midnight hour had passed. Hastily, he made his farewells to his hostess and hurried out to find his carriage. The line of waiting vehicles stretched in front of the Millford home extended well beyond Grosvenor Square and around South Audley Street. However, Adam's carriage was not among them. He kept walking until he came to the mews that backed Upper Grosvenor Street. As instructed, the closed vehicle was waiting in the deserted corner to facilitate a discreet change of costume.

"Copley?" he called softly, but there was no sign of his coachman. He heard a soft moan from within the carriage and the horses whinnied restlessly. Something was wrong. The door opened and a burly figure emerged.

"Decided ter quit yer capers early, did yer, Brand?" The man declared. "Should 'ave enjoyed it while yer could still dance, laddie. Cos, when we're done wiv yer, yer won't be walkin', much less prancin' about, aye lads?"

Adam whirled at the sound of laughter from behind him. Two more bruisers had appeared from the shadows. Guttmacher's men, by the look of them. Desperately, Adam thought of the pistols secreted in the carriage, but there was no way to get to his weapons. All he had was the knife at his belt and his wits. At present, though, neither his blade nor his intellect appeared sharp enough to extricate him from a hopeless situation. With no way out, Adam determined to go down fighting. A marmalade cat arched on a fencepost at the end of the alleyway, yowling at the moonlight. For a brief moment, he felt an absurd hope, but the feline streaked away into the darkness.

"It's scarcely sporting, is it?" Adam said, effecting an air of nonchalance. "Three men, big brawny sons of the Fancy like yourselves, against one man. I would wager that I could take any one of you, two fists against two fists."

The one who appeared to be their leader laughed. "A mort-waisted nob like yerself."

Adam pulled the knife from his belt and held it up to glitter in the moonlight. "I know how to use this, but I'll throw it aside for a chance at a fair scrap. What have you got to lose, gents, I ask you? Even if I win, do you honestly believe I can take you on, one after another and emerge with a whole hide? What do you say, lads, for the sake of sport, eh?"

"Dunno," the leader said, shaking his head.

"C'mon Jack, like 'e says, whatcher got ter lose?" his compatriot asked. "Wicked-lookin' blade 'e's got an' if 'e goes ter cuttin' tain't my purty mug what's goin' in first. I'll be th' one ter take 'im on man ter man, iffen yer afeard, tire 'im out for yer."

Jack roared at the insult. "If there be any takin' 'is nibs on first, it'll be me, Fred. Yerself an' Tom be gettin' yer chances if there's aught left o' him when I'm finished." He spit in his palms and balled up his fists. "Pitch yer knife, laddie, and say yer last prayers."

Adam's house key went sailing into the darkness with a satisfying clatter. He palmed his knife, secreting it in his belt as he slipped out of his jacket. Used now, it would do little good against three men, but later, if he succeeded in whittling down the odds against him, it might come in handy.

Miranda waited with Lady Enderby for their carriage to be brought round.

"I cannot see what is keeping Tom Coachman," Lady Enderby fumed.

"'Tis Lord Brand's absence that troubles me," Miranda murmured. "He had promised to meet us here in disguise."

"Well, we shall just have to leave without him," Lady Enderby sniffed.

A marmalade figure sailed up the marble steps, mewing when it reached Miranda's feet.

"Filthy creature!" Lady Enderby exclaimed, drawing back her skirts. "Get back, Miranda, before it soils your gown."

Unheeding, Miranda bent down, listening to Thorpe's labored mewls. "Go back and help him if you can," she said softly. "I am on my way."

"Miranda," Lady Enderby demanded. "Where are you going?"

"I believe that is my mother's cat," Miranda called back over her shoulder. "She will be dreadfully upset to hear that he has gotten loose. I must fetch him back before he gets lost in London."

Before Lady Enderby could demand that she stop, Miranda had raced toward the lounging group of coachmen. "A guinea to the man who gets that cat," she called, pointing after the rapidly vanishing Thorpe. Immediately, the men detached themselves from the walls and fences, following after the golden feline.

Even hampered by her skirts, Miranda was well ahead of the pack as they rounded South Audley and she nearly lost them as she ran into the mews. The marquess stood over a burly shadow stretched out on the ground as two other men advanced toward him menacingly.

"Adam!" Miranda exclaimed, aghast at the blood dripping from his lip.

"Well, well, wot 'ave we 'ere?" Fred gave a low, long whistle. "Prime goods! Belong to you, Brand? Guttmacher dinnent say nuthin' bout 'er."

"Leave here at once, I warn you," Miranda demanded. "Or else you will be sorry."

"Miranda," Adam groaned. "Run!"

"Nonsense," Miranda said, reaching into her reticule. "I am here to protect you, milord."

"Queer in the attic," Tom said with a leer, advancing on her, "but when a Bedlam wench 'as yer looks, luvie, what's in th' brainbox don't count much, do it?"

A yowling ball of fur flew through the air and Tom fell to the ground beneath the weight of a hissing, spitting cannon-ball. Adam launched himself at Fred.

"Oh, dear," said Miranda, sliding her pistol back into the reticule. With no clear target, the weapon was too dangerous to use.

The sound of a dozen running pairs of feet echoed down the alleyway. It was the coachmen. "There he is!" Miranda called to them, pointing to the writhing mass of clawing cat. "Get him."

At that cry, Jack raised his head, and seeing the brightly liveried throng heading his way, he staggered up and out in the direction of Park Street. With a Herculean effort, Tom pulled Thorpe loose and stumbled to his feet, running as fast as his bow legs could carry him. As for Fred, he took one look at the pointing surging mob and vaulted a garden gate to melt into the shadows.

"Poor, poor puss," Miranda said, lifting Thorpe gently from the hands of an enterprising coachman and placing him on the cushions of Adam's waiting vehicle. She untied the marquess's man and left him massaging his aching muscles while she returned to the milling crowd. "Milord, I have promised a guinea for the first to reach my dear kitty."

Adam snorted, wiping ineffectually at the blood on his lip. "A ten-pound tiger! Dear kitty, my eye."

"We will see to your eye in a moment," Miranda said in an undertone. "However, if you would be so kind as to give a coin to this fellow who wears Lord MacLean's livery, for I believe he came in first, it would be much appreciated. In fact, I think that each of these fine fellows deserves at least a half-crown for their trouble. I shall gladly pay you back, sir, if you would take care of it for me now," she added sweetly.

Adam moaned as he picked up his soiled jacket and pulled out his purse to count out the coins.

As the last of the coachmen pulled his forelock and gave his thanks, Miranda gave him a message. "Tell Lady Enderby that Lord Brand and I will be along shortly. It appears that his lordship got into a bit of an altercation."

"This is entirely improper," Adam muttered as his coachman lit the carriage lights, "not to mention dangerous."

"Why don't you take a walk while I put your master to rights?" Miranda suggested to the man who was moving awkwardly about. "It will take the prickles out of your legs."

"But beggin' your pardon, Miss, what if those bruisers return?" the servant asked.

"We will be well protected; go on with you," Miranda said, pulling her handkerchief from her reticule.

Making sure that his pistols were easily accessible beneath the seat, the marquess nodded his permission and the coachman walked slowly out toward South Audley Street.

"Hold this, please," Miranda demanded, pushing her reticule toward him. "I will need both hands to tend you."

Adam's arm dropped at the unexpected weight. "What do you have in here, lead?" he asked.

"No, iron, actually," Miranda commented, gently wiping at the blood at the corner of his mouth. "Iron shot is proof against magic as well as violence offered by ruffians of the more common sort, such as the individuals we encountered this evening."

Adam's eyes went wide as he pulled the brace of petite pistols from the dainty carry-all. "No wonder you had no room for your purse."

"They are not very accurate over a distance," Miranda said, touching the bridge of his nose delicately. It was not broken, but it would puff before the night was done. "Nonetheless, I can shoot the heart of an ace at twenty paces, so they will do well enough if our friends take a notion to return. Do you think that they intend to come back?"

Adam shook his head, speechless with astonishment.

"I concur," Miranda said. "However, one ought to be prepared for all eventualities, do you not think so?" Without waiting for an answer, she held up her hand. "Watch my finger with your eyes, Adam," she commanded. "It may seem odd, but over the years my family has found the method excellent for determining if there has been damage to vision. I wish to see if you can follow the motion." She moved her fingers randomly, observing as he tracked their progress. Satisfied, she gave a sigh. "You seem to be walking well, if a bit unsteadily. Do you feel as if anything was broken?"

"You had best be getting back to Lady Enderby," Adam said, trying to martial his thoughts despite her nearness.

"After I determine if you have taken any injury. Are you going to cut up stiff about my being unaccompanied? You forget that Thorpe is present," Miranda said, glancing significantly at the cat dozing upon the seat by the open door of the carriage.

"The extraordinary Thorpe," Adam said, wincing as he shook he head.

"Ah, so at last you admit that Thorpe is no ordinary cat," Miranda said, holding Adam's chin steady as she dabbed away the last of the blood.

Adam enjoyed the soft sensation of her skin upon his and considered feigning another ache or two for the continued pleasure of her examination. However, bare shreds remained of Miranda's reputation and although she seemed willing to whistle her name to the wind, he was not, her feline attendant notwithstanding. "Your mother's animal is more intelligent than most," Adam said, turning the subject resolutely from magic. "But it seems small wonder that she has set him to watch you, especially since you have this absurd tendency to place yourself in danger."

"With a brace of pistols in my purse and a dozen men at my heels? And you dare to call *me* absurd? I saved your wretched neck, milord, though you are too chuckleheaded to admit it. If anyone was at risk, it was Thorpe." She stroked the resting cat affectionately.

"And what of wandering into alleyways with amorous men?" Adam asked sotto voce, drawing closer to her. Aloud he wondered, "Is he asleep?"

"The poor dear is exhausted," Miranda declared. "I doubt if a bomb could shock him into wakefulness."

"Shall we find out?" Adam asked, setting the reticule and its contents on the floor of the coach. Giving way to an impulse that had been building all evening, he swept her into his arms, ignoring the soreness as his lips pressed against hers. Hungrily, he tasted her, the salty tang of his blood mingling with the sweetness of her mouth. Pulse pounding, his craving grew until existence was reduced to a maelstrom of sensation. Pain retreated as pleasure invaded, velvety darkness dimming the faint light of the coach lamp. Even the smells of the alleyway were overwhelmed by the delicate fragrance of lilac. But mingled within the tangle of sensuality was a curious sense of tenderness.

Magic. No other explanation was possible for this total bombardment of the senses, this feeling of utter defenselessness. Undone by a kiss that had seemed to plumb the depth of her being, Miranda tried to understand the nature of a spell that could produce such a welter of sensations. The feel of his fingers upon hers seemed to sap the strength from her bones, and the touch of his lips caused an explosion of contradictory reactions—cold and hot, light and darkness as her consciousness seemed to shatter and rebuild itself. In the space of a few seconds, her whole world had spun loose of its secure moorings. Yet that did not frighten her so much as the knowledge that this moment would have to end.

A deep, steady purr penetrated the periphery of Adam's awareness. Reluctantly, he pulled away from Miranda's softness to find a pair of sleepy green eyes staring steadily. "Your chaperone seems to be suggesting that we return to Lady Enderby," he said, taking her hand and bringing it to his lips. "I must seem an ungrateful cur. You saved my life and I have the audacity to chide you for it. Thank you, Miranda."

Thank you. Was that the meaning of his kiss, then? Nothing more than a gesture of gratitude? Miranda's soaring feelings plummeted earthward as she reached forlornly for some feather of dignity. He could not be allowed to see the plucked remnants of her pride. In desperation she took recourse in the prosaic. "How did you know what Thorpe said?" she asked.

"The language of chaperones is a universal tongue," Adam said, striving to match her nonchalance even as he attempted to reconcile this composed woman with the passionate Miranda that he had held in his arms barely a moment before. But no sign of that other Miranda remained, save a slight flush on her cheeks. However, that might just as well have been the token of mortification as the remnants of desire.

Perhaps she was more of a sorceress than she believed. Never before had he so lost control of himself, especially with a woman. Her mere presence was enough to cause him to out-Caliban Shakespeare's fictional barbarian. Even now, he wanted to slam the carriage door on that infernal feline, pull Miranda back into his arms, and kiss her until her cool air of detachment melted. Without incantation or charm, she had managed to transform him into a blundering savage.

Chapter 8

Several heavy applications of the knocker were required before the door of Pelton House creaked open.

"I am sorry, ladies, sir," the out-of-breath butler apologized. "But most of the staff gave notice last week. 'Tis only myself and my wife in this great house."

"Precious little loyalty in the serving class these days." Lady Enderby sniffed.

"Wouldn't say that. Servants need to live, same as the rest of us, Lady Enderby. Can't keep staff if ye don't pay 'em," the old man beside her commented in a creaking voice, thumping with the tip of his cane for emphasis. He handed the butler an old-fashioned tricorne, but kept on his gloves. "At my age, hands are forever cold," he explained.

Miranda watched Adam's performance with admiration. His hobble, unfortunately, was better than half-real and the broken blood vessels on his nose added measurably to the illusion of age. With the addition of a wig, waxy wrinkles, and a mildly puffing eye, his own uncle would he hard put to recognize him. However, his illusion had as much to do with his demeanor as his costume. His voice, walk, carriage, and deportment were entirely in keeping with the character that he had adopted.

"You would do credit to Drury Lane, milord," Miranda said quietly, as the butler went up to announce their arrival. "A pity you feel need to use your skills to cozen an old woman."

"Quite right, my dear," Lady Enderby said.

"'Tis not I who does the cozening," Adam said with quiet vehemence. "Take a look about you, Miranda. Not too long ago, this was considered one of the finest homes in London."

Miranda obeyed, scanning the dimly lit marbled hall. Signs of genteel decay were obvious. Careful scrubbing had not fully eliminated the outlines of missing picture frames, and the few bits of bric-a-brac were painstakingly set about to cover the gaps where larger items had once been displayed.

"She does not gamble?" Miranda questioned.

Adam shook his hoary head. "Only on her delusions, Miranda."

There were footsteps on the stair as Lady Pelton descended to greet them. "Oh, dear!" the sparrowlike woman twittered as she halted on the landing. "Hester, this will not do at all! Monsieur Barone was quite specific that this was to be a select affair with none but a few close friends."

"And I have followed his instructions." Lady Enderby huffed. "This is Miranda Wilton; she is a Wodesby, an unquestionable asset to any traffic with the spirits."

"A Wodesby!" Lady Pelton exclaimed.

Miranda braced herself for the usual gamut of reactions—horror, repugnance, curiosity. She nearly jumped in surprise as the petite lady embraced her heartily.

"How delightful!" Lady Pelton said, standing up on tiptoe to kiss Miranda's cheek. "You must be Vera's granddaughter. We were friends from the schoolroom, your grandmère and I. The Gwynn lands marched with ours."

"Grandmama Wodesby died when I was very young," Miranda said, recognizing Lady Pelton's cadence as the remnants of a Welsh lilt.

"Yes, I remember," Lady Pelton said. "Even magic cannot cure a broken heart and when your grandpapa passed so suddenly, it was as if she could not bear to go on. I know just how she felt."

Harsh lines of pain became more pronounced and Miranda could see the sorrow in the old woman's eyes. She did not know what to say and so remained silent.

"I remember when dear Pelton and I became betrothed. 'Twas the most fearsome experience of my life, I must own. Barely seventeen, I was, a country miss who had never stepped foot outside the county. There I was, courted by a foreign London man, whose language sounded harsh and strange. When I came crying to Vera, she calmed me, made me tea, and read me the cards. Pelton would be the great love of my life, she told me, and she was right!" She smiled in remembrance, then looked uncertainly at the man who stood in the entry.

"Name is Sedgewick, milady," Adam said, lacing his voice liberally with gravel and the creak of age. "Mr. Amos Sedgewick. Hope that you don't mind the intrusion, but when I heard that Monsieur Barone was planning to call upon the spirits, I begged Lady Enderby for the opportunity. Lost a dear one myself and I'd pay well just to hear Edgar's voice again." There was a movement upon the upstairs landing, making it apparent that the conversation was being monitored. "Many's the brandy we'd share at White's and talk over our days on the sea. How he missed his wife, Marguerite, and though he's with her at last, sure he'd want to know how I'm spending all the blunt he left me. No children, y'know."

Lady Pelton sighed. "Pelton and I were never blessed, either, and I must say that his heir has been most unkind. Won't even make me a loan, even though Monsieur Barone's powers are world renowned. That is why I have allowed a few friends to share this experience with me, much as I would wish the monsieur to focus entirely on my dear Pelton, especially tonight. We would have been wed fifty years today. But when needs must . . ." She tucked Miranda's hand into hers and started up the stairs, drawing the young woman along with her. "The other guests have already arrived."

Adam recognized most of the other participants. Lady Westwood was one of the more notorious dabblers in the occult. A particular favorite of the card readers and spirit summoners, she was extremely easy to please. Every charlatan in London knew the peculiar characteristics of her late, lamented pug, Manfred, his favored canine pursuit of leading the footmen on frenzied phaeton chases, his disdain of anything other than the choicest sirloin. A ghostly bark or two from the beyond was usually worth at least half a guinea.

Lord Ropwell's case was entirely different. From the rumors that were circulating, his lordship was motivated by more than mere sentiment. Even while his lady had lived, whispers of scandal had floated on the seas of gossip. Rop-well's jealousy had been notorious both within the bounds of matrimony and without. It was said that he had more than once resorted to pistols before breakfast over imagined tres-passes upon his wife's honor. A former mistress of Ropwell's had been mysteriously disfigured soon after she had informed him that she had taken new protector.

Ropwell was obviously desperate if he was hoping that his late lady would deign to answer him from the hereafter. While the exact circumstances of Lady Ropwell's untimely death were still disputed by the scandalmongers, it was well known that she had hidden the family jewels just before her untimely demise. If those fields that Miranda described existed, Adam had little doubt that Lady Ropwell was gamboling about and thoroughly enjoying her husband's discomfiture. Payment in advance would be prudent, if Barone was expecting to collect anything from his lordship, who was well into dun's territory.

As for Mrs. Bittward, she was a well-meaning woman with too much money and much the same matter in her skull as in Sadler's balloon. An infamous neophyte of current spiritual modes, she would be the most devoted of Hannah More's dis-ciples on Sunday, handing out tracts to all and sundry. By Wednesday, she was praising Guttmacher to the skies, ex-tolling the virtues of his healing powers. Now, on Friday, it was obviously Barone's turn to be the most sought-after soothsayer and by Monday next, she would doubtless be someone else's devoted follower.

Lady Pelton's library had been chosen for the séance. A windowless chamber, darkly paneled, it was the perfect site for disembodied chicanery. Adam stroked his false beard, his bushy wig obscuring his eyes as he inspected the room for the typical accoutrements of the charlatan. Barone had done his work well, not an obvious device in sight. Adam was just about to go to the shelves on the pretext of examining the books, but the conjurer chose that moment to make his en-trance.

Dressed in unrelieved black, Barone made an impressive sight. His wife, also darkly garbed, arrived just behind him.

Adam concealed a smile. The magician's chosen method was now apparent.

"Lady Pelton." Barone raised the old woman's hand to his lips. "I have consulted with the spirits and they are much agitated. I fear we may not be able to continue tonight."

Miranda cast a stealthy glance at Adam, wondering how Barone could possibly have discovered his disguise.

Lady Pelton was aghast. "But surely Beelzebub—"

"'Tis not Beelzebub this time," Barone said smoothly. "I know Beelzebub goes to Brighton this evening. However, my guides demand some personal token from you, to assure them of your sincerity. They have chosen your necklace."

"But that is all that I have left," Lady Pelton said, stricken, putting a protective hand over the diamond piece. "Pelton gave this to me on the first anniversary of our marriage."

"So I have told them, milady," Barone said solemnly. "I tell them it is precious to you, but they demand no less for their service. So I fear we cannot speak to your *chèr* spouse."

Miranda watched as the elderly woman struggled, fingering the necklace nervously as she tried to decide between the sentiment of a lifetime and the pressures of the present. Barone's expression was outwardly sympathetic, but the light of greed shone brightly in his eyes.

Adam sidled closer to her. "No harm, Miranda?" he asked softly.

"There is a thin wire running from the seat at the head of the table," she whispered. "Black against black is tantamount to invisibility."

Adam nodded almost imperceptibly, his mood rising as he realized that she was effectively declaring her allegiance.

With trembling hand, Lady Pelton unclasped the necklace and put it into Barone's grasping fingers. "Are the spirits satisfied now, Monsieur?" she asked, twin tears sliding down her wrinkled cheek. "Will they let me speak to my beloved Pelton?"

Barone inclined his head in a listening attitude as he placed the necklace in his pocket. "They are pleased with your gift, milady, and even now they go to seek your husband beyond the veil. *Vite, vite,* we must be seated. Lady Pelton, to my

right, my wife, then Miss Wilton. Monsieur Sedgewick, you
will take the place on Miss Wilton's right; Lady Westwood,
then Lord Ropwell, Madame Bittward, Lady Enderby and
then our circle will be complete."

The company seated itself according to his direction.

Miranda tripped on the carpet as she started toward her
seat. Adam frowned as Barone caught and steadied her, his
hands lingering a shade too long. Ruthlessly, Adam repressed
a Caliban-like urge to take Barone by his neck-linen and
shake him till his teeth rattled.

"*Pardonez-moi, Monsieur*," Miranda apologized, looking
deep into his eyes. It was like looking into a cesspit, full of
dirty thoughts and filthy deeds, but he was fully distracted, as
she had hoped, while her hand slipped into his pocket.

"But of course, Mademoiselle Wilton," he said, momentarily dazzled by her smile.

"The hour is growing late, *chèr*," Madame Barone said, an
edge in her voice. "We must begin."

At his nod, his wife blew out the candles one by one and
the room was plunged into total darkness.

Barone's call cut through the black. "Spirits, hear me!" he
roared.

"He must believe them deaf," Adam murmured. Those Caliban urges were coming upon him again. Even the smell of
Miranda's perfume in the darkness was enough to rouse the
buried brute, recollecting the softness of her touch, the
warmth of her lips.

A delicate chiming filled the air. "Lady Westwood,"
Barone's voice slid down the register. "Does the name 'Manfred' have any meaning for you?"

"Oh yes, Monsieur," Lady Westwood sang out eagerly.
"How does Manfred do?"

"This message, I do not understand. It is most strange, almost like, like . . . the barking of *un chien*. He says that there
are many phaetons where he is, milady. Did this Manfred
enjoy handling the reins?" Barone asked in feigned puzzlement.

"Oh, no," Lady Westwood giggled. "Manfred chased
phaetons. He was a dog, you see."

"Now it makes sense, milady. He speaks of sirloin every day," the conjuror went on.

"Tell him that I have kept his room just as he left it," Lady Westwood said.

"I shall . . . no, his bark is fading, milady. Another spirit takes his place."

"Botheration!" Lady Westwood exclaimed. "Perhaps tomorrow night? Surely we could make an arrangement. I must tell Manfred the news about Lady Harper's nasty cat."

"Madame is no longer in her seat," Miranda informed Adam under cover of Lady Westwood's complaints.

The chiming clamor came again from the center of the table.

"Another change in spirits," Adam murmured.

"James?" A feminine voice spoke from the farthest corner of the room. "James, are you there?"

"Felicity?" Lord Ropwell asked. "Is that you?"

"You wish to know about the jewels, James?" The disembodied tones echoed in the room.

"It was very naughty of you, Felicity," Ropwell declared, unable to control the hard edge in his speech. "Where are they?"

"You are unkind, Ropwell; I think that I will go away."

"Felicity! Felicity!" Ropwell roared. "Tell me where you hid them, you bitch!"

"I am sorry, milord," Barone said. "Spirits are such fickle creatures. You must speak to them kindly or else they will flee. Your Felicity has gone."

"Get her back!" Ropwell demanded. "I will double your price, damn you. Get her back!"

"I do not think that Lady Ropwell will return this evening," Barone said firmly. "I would suggest that a private séance would be best for you, milord. We will talk of this later." He pulled gently at the wire, causing the chimes to sound lightly. "Meanwhile, monsieur Sedgewick, I have a word from a man named Edgar."

"Not Edgar Penstreet!" Adam cackled.

"The same. He says that he still recalls those delightful evenings at White's and your days together at sea."

"Does he, now?" Adam said, keeping his sarcasm under firm rein.

"He wishes to speak to you again, Monsieur, at further length, but he must go now, for Marguerite calls."

"Just like that, Marguerite was. Always drawing old Edgar off just as the conversation got interesting," Adam said, rising from his seat quietly. Somewhere in the corner of the room was Madame Barone. Now that Mr. Penstreet had been called upon and was not likely to be addressed again, Adam could safely attempt to locate her. Luckily, the chamber was sparsely furnished, diminishing the chance of an inadvertent spill.

"Mrs. Bittward, it was the spirit of your husband that you wished to address *n'est-ce pas*?" Barone asked. "You were quite anxious to see how he fares."

"Yes, I have always wondered about Bernard," Mrs. Bittward declared. "Can you summon him for me?"

"Concentrate upon him, Mrs. Bittward," Barone demanded, pulling the wire to start the clamor. "Concentrate."

Softly the notes of a flute rippled from the corner. "Your husband, he was fond of music, yes?" Barone asked.

"It was his passion," Mrs. Bittward stated excitedly. "Though he was more appreciative of violins than flutes."

"He is surrounded by music, I see, Madame. Angelic choirs, heavenly harps," Barone added.

"Bittward? He is in heaven, you say?" came Mrs. Bittward's startled question.

"Yes, Madame," said Barone, embroidering upon the story. "He hears the angels sing daily and wishes that you could hear the glorious music!"

"No!" Mrs. Bittward cried, rising from the table. "That is impossible, impossible, I say. You lie, Monsieur! You lie!"

"Calm yourself, Madame," Barone said, his voice rising in agitation. "You are provoking the spirits."

"You charlatan!" she exploded. "Bernard was a sinner whose vices knew no bounds. He died in a brothel and the loose women wept for joy, I was told. If he is anywhere, he is in the deepest pit of hell. Heaven, indeed!"

"Redemption is possible for all, Mrs. Bittward," Barone said, trying to recover control of the situation.

" 'Wishes that I could hear the glorious music!' Indeed! The man who filled our box at the opera with his lightskirts?" Mrs. Bittward bellowed, but the force of her roar was momentarily transcended by a shriek that came from the corner of the room, followed by the sound of scuffling.

Miranda took the cue. She ran to the door and pulled it open, letting light shine into the shadows.

"Demons!" Lord Ropwell yelled.

"Beelzebub," Lady Enderby screamed.

"Madame Barone," Miranda said calmly. " ' T w a s she that was causing those manifestations." Using a taper from the hall, she lit the candles upon the table to reveal the erstwhile Mr. Sedgewick, his wig askew, holding the struggling Madame Barone.

"Brand! You are supposed to be Brighton bound!" Barone squealed.

"And miss the opportunity to see you and your charming wife once again?" Adam asked, trying to keep the woman's wrists firmly in his grasp. "Once I heard that you had reneged on our little deal, I sent Prinny my regrets."

"Unhand my wife, Brand," Barone demanded.

"Gladly, if she will keep her hands from me." Lord Brand complied, skillfully catching her escaping wrist before she could deliver a slap. His face had already taken enough abuse for the evening. "Lord Ropwell, ladies, take note of the flute in Madame Barone's fingers; also recall the direction from which those noises that you heard came."

"Pay no attention, mesdames, monsieurs," Barone pleaded. "Lord Brand has sworn to ruin me, for he hates those of us who commune with the spirits. He will use any pretext."

"And I suppose Lord Brand is responsible for this?" Miranda asked angrily, pulling on the wire near Barone's chair. The tinkling noise that they had heard to announce the arrivals of spirits sounded beneath the table once again. "Check below here and you will see the source," she added. "A simple set of chimes."

"Lady Pelton's jewels, Barone," Adam demanded, his hand

out. "And the money that you swindled from these people, or
else I shall call in the magistrate."

With a scowl, Barone took the purse from his pocket and
threw it upon the table. "You will regret this, Brand."

"The necklace!" Adam insisted.

Barone felt in his pocket, then frantically dug deeper. "It is
not here."

"Perhaps the spirits took it?" Lady Enderby suggested.

"Are you looking for this?" Miranda asked, the diamonds
twinkling in her palm. Stepping to the other side of the table,
she fastened the necklace around Lady Pelton's neck. "I have
held this since the beginning of the séance, so either your
greedy spirit guides are incredibly stupid or, as we have just
proven, they are the products of deceit and subterfuge. Get out
of here, Barone, and do not dare try your game in London
again. For if Brand's enmity does not suffice, I shall see to it
that both the Wodesbys and my Du Le Fey cousins place a
curse upon you."

Madame Barone blanched. "You are a relation of the comte
Du Le Fey, Mademoiselle?"

"Étienne, le comte, is my cousin, Madame. Though our two
countries are often in conflict, I am sure that a malediction
upon a worm like your husband would not impinge on Étienne's sense of patriotism," Miranda said.

Madame Barone grabbed her husband's arm. "Come *chèr*,
we must leave at once."

"But our equipment," Barone protested.

"Equipment, Philippe can make for us new," his wife said,
dragging him along. "But that one," she glanced nervously
back over her shoulder at Miranda. "That one needs no wires
or device to summon demons. The Gypsies, even they speak
the name Du Le Fey with respect. We shall bother your
friends no more, Lady," she declared with a bob of her head.

"I take your word, Madame," Miranda said. "And in the
event that your husband forgets himself, I have three hairs
from his head. I pray that there will be no need to send them
on to my cousin Étienne."

"*Non, non*, Mademoiselle, I assure you," Madame Barone
said, her face grey as ash. With a final tug, she pulled the

shaken conjurer from the room, slamming the door shut behind them.

"Three hairs indeed!" Adam said with a hearty laugh, regarding her with undisguised admiration. "You have hummed them completely."

"Actually, I only did get two hairs," Miranda admitted shamefacedly. "Enough to make Barone decidedly uncomfortable, but not sufficient for a full-blown malediction."

"You are a witch?" Ropwell asked.

"Of course, she is!" Lady Enderby declared stoutly. "All the Wodesbys are."

Adam saw Miranda's stricken look and knew that she was about to explain that witchcraft was not the destiny of every Wodesby. However, they were all distracted by the sound of a sob. Lady Pelton was standing in the corner, weeping softly, touching her necklace as if uncertain of its reality. "I would have given it up gladly," she sniffed. "A few words were all that I wanted. I had thought that first postponement of the séance the night of Lady Enderby's party was destined. Tonight . . . when Pelton and I would have been married half a century, it would have meant the world to me to speak to him."

"But you would not have heard the words that you longed for, Lady Pelton," Adam began.

"Yes, I know now that Barone was a fraud," she said, her nose twitching like a rabbit's as she sniffed. "And I thank you, milord, and you, Miss Wilton, for saving dear Pelton's gift from that rogue's hands. At least I still have something left to barter when I find a true seer."

Adam caught Miranda's troubled look.

"You would do this again?" Miranda asked.

"I must speak to Pelton," the older woman said desperately. "All those years we were together, I never once told him how much that I loved him, how happy he made me. Then I woke one morning to find him gone."

"I am sure he knew," Adam murmured.

"How can you be certain, when I am not?" Lady Pelton asked, doubt in her eyes. "How many of us keep our feelings to ourselves, in our heads, but never on our tongues, always assuming that those we love understand what is inside. Many a marriage have I seen fail not because of words but because of silence."

"And that is all that you wish?" Miranda asked.

"No more than that," Lady Pelton said quietly. "It may seem naught to you, but it is everything to me."

Miranda nodded her head thoughtfully. "Yes, I can see that." She walked away from the table, weighing the situation. Mrs. Bittward, Lady Westwood, and Lady Enderby gathered around Lady Pelton, clucking their sympathy as Lord Ropwell helped himself to brandy in the corner.

"There will be another Barone to get his claws in her." Adam said, following Miranda to the corner of the room.

"Unless she can talk to her husband," Miranda said, picking up a book and leafing through it distractedly. 'To my dearest Loulou,' the inscription read, 'from her furry Pelt.' "Did you know Lord Pelton?" she queried.

"They made an odd pair," Adam said. "He was a bear of a man, as large as Lady Pelton is tiny. A deep-voiced fellow who rarely spoke and when he did, his speech was marred by a stutter."

"Could you imitate him?" she asked, an idea beginning to materialize.

"I vow, I can almost hear the gears whirring in that brain of yours. What are you thinking of, Miss Miranda Wilton?" Adam asked his eyes narrowing.

"Do you recall Uncle Ned and the missing teapot?" By the suddenly wary look in those brown depths, Miranda could see that he was following the drift of her thoughts.

"Are you asking me to take part in a sham, or do you believe that you can truly speak to the hereafter?" Adam asked apprehensively.

"I have told you time and again that I am no witch," Miranda said patiently. "And you may stand on principle, milord, if you so desire. But will you, nil you, I will try to assist that woman, by myself if need by, though the results might be far less effective."

What she suggested went wholly against his principles. But the soft sound of Lady Pelton's weeping tugged at his heart.

What would it be like to love someone so fully? he wondered. Dim echoes of an eight-year-old boy crying in the emptiness of the nursery reverberated. Visions rose of his father's growing desperation and rage as charlatan after charlatan failed to deliver the promise of eternity that he so craved. Yes, there would be another Barone, and another and another until they sucked the old woman dry, just as they had drained his father. Yet how could he lend his name, his credence to something he could not countenance? "What is it you wish me to do, Miranda?" Adam asked.

"Tell her what she needs to hear, what your father would have wished to hear all those years ago," she whispered, her eyes sparkling with enthusiasm.

Adam regarded her uneasily. "Would you have me transmit fantasies of your Elysian fields, Miranda?"

"They exist, Adam, for everyone," she said, feeling the pain of his disillusionment. "And though our dreams of that far country may differ, we will all reach that boundary some day and face the Light. I believe that with all my soul and I think that if you reach far enough inside yourself, you believe it, too."

"That was long ago, Miranda," he said, with a lopsided smile, "a little boy's wish of angels and a heaven where they served cream cakes thrice a day."

He could not keep the wistfulness from his voice and Miranda felt a sudden desire to reach out to him, to hold the child that he had been and—though he did not realize it—the child that he still was. "She believes," Miranda said, nodding toward Lady Pelton. "Can that be sufficient for now, Adam?"

"You realize, of course, that this will seal your reputation as a sorceress in the eyes of the Ton," Adam said. "No matter that you may deny it after this."

"What the Ton thinks holds little interest for me," Miranda said, her smile slipping to melancholy. "Those who matter will still know the truth. All the wishes in the world cannot make a hazel rod out of a willow, Adam. Now will you help me? You are the one man no one would suspect of collusion."

He wanted to agree, but the very reason that she cited was the most compelling consideration against his cooperation.

Adam shook his head. "To put my imprimatur on a séance, to collaborate in a deception of this kind would go against all that I have stood for these years past. I cannot, Miranda, even for Lady Pelton's sake. Moreover, I could not lie to her, assure her of an eternity that I doubt exists."

His look was a plea for understanding and Miranda swallowed her disappointment with a curt nod. "Very well, then. At the least, can I have your word that you will not interfere."

"I will even leave, if that is what you wish," Adam said.

"There is no need for that," Miranda told him. "You may stay if you choose, so long as you do not spoil things. There is naught in my plan that requires anything more than simple belief and so long as you do not interfere with that, I will be content. Just do not be surprised by what you might hear, milord."

"I will not obstruct you," he said, inexplicably hurt by the distance in that "milord."

"I expect no more," she declared with an incline of her head, before she went to sit beside the weeping woman. "Lady Pelton, I have been mulling over your situation. My mother would not wholly approve of what I am about to offer, for I am a spinster. To walk among the spirits, one really ought to be well attached to this earth by ties of a spouse or children. But due to your circumstances, I think that your husband may be reached with a degree of safety. 'Twould be your fiftieth year together, after all."

"Would you call upon Pelton for me, my dear?" Lady Pelton asked, raising her rheumy eyes hopefully.

"I will do what I can," Miranda said, with enough evasion so that she was not lying outright.

"Take this, then," the old woman said, reaching back to unfasten her necklace.

"No, Lady Pelton," Miranda said firmly. "I ask nothing from you other than your solemn promise. If you speak to your husband tonight, then you must content yourself with what you hear. Never attempt to raise him from eternal rest again."

"Very well," Lady Pelton said. "As long as I say what needs to be said."

"Excellent," Miranda agreed. "Now we must hurry and gather round the table, for all must be done before the cock's crow. Place the necklace in the center, Lady Pelton, since that item obviously holds sentiment for both you and your late lord."

Lady Pelton obeyed, laying the diamonds to gleam at the center of the table.

"All of the candles must be doused," Miranda instructed, "except for the branch in the middle."

"Light, Miss Wilton? Most charlatans demand absolute darkness," Lord Brand said, his tone at its most sarcastic.

"Then perhaps I am unlike most charlatans, Lord Brand," Miranda said, keeping herself calm, thinking that she should have tossed him on his ear when he gave the opportunity. Yet when she met his eyes, she saw something curiously conspiratorial in that dark field of brown. Could he be trying to give her credence by casting doubt? An uncooperative, skeptical Lord Brand would certainly be more credible than a quiet consenting one, and illusions performed under scrutiny were less subject to doubt than those done under cover of darkness. Whatever his intent, his remark had served to point that up.

"Shall we join hands?" Miranda asked. She felt Lady Pelton's thin fingers slip trustingly into her palm and on the other side, Lord Brand's broad hand enveloped Miranda's own, a gentle, reassuring pressure confirming her suspicions. Though he might not help outright, he would not hinder.

"Tell me your first name, Lady Pelton, and then your husband's," Miranda urged.

"Louisa and Augustus, Miss Wilton," she supplied.

"Think, Louisa, think upon your Augustus," Miranda urged. "Remember the sound of his voice, the touch of his hand; feel it in your thoughts."

Lady Pelton closed her eyes and a sweet smile lit her face. "I see him before me, Miss Wilton."

"Keep that image in your mind and we shall call him." Miranda's voice fell to a deep sing-song. "Augustus, for the sake of the love that you bore Louisa, come to us. Fifty years ago tonight, remember the joy of your youth and come to us."

Lady Pelton sighed softly and joined in the refrain, "Come to us."

"Recollect the vigor of health, the burdens of sickness, come to us."

"Come to us," Lady Enderby intoned.

"For all that you shared in sorrow, come to us."

"Come to us," Mrs. Bittward chanted.

"For the love that you cherished, come to us."

"Come to us!" Everyone but Lord Brand demanded.

Adam watched with detached fascination as the participants became caught up in the rhythm that Miranda had established. Even fragmented, the familiar words of the marriage ceremony tapped all the force of each individual's memory. The beat that she set was like the pulsing of a heart, causing the phrases to build into a powerful invocation binding them all to one purpose. Then he heard the voice coming from the center of the table.

"Nettie's th' name, sent t'guide yer I was," the voice declared.

Adam observed Miranda, but her lips were not moving. Her expression was rapt, but there was a twinkling challenge in her eyes as they caught his glance. He had met a few magicians who had possessed the amazing ability of casting the voice, but none who could do it without any obvious signs of motion. There was naught but a slight ripple of her throat to indicate that Miranda was providing the female version of Uncle Ned with her ghostly voice. Even if he were out to trip her up, it would be difficult to prove that there was fakery afoot.

"Got a lidy name o' Loulou wiv' yer?" Nettie asked.

"Obviously, a misguided spirit guide," Ropwell commented.

"Hush, Ropwell! Or leave," Lady Pelton demanded, then turned to address the branch of candles. "I am Loulou," she said, her lip trembling. "But there was only one person on earth who called me by that name."

"Yer furry Pelt sends 'is love, 'e do," Nettie said.

Lady Pelton's hand squeezed Miranda's tightly. " 'Tis Pelton," she whispered excitedly. "That was what I called him."

Miranda nodded. "Nettie, can Lord Pelton speak to us?"

"Dunno, 'e kin try, but t'ain't easy when yer been gone long as 'e 'as and ain't used ter blabbin'. New dead's what I am, so's 'tis easy fer me. But 'e kin 'ear yer, every bleedin' word, beggin' yer pardon, Miss."

"Say what you wish to, Lady Pelton," Miranda told her.

"Pelt, I love you," Lady Pelton called tremulously into the heart of the light. "I miss you so dreadfully and every morning when I see your pillow empty, I regret waking."

Suddenly, the room grew chill and though there was no draft, the flames flickered wildly. Yet the candlelit glitter from the diamonds seemed to intensify, fragmenting into shattered shafts of light.

"I . . . w . . . w . . . wait . . ." The disjointed words seemed to come from within the flame. "For . . . you . . . L . . . Lou . . . l . . . lou . . ."

How in the devil was she managing this? Adam wondered. Miranda sat wide-eyed, as if she too were startled by this turn of events. Lady Pelton rose slowly from her seat, her eyes soft and dreamy. Her stooped shoulders straightened perceptibly as if a heavy burden had suddenly been lifted, and for a moment it seemed that the weight of years fell from her. Her tiny hand lifted to touch her cheek.

"Thank you, Pelt," she whispered softly. "As long as I know that you will be there waiting, I can endure."

Then, as abruptly as it had come, the cold feeling was gone and the flames ceased their dance. Miranda slumped back in her seat, her eyes glistening with unshed tears. Her hold on Adam's had slackened.

"I have never seen the like." Lady Westwood was the first to break the silence. "And many a séance I have been to. You are to be congratulated, Miss Wilton. When will you be able to contact Manfred for me?"

"I will give you five hundred pounds, Miss Wilton." Lord Ropwell leaned over the table eagerly. "Five hundred pounds if you can convince Felicity to tell me where she hid those jewels."

"Remarkable!" Mrs. Bittward declared. "A most amazing

experience. It was like being caught within a block of ice, was it not, Lady Enderby?"

"Like the middle of winter," Lady Enderby agreed. "Do you not think so, Lady Pelton?"

The elderly woman shook her head. "I was warm, for the first time since Pelton died, the chill was chased from my bones. And I felt as if . . . as if he leaned over and . . . and . . . kissed me on the cheek as he was often wont to do." A smile lit her wizened face. "Thank you, Miss Wilton. You have given me the hope I need. Miss Wilton!" Lady Pelton touched the young woman's shoulder in alarm.

But Miranda did not respond. She stared straight ahead, as if seeing some distant vision. Adam lifted up her limp hand and came to the rapid realization that this was not part of her performance. It was like holding an ice sculpture. "Miss Wilton," he called.

"What if she has loosed her tether to this world, Lord Brand?" Lady Pelton cried. "I have been so selfish. I should never have asked her to attempt so dangerous a feat."

"Miranda," Adam called, holding her cheeks between his hands. Although he did not subscribe to her creed, he had seen the tremendous power of credulity. If she truly believed herself to be wandering in those faraway fields . . . "Miranda!"

Chapter 9

Miranda blinked like a just-wakened sleeper. "Adam?" she asked, tears slipping unheeded down her cheeks.

"I am right here, Miranda." Adam chafed her fingers. Folding her palms within his own, he breathed upon her hands, trying to bring warmth to the chilled extremities. "Ropwell, bring me some of that brandy, if you've not drunk it all," he demanded, watching as her pupils began to lose their dilated look. He loosened his hold on her momentarily to pull off his jacket and drape it around her shoulders.

Lord Ropwell responded with alacrity. "Wouldn't want to lose our guide to the hereafter, would we?" he said with false heartiness.

Squatting beside her, Adam put the glass to her lips, holding her shoulder to keep her steady. "Drink slowly," he told her and breathed a quiet sigh of relief. Color was returning to her cheeks and the disturbing empty gaze was gone. Instead he saw a profound sadness. He wanted to question her, but now was not the time.

"Miss Wilton, about the jewels—"

Adam silenced him with a scowl. "Leave her be, Ropwell," he commanded coldly.

"What right do you have to speak for her, Brand? You ought to be at Guttmacher's unmasking the fraud. I have a substantial sum bet in your favor."

"I am flattered by your confidence," Adam said, not bothering to mask his sarcasm.

"Does it bother you so much?" Ropwell asked with a sneer. "Now that it appears that the exception has been found to your prosaic rules? Pray, how do you explain what just happened here?"

"There are always alternatives. Many things are not what they appear to be," Adam said, not at all convinced himself. Something had happened, something unusual, and though he had not experienced a change of heart, the idea that there might be possibilities beyond his ken filled him with sudden doubt and unreasoning fear. If her truths were within the realms of reality, she had taken a terrible risk. The mere thought of her making the attempt again for Ropwell's greed was beyond bearing. "At present, though, I think that Miss Wilton's well-being is paramount."

"So it is," Ropwell said. "If I may call upon you tomorrow, Miss Wilton?"

Adam was about to tell Ropwell that he might go to the devil first, but Lady Enderby spoke before him.

"I am sure that the Wodesbys would be delighted," Lady Enderby declared.

With a satisfied nod, Lord Ropwell made his farewells.

"Mama will not receive him," Miranda said weakly.

"Of course she will, Miranda," Lady Enderby said smugly. "His bloodlines are unexceptionable and he is quite eligible, especially if you find those baubles for him. The Ropwell jewels are worth a veritable king's ransom. Marriage would not be a high price to pay for their recovery."

"I see," Miranda said, taking a restoring breath. Her veins felt as if they had been filled with iced water, but anger was warming her rapidly. "And since I am at my last prayers, Ropwell might well be the best that an aging spinster can hope for. I would be addressed as 'your ladyship' after all," she said steadily.

"I knew you had a head on your shoulders, gel," Lady Enderby said approvingly.

Miranda's expressionless face would have done credit to a card sharp, and her cool, practical tone was unnerving. Would she actually consider a man like Ropwell? Adam wondered. Rumors were rife that Ropwell had assisted his lady in her fatal headlong tumble down the stairs. "Ropwell's stinking repute would have the fishwives in Billingsgate holding their noses. You would do better to rely on that fellow in the country, Miss Wilton, the man of your dreams."

The man of your dreams . . . No worse phrase could have been chosen. "My dreams are no business of yours, Lord Brand!" she snapped, pain slicing through her. She knew that he spoke out of honest concern, but the fact that he could so easily consign her to the arms of an unknown cut her to the core. It was no fault of Adam's that he haunted her nights and the revelation of heart that she had confronted on her journey through the dark was still too new, too raw to cope with. "I am sorry, milord," she said, avoiding his gaze. "Once again I must plead weariness, a poor excuse for rudeness, but it has been a rather eventful evening."

"I find it something of a wonder that you can speak at all," Adam said, recalling all that she had been through in the course of the night. But now the strain seemed to be taking its toll, from the quiver of her shoulders to the decidedly clammy feel of her hands. She looked terribly brittle, as if she might shatter at a touch. Adam seized upon exhaustion as an explanation for her momentary lapse into the semiconscious. "Let us get you home, Miranda," he said helping her to her feet.

The gentle tone of his voice was almost her undoing. She wanted to crumble into his arms, to be held and to savor every sensation from the clean, masculine scent of him to the roughness of his late-night stubble. But pity was not what she longed for and that appeared to be the extent of what he was offering. Somehow she forced herself to stand. Mechanically, she set one foot before the other until, at the end of an eternity, they reached the carriage.

As Adam helped lift her into her seat, Thorpe rose swiftly from the cushions and regarded him with a distinct look of feline disapproval. "She is falling off of her feet," Adam growled and then shook his head in disbelief. He was justifying himself to a cat.

Lady Enderby settled herself in and the carriage clattered off. "A ghost," she prattled, her jowls quivering with excitement. "Even you must credit it, Lord Brand."

"Drafts," Adam hedged, "you could fly a kite in the winds that go through some of these old houses."

"There is not so much as a breeze in the air tonight," Lady Enderby countered. "And what of Lady Pelton? She felt her late husband's touch?"

"She felt what she wished to feel," Adam replied, eying Miranda anxiously. Her face was still unnaturally blanched and despite the jarring, jolting motion of the vehicle, she appeared to be slipping into sleep.

"Meowrrrr!" came the alarmed cry.

"Was I nodding off?" Miranda asked, forcing herself to sit bolt upright. There was a peculiar comfort in his jacket, the scent of him. Warmth enfolded her, as if she were in his arms again, lulling her, making her vulnerable to the fatal seduction of sleep. "Do not let me drowse," she begged them. But Adam merely smiled, unaware of the danger.

"I should say not, considering how the night is in its infancy," Adam said, with a tender smile. She looked oddly appealing, tousled and half-asleep, and he allowed himself to imagine that face against a pillow, just touched by the dawn. "Another hour and the roosters will be rousing themselves. Sleep if you want to; we are but a few streets from your home."

"You do not understand," she whispered, desperately fighting the tide of drowsiness. She dared not sleep, not till the cock's crow. Her eyes blinked wide, but slowly the lids began to drift closed. Thorpe yowled again, reenforcing the warning this time with a slash of his claws.

Adam hauled Thorpe away by the scruff of his neck. "Are you all right, Miranda?" he asked.

"Nasty creature!" Lady Enderby said, shrinking back.

"It is no more than a light scratch, I assure you," Miranda said, bending to clutch her ankle as the pain momentarily chased away sleep. "Leave him go, Adam. He has achieved his purpose and will do no more harm."

"And what purpose is that?" Adam asked, knowing full well that the Wodesby answer he might hear would not be to his liking.

"And keep hold of that vile beast, Lord Brand!" Lady Enderby implored as the carriage slowed. "Or better still, I shall open the window and you may throw it out."

"Harm a whisker on Thorpe's head and you will answer to me," Miranda said, casting a black look. To her surprise, Lady Enderby cowered in the corner.

"We are at the door of Wodesby House," Adam informed them drily. "If you would prefer, Lady Enderby, I will escort both the cat and Miss Wilton."

"B-b-but, I really ought to speak to Adrienne and explain—" Lady Enderby began.

"I will make any necessary explanations to Lady Wodesby," Adam offered. "You need not wait here."

"W-would you, Lord Brand?" Lady Enderby said, unable to conceal her relief. "I must confess that I am a trifle overset."

As soon as Adam, Miranda, and Thorpe had alighted, Lady Enderby's carriage clattered off at breakneck pace. The cat ran to the door and started to yowl.

"She did not even wait . . . until we crossed the threshold," Miranda said. "And she has the gall to prate . . . about manners."

"She fears you now, Miranda," Adam said, putting his arm around her waist. Her hair brushed against his cheek as she leaned against him for support. Slowly, he helped her up the marble stairs to the great oak door. "You have assumed the status of a witch, as least in her eyes. Is that not what you wanted?"

She pulled her elbow from his grasp. "I am no witch, damn you!" A sob caught in her throat. "And now I know that I never shall . . . be one. Tonight when Pelton's ghost . . . put in an appearance, I thought that I might . . ." She faltered and Adam reached out to keep her from falling.

Dominick opened the entrance, his impassive expression fading at the scene before him. He saw Adam reaching for Miranda, her face tearful, her skirt disheveled and bloody. The Gypsy's knife opened with a soft snick, moonlight shining silver upon thin steel.

"You can cut my throat later if you want to," Adam told him, adding a Romany curse for good measure. "But now, your mistress needs help. That bloody tiger of Lady Wodesby's clawed her in the leg and between the tabby, Lady Enderby, and the ghost, she's halfway to a haunt herself. If you don't believe me, ask the cat." He swept Miranda up, carrying her into the entry. Thorpe followed, yowling at a panicked pace.

Miranda moaned softly as her face skimmed against his stiffly starched linen. Just the same, she felt warm and safe, enfolded by his strength. If it was destined to end so, then she would not fight the weariness anymore. There were worse ways to die than to drift away in his arms.

"By The Merlin!?" The thunderous oath echoed down the stair. "A man cannot even get his coat off in this place before his ears are assaulted. Calm yourself, you blasted feline, if you wish to be understood."

Adam looked up to see a man in a caped greatcoat rapidly descending the stair. Dressed entirely in black, the stranger seemed to be cut from the fabric of the night itself. His hair was dark as Newcastle coal, relieved only by a streak of white that ran through the center of his untidy Brutus. An enormous black mastiff followed silently in his wake, halting at the landing to regard the scene below with blazing yellow canine eyes, before uttering a single bark.

"You heard Angel, Dominick," the stranger said, his emerald eyes widening in alarm. "Get Tante Reina and quickly. Perhaps she will have some means of helping stave off sleep."

Dominick hastened to obey.

"Put my sister on her feet, sir. Immediately!" the stranger demanded, hurrying to Adam's side.

"You are her brother, Damien, I take it," Adam said, a sinking feeling in his gut. So much for his hopes that Wodesby might exert a steadying influence. Another Bedlamite, with a talking dog to boot. "I am Adam Chapbrook, Lord Brand. This is not what it might appear, Lord Wodesby."

"Few things are what they seem to be," Damien commented, as he hurried to Adam's side. "Now put her down, if you please."

"Are you mad, man?" Adam asked. "Can't you see that she's exhausted?"

"Explanations later," Damien said. "Set her on her feet. We must keep her awake or we may lose her."

"He is right, Adam," Miranda murmured. "If I sleep now, I may sleep forever."

As Tante Reina came rushing into the entry, Adam began to catch the contagion of dread. In all his months with the Gypsy caravan, through the myriad of illnesses, accidents, and deaths that the traveling people were subject to, he had never seen the old woman's expression so dire.

"Walk with her, Lord Damien; help bind her to this earth until the cock's crow or else her soul may go seeking for the Light," Tante Reina demanded. "Talk to her, Gajo. Pray, if there are any gods that you believe in, pray that this night is soon ended."

The mastiff gave a series of sharp yips and Thorpe yowled in protest, unsheathing his claws.

"This is no time for recriminations," Damien said, pulling Miranda's arm about his shoulder as he addressed his dog. "I doubt you could have done better, Angel. Thorpe did all that he could."

"Her eyes are closing," Adam said as he draped Miranda's other arm around his neck. "Can you not use a spell or charm or some such?"

"I would not have guessed you to be a believer in the power of magic," Damien said, looking at Adam curiously.

"I am not," Adam told him, as they urged Miranda forward. "However, I do place a certain faith in the power of the mind. More than once I have witnessed remarkable feats accomplished with nothing more than strength of will. Your sister obviously places great store in this magical philosophy."

"And therefore, you regard her danger as real," Damien observed, regarding him with a measure of newfound respect.

"Damien?" Miranda's eyes snapped open momentarily. "How . . . how . . . did you come?"

"Mama's summons, of course, garbled though it was," her brother said. "And I was about to go up and see her. My coat is yet on my back, as you may note. Then you walked in, trouble on two feet as always, my hellion sister."

"As if you and your hound are not a pair of imps infernal," Miranda whispered as they started across the marble floor. "I saw the Light, Damien; it was beautiful beyond imagination."

"Your magic has quickened, Randa?" Damien asked, joy in his words. "I vow, Mama will be overcome with delight."

Miranda shook her head weakly. "I am no . . . no . . . more a witch than I was this morning. In fact, less, for when I woke today, there was s-s-still that small hope, that somewhere hidden deep, was that tiny s-spark of enchantment. That was why . . . why . . . I willed myself to go with Lord Pelton's ghost."

"A reckless deed, Randa," Damien said, halting in his tracks, his countenance contorting with horror, "to attempt a journey with a spirit when you have no certain means of return is tantamount to suicide."

"Do not scold, Damien, I had . . . had . . . to know," she murmured, forcing her tongue to form words when her mind was demanding rest and a return to the glory of the Light. "All my life, I have been waiting, every day waking with the secret fantasy that perhaps I would be whole when the sun set, to be . . . to be . . . like Mama, like you."

Adam heard the ache in her words and was about to tell her how nonsensical her notions were, but she began to speak again.

"There are any . . . any . . . number of stories in the chronicles," Miranda informed them. "I told you, Adam, about spirits similar to Pelton's. He had un-unfinished business, you see, and was merely waiting for an opportunity to visit his lady." She gave a bark of unhappy laughter. "Even a scoundrel like . . . like . . . Barone could have raised him, had there been but an ounce of sympathy in his invocation. When I felt Pelton's spirit, I knew that this might very well be the only . . . only chance that I had. When he crossed the void, I attached myself to . . . to him in the hope that he could take me to the Light . . . the Light."

The pupils of her eyes narrowed to pinpoints. Damien halted and shook her shoulders. "Speak, girl, speak if you would stay with those who love you."

"M-many a mage or witch has bonded with a spirit thusly," Miranda continued, tripping over the syllables like a drunkard with three sheets to the wind. "And in that journey to the r-r-realm of souls has come back with r-renewed power. Even m-mortals have hung near death and c-caught glimpses of the Light. If there was some hidden m-magic within me, the Light would surely have revealed it."

"And most of those soul-travelers have never returned to tell the tale of their seeking," Damien said, pain in his expression.

"Were you so eager to find your doom, Randa, that you were willing to risk all?"

"I could do worse than to end my existence bemused by glory," she shrugged feebly. "How can you bear to leave it, Damien, when the bliss is upon you and you can see to the edge of Eternity?"

Adam heard Damien's sharp intake of breath. Miranda shivered and he moved closer, trying to warm her body with his own. Nonetheless, she seemed to be growing colder. As they walked, he used his free arm to rub her hand, reaching up to the chill expanse of her bare arms beneath his jacket. "She's freezing, Wodesby," he said. "Do something, man."

"We are doing all we can. She was better than halfway to oblivion," Damien said, shaking his head in disbelief. "How close were you to the Light, Randa?" he asked.

"Close enough to see myself p-plainly, to know that there was n-n-not even a spark of magic within me. I am a cripple, Damien and I n-n-never will be otherwise. I wanted to s-s-stay there." She did not mention what else had been revealed within the shadows cast by the Light. That would remain her own secret source of torment.

"Merlin's Beard," Damien whispered.

"But you came back," Adam said, coaxing her to continue speaking.

"Yes," she said, the single syllable torn from her as she regarded him with anguished eyes.

"What power was it, Miranda, that tempted you to return from the verge of oblivion?" Damien asked, watching her expression carefully.

"I heard my name," she said softly, "a voice calling me back from the brink. It was like a thread, leading me back through the dark labyrinth of the Void and I returned, even though I did not want to."

"Mama?" Damien questioned hopefully.

Miranda shook her head. "No, she could never have called through the Void, not weak as she is."

"Then who?" Damien asked, wondering who else might have exercised such powerful magic on his sister's behalf.

Miranda closed her eyes against a sudden rush of tears.

Never before had she realized the full extent of her emptiness. She had thought that she could live satisfied with the crumbs of contentment, fabricating an illusion of fulfillment in her hopes of a home and children, the importance of her work with the archives.

But now, now she knew that her visions of the future were no more than delusions, shattered by the sound of her own name. In the glow of the Light, her heart had been plainly revealed. Nothing less than the force of love could have pulled her from the dark void. But while love tied Miranda inexorably to Lord Brand, Adam seemed entirely free of anything more than the most casual of feelings toward her. Dimly, in the distance, she saw the glimmer of the Light, beckoning to a place where there was no pain.

"Open your eyes, Miranda," Adam demanded. "You must stay awake."

"Why?" she asked, trying to focus as she looked up at him.

Adam could barely contain his anger. What had they done to her, these Wodesbys, with their strange pretensions? How could it be that she felt that she had nothing to live for? "What of the man you profess to care for?" he asked, gently putting a hand to her cheek. "Would you abandon him so easily?"

Miranda was confused for a moment, wondering who he could mean other than himself. Martin, she reminded herself painfully. He was telling her to live for the sake of Martin Allworth. "The m-man of my d-dreams," she whispered softly, closing her eyes with a breathy sigh.

Angel howled.

"Randa!" Damien took her by the shoulders and shook her.

Tante Reina hurried to the library window and pulled the draperies wide. "Is well, Lord Damien!" she called, pointing toward the sky. The first rose tinged traces of dawn were creeping over the treetops. "Let her sleep, milords. Rest now will not harm her."

"But will it mend her?" Adam asked, regarding Lord Wodesby with smoldering rage. With a glare of defiance, he lifted Miranda into his arms, letting her settle against his chest with a soft, incoherent murmur. "That makes twice tonight, she has put herself in danger for the sake of that arcane

Wodesby heritage. Her quick wit saved my life, sir, though she could well have lost her own in the process. Now show me where to put her and then show me the door."

She moved, her hair brushing against his chin and he looked down at her, saw the traces of tears on her cheeks. Adam's throat tightened angrily as he met Lord Wodesby's enigmatic gaze. Silently, Miranda's brother led Adam up the stairs to her chamber, the dog and cat padding behind them. With the utmost care, Adam laid her upon the pillows, smoothing back the hair from her face as he slid his other hand from beneath her. The rays of the rising sun touched her, emphasizing the pallor of her cheeks, the dark shadows beneath her eyes. She moaned softly as his hand withdrew.

Adam could remain silent no longer. "Your sister is a rare woman, sir. Miranda has a beauty that goes far beyond her face and form, a compassionate heart, a gentle grace, intelligence. She is everything that is desirable. Yet she regards herself as a cripple, Wodesby, a cripple, because of this strange legacy that you claim."

"You go too far, Lord Brand," Damien said, his countenance closed. "You speak of matters that are none of your concern."

"I may not understand the whys and wherefores, milord, but I do believe that your sister damned near died tonight," he said, watching as she curled up like a child, clasping her knees with one hand, the other limp upon the pillow. "And if she feels that she is less than whole, you Wodesbys are to blame for it. Why, a woman of her quality would have long been married, with a tribe of children at her skirts, were it not for this ridiculous myth that swirls around you. By the time the sun sets tonight, the entire Ton will have heard of the events at Lady Pelton's table. If they did not brand Miranda as a witch before, they will now."

For a fleeting moment, Adam saw past her brother's guarded expression to the wellsprings of sorrow in those green eyes.

"Poor Randa," Damien said, going to the bedside to stare down at his sister. "All of the burden and none of the joy."

"Damn you, Wodesby," Adam said. "Do you or your mother have any inkling of what she has already endured and will suffer yet, once the rumors fly?"

"The stares? The behind-handed whispers? The fear, or the false friendship that is offered for the sake of the power inherent in our name? The soldiers who cross themselves hastily, when they believe I cannot see?" Damien asked coldly. "You cannot damn a Wodesby, Brand, for 'tis a known fact that we are accursed from the womb. I assure you that my mother and I both are well aware of the lack of understanding that is engendered by the patrimony of our name. But at least we have the compensation of our Gifts. Miranda, unfortunately, lacks—"

"Nothing!" Adam roared. "Your sister has gifts that you do not recognize as such, but I will not hear her called a cripple again, sir, not even by her brother."

Damien smiled wearily and for the first time, Adam could see a resemblance to his fair-haired sibling. "You did not let me finish, Brand. What I meant to say is she lacks confidence in herself and perhaps, I am partly to blame for that, as for so much else. When our father died, I . . ."

Wodesby shook his head and once again, those green eyes were transformed into pools of pain.

"But that is a very long story, too long after so lengthy a night. Go home, Brand, and sleep, for you could, no doubt, use it. I thank you, on behalf of my sister and indeed all of us. You have the gratitude of the Wodesbys."

"I don't want your gratitude, Wodesby," Adam retorted, his anger diminished but not drained. "Any more that I want your mama's seal of protection. It is Miranda that concerns me. She deserves far better than she is getting."

"Yes, she does, and if you would do me the honor of returning, I think that you also are deserving of some explanations," Damien agreed, his brow rising. *Under Wodesby protection?* It was increasingly obvious that it would be a long time before there would be a pillow beneath his head. Mama had some explaining to do. "As you can see, I still have bits of Portugal clinging to my boots."

Adam nodded, taking one last look at Miranda as Tante Reina bustled in. The young woman's hand was hanging off the bed and he lifted it to the pillow. "May your dreams be sweet, Miranda," he whispered.

Damien watched as the corner of his sister's mouth curved in a peaceful smile. He had little doubt now just whose voice had summoned her back from the beyond. An Outsider, and to make the tangle more convoluted, an unbeliever. Yet, as the mage searched himself he could see no vision of a resolution to this dilemma in Brand's future. But then, clarity of thought was an absolute necessity for a Seer and there was too much emotion clouding his mind. Damien stifled a sigh as the two of them left his sister to Tante Reina's ministrations and Thorpe's watchful eye. "She will be well, Brand," he said, answering the man's unspoken question. "What she requires most right now is the same thing that I desperately need: sleep."

"I would imagine so," Adam said, noticing Lord Wodesby's travel-worn appearance for the first time as they walked down the stair. Even the mastiff that padded after them looked as if it had traveled leagues. "You are new come from the Peninsula, milord? I cannot believe that your mother's message reached you so quickly; she sent for you but a few days ago."

Once again, Wodesby's raised brow put Adam in mind of Miranda.

"I see that I have much to explain," Damien said with a sigh. "My mother called me through the Void, Lord Brand, an undertaking not lightly done, for it requires a tremendous strain upon the Gift. As soon as her mind touched mine, I took my leave of Wellington and came home by the fastest possible route."

"Broomstick?" Adam could not help the question, his lip quirking.

"That, Lord Brand, is a myth," Damien said with a semblance of a smile. "And I confess myself somewhat glad that such flights are confined to legend, since I can imagine nothing more uncomfortable than a prolonged flight with nothing but an old besom to buttress my behind. No, I used more conventional modes of travel: a fast horse and a sailing vessel, though I must admit to conjuring a bit of fair wind to speed me. But I forget, you do not believe in such things."

"Of course not," Adam replied automatically, but a shred of doubt began to niggle at his brain. How on earth could Lord Wodesby have received his mother's summons so quickly, unless . . . ?

"At your convenience, Lord Brand," Damien said, opening the door. "I will have Dominick give your man some of Tante Reina's salve for your wounds. I will not ask how you came by them; I will await the story tomorrow."

"Or today," Adam agreed, looking up ruefully at the rising sun, all at once recollecting Lord Ropwell's promise to call. "Are you familiar, Wodesby, with a man by the name of Ropwell?" he asked.

"I vaguely recall him," Damien said, his brow furrowing uneasily. "A viscount? Ropwell. There is a bad feel about that name."

"I would not be surprised if the rumors have reached clear to Portugal," Adam said in disgust. "Suffice it to say his reputation is less than savory. Unfortunately, his title wholly outweighed his repute in Lady Enderby's estimation. She informed him that your mother would be delighted to receive him, although I suspect that his intent is less on wooing your sister than using the power that he believes that she possesses."

"Thank you for the warning," Damien said, more certain than before that Lord Brand's feelings too, were engaged, though he seemed wholly unaware of his attachment. Matters were growing more complex by the moment. What manner of muddle had his mother gotten them into now? "I will deal with Ropwell. Ah, there is Dominick now."

The Gypsy reined in the Wodesby carriage and brought it to a halt before the front door.

"There is no need for the ride, sir," Adam said. "'Tis but a short distance and I think that the walk might do me good. But I will take the salve. Nasty stuff, as I recall, but I have never seen an ointment that heals wounds more rapidly."

"As you wish," Damien said, inclining his head in agreement. "A good walk often leads to the resolution of questions."

Adam looked at him, startled.

"One need not be a magician, Lord Brand, to recognize confusion on a man's face," Damien said, with a parting salute. He turned, but kept the marquess in the corner of his eye as he took the jar from Dominick and strolled briskly up the street. "Follow him, Angel," the mage directed quietly. The mastiff gave a soft whine. "I am fagged myself and you were the one questioning Thorpe's competence. 'Fumbling feline,' was the phrase you used, if I recall. Now off with you, unless of course you truly wish to join me in a tête-à-tête with Mama."

Angel loped swiftly out the door.

"Thought not," said Damien with a rueful look as he swung the door closed and started slowly back up the stair.

"Wodesby? What in the devil took you so long?"

Damien blinked, staring for a moment at the man at the upon the top landing. Between the dim shadows of morning light and his weariness, he thought that Lord Brand had somehow returned. But as his eyes adjusted, Wodesby realized that the distinguished apparition had hair of silver. "And who in blazes are you, sir?"

"Lawrence Timmons, at your service," Lawrence replied with a bow. "Please forgive my abruptness, but I am quite concerned about your mother. She was beginning to worry."

"Was she?" Damien said, his brows knitting together like thunderclouds. "Well, I confess, sir, that I am beginning to be a trifle concerned myself."

Damien stared out the window over the quiet herb garden, identifying the various plants as his mother's voice washed over him. It had been high tide and storm since he had set foot in the door of her bedchamber, demanding explanations. Thankfully, the waves of her anger were beginning to ebb.

". . . Do not dare to bark at me, Damien Nostradamus," Lady Wodesby warned, setting her morning chocolate on the tray with a hazardous clinking of china. "Mage of Albion you might be, but I am still your mother and Mistress of Witches, and you will not forget it again! The false values that young men learn these days," she muttered. "Treating women like chattel, ordering us about like inferior servants. One would think that they were Bearers of Life, with all their airs. I cannot think where you might have picked up these manners. Certainly, it is not what I have taught you. Muddying my Aubusson rug at the crack of dawn and daring to read me a lecture. And Lawrence, how you embarrassed him!"

"What was I to think, with a man coming down the stairs in the wee hours of the morning?" Damien replied, turning to face her. "And then guarding you from me, like a dragon 'pon a treasure trove."

"Dear Lawrie," his mother said, "could you blame him when you came roaring into my chamber hurling unconscionable accusations? You are quite fearsome, my boy, when you are hot with anger. Once you had calmed down, he did agree to leave. Besides, we did nothing more than talk the night away, like children in the nursery. We are old friends."

There was a look in her eyes that Damien could not like, a special soft glow that he had not seen since his father's death. With a twinge of foreboding he realized that there was much more than friendship in his mother's voice when she spoke of Lord Brand's uncle. "He has no right to interfere in family business," Damien said, attempting to change the subject. "But I must say, the man showed great sense. He fully agreed that you ought not to have your cards back until you fully recover."

"I need them, Damien. You can see for yourself, I am much improved," she snapped and a burst of flame flared from her fingertips.

"You tire yourself with needless display, Mama," he said, stifling a yawn. "When you are well and able enough to divine their location on your own, you may use your cards. Lucky for you that Thorpe and Miranda had the good sense to conceal them, else I doubt that I would be talking to you this side of the Void."

"Or perhaps I could have mitigated last night's disaster," Lady Wodesby said tartly.

"Or perhaps you could have done nothing," Damien said, reaching to clasp her hand, knowing that her annoyance stemmed almost entirely from worry. He sat in the chair beside the bed. " 'Only a fool believes that he can fool with Fate.' So you yourself have told me, time and again."

"Ah, my son, I must be growing old, if you are throwing my own advice back in my face," his mother said, leaning back upon the pillows.

"Old? Never? Did I not know better, I would say that there was a spell of eternal youth upon you, Mama. If you would note which one of us has the hair that is turning white," Damien said, tugging significantly at his blanched forelock.

"And you dare to accuse me of taking risks, my boy, when you help Wellington to turn the tides of battles? By the time Napoleon goes down to defeat, I suspect you may be as hoary headed as the first Lord Wodesby," Lady Wodesby declared with a shake of her head, raising her hand to stave off argument as Damien opened his mouth to speak. "But we can save our usual quarrels for later, Damien. You say that Miranda is in love with him?"

"She was within the Light, Mama," Damien said. "Even you or I would have had difficulty resisting that lure, unless some very great power pulled us back, the one tie that is stronger than death. Can you think of any other reason for her to return to the here-and-now?"

"She did seem to be growing fond of Lord Brand," Lady Wodesby said thoughtfully.

"How could you allow it?" Damien asked, rising from the chair. "He is not one of us, of the Covens. You, of all people, should know how important it is—"

"Do not dare to tell me of my obligations to the Blood!" his mother blazed. "I married for the Covens and though I grew to love your father dearly, he was not the man my heart had yearned for, any more than I was his first wish. Yet we made our alliance and did a good job of it too, I'd say," she added, her voice gentling at Damien's shocked expression. "I pray, my son, that you never need to make the choice between love and duty. And since I have discharged mine, I may choose to satisfy myself now."

Damien chose to ignore the discomfiting portents of her last phrase for the moment. "We are discussing Miranda, Mama."

"So we are," Lady Wodesby said with a deep sigh. "Your sister is nine and twenty, Damien. In case you have not noticed, there are no young mages begging for her hand."

"Impossible; she is a Wodesby," Damien said, rising from his chair to look out the window once again, but he could see nothing more than the scenery. There were no visions, just a sense of dread. Something was about to happen, but he dared not reveal that vague unease to his mother. Too much strain was already upon her and with her cards forbidden there was naught that she could do to alleviate the situation. "Miranda should have been handfasted long ago. I have neglected my duty, and now I will see to it."

"Do you think I have not tried?" Lady Wodesby asked sadly. "There is not one man willing to take the risk, not when there are so many other eligible witches to choose from. Miranda has no magic. But she may yet marry, Adam. I have seen signs of a wedding in the cards."

"Surely, then, there must be someone," Damien said, passing the sons of the Covens in mental review.

"Is that the measure of what you want for your sister? Someone? Anyone, so long as the Blood runs in his veins? Is that what we have come to, Damien?" she asked, her bitterness coming to the fore. "Is this power that we prize worth so high a cost? In seeking that piece of the divine, we have come to deny that which makes us human. Breeding like prize mares and stallions, destroying those that are not an asset to the herd by letting them wither away in celibate solitude or forcing them to choose a man like Martin Allworth in desperation."

"Allworth? Surely she would not have turned to Allworth?" Damien said in disbelief.

"She wants what every woman seeks, son, mortal or witch, and we cannot fulfill that need for her within the Covens. If Miranda was seeking for her doom last night, then we are to blame."

"That was what Brand said," Damien murmured, suppressing a pang of guilt. To be the Mage, brother, and son was nigh on impossible. Where did Miranda's best interests lie and what was the choice most suited to maintaining the welfare of the Covens? And his own mother, speaking of an Outsider with that dreaming gaze? Even though Damien found himself liking the man, such an alliance seemed unconscionable, especially for the Mistress of Witches. "We must find her a husband."

"Aye, I know that as Mage of Albion it is your right to force some young man to take her to wife. Your sister knows her duty and she will wed him. But in doing so, would you deny her the sole chance she may have to experience the only Gift that all mortals may share?" Lady Wodesby asked, her eyes misting. "And have her tied to a husband who may well hate her for what she is not? It could only have been Brand who called her back from the brink."

"Still, he may not love her, even if that is where Miranda's affections lie," Damien pointed out, attempting to deny the obvious truth.

"I can determine that," his mother said eagerly, "if you return my cards to me."

"Why is it that the Wodesby women are so eager to throw themselves into oblivion?" Damien asked more in irritation than facetiousness.

"The Wodesby men!" Lady Wodesby answered without missing a beat. "By The Merlin, you are just like your father, stubborn as an oak. My Tarot, if you please."

"I will never be half of what Father was, for all we might wish it," Damien said quietly. "But I will not allow you to kill yourself trying to foresee the details of Brand's fate, for I know you will not content yourself with knowing his heart. My powers, such as they are, will have to suffice for now." He went to the door.

"Damien, you must not blame—" Lady Wodesby began, but it was too late. Her son had gone from the room. Even if he had remained, she doubted that the boy would hear her anyway. He was too much like his father in that respect as well, taking upon himself burdens too great for one man to bear. "Have I failed them both, Thorpe?" she asked sadly, pondering old pain, half-healed wounds.

But for once, her familiar had no comfort to offer her. The feline was asleep by the fire, dreaming of catnip fields.

Chapter 10

"Mirandaaaaa . . . !"

Adam's scream echoed in the darkened chamber as he sat bolt upright, his chest matted with the sheen of cold sweat. Gulping air like a half-drowned man, he untangled the sheets that but a few moments ago had been ghostly fingers attempting to strangle him. It had been naught but a dream, but never before could he recall a dream so vivid.

He slipped into a robe and pulled the curtains wide. The sun was nearing its nadir, the afternoon almost spent. According to the gilded hands of the clock on the mantel, the hour of five was half done. He had slept for nearly eleven hours, yet he did not feel the least bit rested.

Odd snatches of dreams drifted into his recall, visions of Miranda, lost in a dark tunnel, the shade of Augustus Pelton tugging her along by the hand. Before them was a blinding glare, like a summer sun reflecting on the water and the ghost was walking straight into the inferno. Even now, with eyes open wide, Adam's heart began to pound like a tinsmith's hammer and the metallic taste of fear rose acid on his tongue. It had seemed so real, so very real. But then, his dreams had become entirely too vivid of late, disturbingly so. Though she claimed to have no part of the Wodesby heritage, Miranda had ensorcelled all of his nights since their first meeting.

Of late, it seemed that the line of separation between illusion and reality had become perilously thin. The Wodesby insanity seemed to be seeping into his well-ordered world of logic. Indoor breezes on a still night, shades that chilled the bone and warmed an old heart, cats and dogs having words with each other, messages sent through the ether by mind.

Barely a week before, he would have laughed, dismissed it all as the absurd fabrications of a liar or a Bedlamite. But now, he could neither mock nor ignore that which he could not explain.

Even more disturbing was this odd constriction in his chest every time his thoughts turned toward Miranda. He found himself worrying about her, consumed with a fever of apprehension that was well beyond natural friendly concern. Never before had a single kiss become so fixed in his mind and he found himself reviewing every minute sensation, from the feel of her skin, to the feathery tickle of her breath upon his cheek.

The Caliban in him ran rampant, imagination transforming those brief moments into elaborate fantasy. But this elemental hunger clearly exceeded mere erotic need. Adam wanted more than the taste of her lips. Somehow, the sound of her laugh, the sight of her smile, the smell of her sweet scent had attained the disturbing status of near-necessities. It was shocking to realize that the beast raging inside of him would be content just to hold her in his arms, to hear her voice, to be with her.

Common sense demanded that he put as much distance as possible between himself and the Wodesbys. However, there was nothing rational about these strange emotions that defied all laws of logic. As Adam stared out the window at the setting sun, trying to reconcile his contradictory collection of feelings, the familiar odd tingling began at the back of his neck.

Down he searched into the gathering shadows of the mews, almost expecting to see Thorpe's cat's eyes staring back up at him. But there was not a feline in sight—no wonder, with that huge dog prowling in the alleyway. A mastiff, black as onyx. It would seem that his marmalade nurserymaid had retired to be replaced by a guardian Angel.

He tore the window open. "Go home!" he roared. "Go tell your master I will not be hounded! Do you hear me?"

But the dog just stood and stared upward at him, with a look suspiciously like laughter.

Adam belted his robe as he pelted down the stairs, running like a madman, his bare toes stubbing on the stones as he opened the garden gate to face the dog. "I am not a sheep to be tended, do you understand? Do you understand?"

The mastiff wagged his tail and panted in a perfect imitation of a dumb canine.

"Oh, no, you don't," Adam said with a shake of his fist. "You do not fool me in the least. Tell Wodesby I have had enough, you hear? Enough!"

"What on earth are you doing?"

Adam turned to find his uncle staring at him with a mixture of amusement and bewilderment. "I . . . I . . ." he stuttered.

"It seemed as if you were having a bit of a tiff with that dog over there," Lawrence observed, leaning on the doorpost casually. "However, it would seem to me that the canine's comportment is superior. She, as you may observe, is fully dressed in the manner of her kind. However, you . . ." His gaze took in the barely decent concealment of Adam's dressing gown. "You would do well for a few more fig leaves, dear boy. My, my, I had never suspected that a blush might extend so far."

"I am going mad," Adam murmured.

"About time it happened." Lawrence laughed, watching as his nephew turned and fled into the house. "Sanity is not all that it is cracked up to be, eh, Angel?"

The mastiff wagged her tail in agreement.

"Your master thanks you for your vigilance and asks that you return home for a well-deserved rest," Lawrence said, tipping his hat in salute. "I will accompany you back to Wodesby House."

With a tired bark of acknowledgement, Angel set off for home.

Lady Wodesby reached out, gently touching her sleeping daughter's cheek.

"Adam?" Miranda murmured, her eyes flickering open.

"I did not wish to wake you, my dear, but midnight is nigh," her mother said. "You really ought not to be asleep when the heart of the night comes. 'Tis doubtful that the Light will beckon now, but far better to be sure than to risk losing you again."

"The Light," Miranda whispered, feeling an ineffable sorrow.

"You will return one day, Miranda," Lady Wodesby said, putting a comforting hand on the young woman's shoulder. "But at the proper time, when your days are full in number. It was fortunate indeed that Lord Brand was present."

"So you know," Miranda said, closing her eyes so her mother could not see the full extent of her pain. "I almost wish that he had not called me back. For now I cannot face the thought of a farce of a marriage to Martin Allworth any more than I can deal with the prospects of a life without Adam."

"Damien will come to accept a liaison with an Outsider," Lady Wodesby said, a stubborn set to her chin as she clasped Miranda's hand. "He will have to."

"If that were only all," Miranda said, bitterness rising like bile. She pulled herself up to a sitting position. "The Mage waves his hand and *voilà!* Everything is in order. Well, the world out there is not governed by your magic these days. The Marquess of Brand has a bevy of eligible young women to choose from, the last of them far more acceptable in the eyes of society than a daughter of the House of Wodesby."

"Unless he loves you, as I believe he does," Lady Wodesby said.

"How could he?" Miranda asked, disbelief turning rapidly to suspicion. "Unless . . . Mama, you have not given him one of your potions, have you?"

"Ah, my dear!" Lady Wodesby breathed a sigh at the agony in her daughter's eyes. "Our family has done you ill indeed, if you can believe that you would need a philter to capture a man's fancy. You may assure yourself, what Brand feels for you is not born from anything that I have brewed. He has been waiting for you to waken."

"Adam is here?" Miranda asked, the last traces of sleepiness vanishing, to be replaced by trepidation. What would he think of her now? "Tell him that I am still asleep, Mama."

Lady Wodesby's brow furrowed. "Child, you may lack magic, but I had never before thought you in want of courage. Brand has nearly worn a path through the library carpet with his pacing, though both your brother and I have assured him that rest was the only requirement for a complete recovery. He saved your life, my girl, though he does not know it. At the least, you owe him your thanks. Now I will help you dress. You ought to be up to it, since you made your journey under power of the ghost's magic and not your own."

From her mother's determined look, it was clear that Miranda would be dragged from the bed if necessary. Cautiously, she set her feet upon the floor.

"No dizziness? No weakness?" her mother asked, keeping a steadying hand on her daughter's shoulder. "How do you feel?"

"Ravenous," Miranda replied.

"A good omen," Lady Wodesby said, with a relieved look. "If you are hungry, 'tis clear that you have both feet back in this world. Damien and I have already dined; however, Lord Brand barely touched a morsel. I shall tell Tante Reina that the two of you are ready to sup."

"He is only being kind," Miranda murmured.

"I have never known kindness to interfere with a man's appetite," Lady Wodesby said, pulling a gown from the wardrobe and eying it critically. "This blue should do nicely. Nor would mere concern warrant reading your brother a sermon upon your virtues as Brand did just a few hours ago. I was certain that the roar would rouse you."

"Adam dared to deliver a lecture to Damien?" Miranda shook her head in astonishment as she slipped into her shift.

Lady Wodesby chuckled as she pulled the dress down over her daughter's head. "I vow, I have not heard the like since your papa's passing. According to Thorpe, Damien sat meek as a pup who has mauled his master's slipper while your Adam took him to task. Angel was growling under her breath."

"He is not my Adam," Miranda said, flushing from her brow to her collarbone. "And likely never will be."

"It takes no wizardry to bewitch a man," her mother observed, fastening up the row of buttons. "However, if you are determined to despair, you are entirely correct; you will never play the role of his Eve." She turned Miranda round to face her. "Do not hold yourself lightly, my dear, or fear to take a chance. There is naught worse than living with the knowledge that love might have been yours if only you had reached out to grasp it."

"What if he comes to fear us when he realizes the truth of the Wodesby blood?" Miranda whispered, hardly daring to voice her worry. "Or worse still, what if he disbelieves, and despises me for taking part in a farcical séance?"

"Then he is not worthy of you," Lady Wodesby said, staunchly, drawing her daughter close. "But I think you underestimate him, just as you underestimate yourself."

The clock in the corner struck the midnight hour as Damien rose and gestured toward the shelves of the enormous Wodesby library. "So you see, Lord Brand, the practice of magic is something of a science, with its own set of governing rules, as logical in their own order as any of Newton's theorems. But just as one must have Leyden jars to store the force of electricity, one must have the proper vessel to handle magic."

"The Blood?" Adam asked, wondering how young Wodesby was managing to keep himself upright. As far as he could determine, the man had not yet slept and exhaustion was taking its toll. Still, there was too much at stake to do the pretty and let the fellow take to his pillow.

Damien nodded. "And knowledge. An untutored witch can be a dangerous force, milord. But knowledge without the Blood—"

"Like Miranda," Adam ventured.

"Make no mistake, milord," Damien said, his eyes flashing with sudden fire. "Though she has no Gift, my sister is of Blood as pure as my own, in direct lines from The Merlin himself."

Intimations had been strewn throughout the conversation, but the challenge in Wodesby's expression made his meaning clear. "I do not deny her place in your magical peerage, Wodesby," Adam said cautiously. "I only seek to understand. In the normal course of events, what would happen to a woman of your people who shared your sister's circumstances?"

"A match is arranged," Damien declared, deliberately making it sound like a fait accompli.

Though Miranda had mentioned that there was a suitor waiting in the wings, it was somehow different to hear her brother state it outright. "So, you would not entertain Ropwell's suit?"

"It did not take long to ascertain his true purpose," Damien said, his lips thinning to an angry line as re recalled the interview. " 'Twas as you said; he is seeking the jewels that his wife hid away. Offered me a share if Miranda could find the cache, as if I would deign to take money from a murderer. I saw blood on his hands."

From the fury raging in the Mage's eyes, Adam found himself close to believing that Wodesby's claim was literally true. "Would that the authorities have such discerning sight. Unfortunately, it seems that the missing Ropwell treasures will be his only punishment." Then, suddenly, the green of the younger man's eyes deepened to the color of an unfathomable sea.

"No, there will be retribution," Damien said slowly, the familiar shimmer of the Vision coming upon him as the dim shadows of future events began to take shape in his mind's eye. Foreboding filled him and he struggled to see more distinctly into the time of Will Be. But weariness was too heavy upon him for clarity of focus. Only Ropwell, transfixed by some unknown terror, was discernable, but there were others with him, innocents who somehow shared his danger. Damien closed his eyes against the horror, the recurring sense of helplessness. No matter that he had been a Seer since the age of thirteen. Twenty years of visions had not inured him to that terrible feeling of impotence.

Wodesby opened his eyes and the deep sadness in the young man's expression filled Adam with sympathy and an uneasy feeling. Had the Mage discerned some fragment of the future? "Do you see anything regarding Miranda?" Adam asked.

Damien shook his head, steeling himself against the first

flash of searing agony. Never before had he experienced a Vision in such a state, and now he was about to pay in pain. He had to lie down before the full onslaught, yet at the least, he felt obliged to calm the obvious worry in Brand's eyes. "I did not see her," he said evasively, struck by a pang of guilt. It said much that Miranda had been Brand's first concern. "But it appears that Ropwell is destined to receive his just due."

Every Gift had its cost, Miranda had told him. What was the price of prophecy? Adam wondered. Somehow, he could not imagine a Seer's knowledge as anything other than an unbearable burden. Angel rose from her place by the fire and went to nuzzle her master with a low bark of canine anxiety.

"You will have to excuse me, Brand," Damien said, rising with effort and walking to open the library door. "I can no longer see or think clearly. Angel will escort you home."

"As I explained to you earlier, I see no further need for your protection," Adam said, wanting to offer his help but knowing that Wodesby would likely refuse it. "If Guttmacher was the Tailor that your mother perceived as a threat, then Miranda foiled his plans and the ghostly encounter that Lady Wodesby predicted has seemingly occurred. So it would seem that the dangers have passed."

"Indeed." Damien inclined his head in agreement, feeling inwardly relieved that matters had been simplified. In truth, all debts were balanced; Brand's inadvertent deliverance of Miranda reckoned equal against the rescue that she staged— a life for a life. Moreover, it would be far easier to steer Miranda away from an ill-advised liaison if Brand were not at the end of a Wodesby tether. A shame, it was, that the marquess lacked the Blood. Damien found himself rather liking the Outsider. "Very well, then, I will call off our watch, if that is what you wish. However, should you ever be in need of our shield or aid, Brand, you have only to call."

Adam's solemn nod was a barometer of the measure of change in him. Just yesterday, Wodesby's regal offer might have garnered him a disbelieving smirk if not the outright laughter that had greeted his sister's promise of protection. Less than a week had passed since he had first met with Miranda, eating and talking in the warmth of the kitchen. But it almost seemed as if that had been some other man. "And Miranda? If there is any change, you will notify me?"

"Of course," Damien told him, trying to convince himself that separating his sister from the marquess would ultimately be best for both. "She will be fine, Brand."

"I can find my own way out," Adam said, his mind wandering back to a time when he had heard similar promises. "Your mother will be fine, Adam," his father's voice echoed. "There is no need for worry . . . no need . . ." Although it was foolish, the marquess wanted to hear that assurance from someone else's lips.

While Lord Wodesby was all that was amiable, Adam had sensed a reserve that seemed to border disturbingly upon disapproval. No wonder, considering the home truths that he had voiced during the interview. But there had been something more in the discussion than the simple umbrage of wounded pride; there was a distance that was courteous but cool. "If you do not mind, sir, I will go down to the kitchen and make my farewells to Tante Reina. I would not want to give her insult."

"Only a fool would insult Tante Reina," Damien said with a sleepy semblance of a smile. "May Fortune favor you, Lord Brand."

"And you, Wodesby," Adam returned.

"When it comes to her servants, I fear that Dame Fortune is not a kind mistress," Damien said, his eyes clouding with recall as the full weight of his responsibilities came to rest upon his shoulders. A husband would have to be found for Miranda. However, the Mage had the unsettling premonition that it might be simpler to split the Channel with a staff than to find a man who could make her forget her infatuation with Brand.

Adam watched anxiously as the young man climbed the stairs, grasping the baluster as if the polished wood rail alone kept him upright. His shadow of a hound trailed close behind, like a nervous nurserymaid, until they reached the upstairs landing.

"Meowrrr!" Thorpe purred softly, rubbing at Adam's ankle to capture his attention.

"My regrets, Thorpe. I still cannot converse in feline," Adam apologized.

Thorpe swished his tail like a furry flag. He padded toward the kitchen stair and looked over his shoulder impatiently.

"You wish me to follow?" Adam asked.

A satisfied mew was an obvious "yes."

Adam shrugged. With any luck at all, he would find the old Gypsy woman and confirm Miranda's condition. As he trailed the cat down the steps, the Mage's words whirled in his mind. Magic! Not the manipulations of mountebanks or the cheats of charlatans, but a force as natural as gravity or electricity. Difficult as it was to credit, the evidence was mounting in favor of the existence of those marvelous abilities. He felt like a blind man trying to grasp the concept of color, unable to comprehend even the simplicity of light and dark.

But his newfound frustration was as a pinprick to a cutlass wound. Miranda had lived her entire life encompassed by rainbows that she could not see, knowing that she was missing that special sense. At least Adam had been blessed in the bliss of ignorance. Even now, he could only guess at the extent of his handicap. No wonder at all that she had gone seeking after that special sight. Indeed, from what Lord Wodesby had let slip, the marvel was that Miranda had returned at all. The thought of losing her filled Adam with a sudden panic. What if they were hiding the truth? Dread swiftened his pace and he took the treads two at a time, heedless of the dimly lit stairwell, all but stepping on Thorpe's tail in his breakneck haste.

As they reached the kitchen, Thorpe looked over his shoulder, his indignant growl an obvious rebuke before stalking away haughtily. But Adam paid him no mind. All of his fears and doubts vanished under a spell of true enchantment.

Miranda sat at the rough-hewn kitchen table, her hair tumbling down her shoulders in a gleaming fall of gold.

"There you are, Adam. I see that Thorpe has found you at last," she said, rising and gesturing toward the place set opposite her. "Mama said that you had barely touched a morsel at supper. You must be as hungry as I."

Like a Raphael Madonna, an aura seemed to surround her,

suffusing her face with a soft glow, as if that otherwordly
Light somehow lingered, bathing her in its radiance. "Miranda," he whispered, crossing the room, recalling the pale,
chilled shadow she had been a few hours before. Tentatively,
he raised a hand to her cheek, half-expecting his fingers to
pass right through her, but the soft flesh that met his touch
was warm and unquestionably alive. She looked up at him in
puzzlement.

How could he explain this need? Adam wondered, as his
hand wandered upward, tangling itself into the silken strands
of her hair. Once again, Adam tried to convince himself that
what he felt was not more than a combination of compassion
and Caliban's savage cravings. But the truth, when it fell, was
like a hammer blow shattering the mirror of his illusions.
Though it defied all logic, he had somehow fallen in love with
Miranda. Emotions simmered within him like a brew in a
cauldron; swirls of desire, molten yearnings, and seething
fears somehow blended with warm tenderness, sweet anticipation, and seasoned with a touch of hope.

"I was afraid for you," Adam whispered, trying to remember that she was promised to another, doubtless one of her
own, a man of the Blood. All at once, the undercurrents of his
conversation with Wodesby became clear. It was a disconcerting feeling, to say the least. For the first time in his life, Adam
was outside the charmed circle, his title and fortune worthless
in the face of this exclusive aristocracy. Confound it! Miranda
was of the Blood, beyond an Outsider's touch. Yet his own
blood was singing in his ears, demanding that he take her into
his arms.

Touched by wonder, Miranda looked up into his eyes. Deep
within those earthen depths, she saw a faint glimmer and
knew that she beheld a spark of the Light, the bright core of
the soul that only love may glimpse. Once more, she felt the
tug of the gossamer cord that had bound her to him. Though
she might have to wait a lifetime to see the fullness of glory
again, there was splendor in the feel of his fingers upon her
cheek, tracing a line of fire to her mouth.

Longing burned, as every fiber of her spirit seemed to tremble in expectation. When she stepped into the charmed circle

of his arms, she knew with utter certainty that this was where she belonged. His hands were the touch of destiny and eternity exploded in the shattering sensation of his kiss. His lips claimed her, gently at first, then with a deepening passion. Miranda surrendered to the tide of emotion, wondering at the host of contradictions that seemed to fill her. Apprehension and certainty, joy and sorrow, ecstasy and pain warred within, like the chaos before creation. Yet somehow, in the midst of the tempest, she felt a curious sense of serenity. This was what she had been born to do, to love this man until the Light claimed her. For the first time in her life, Miranda knew the fulfillment that was magic.

It was as if Adam had never before kissed a woman. Like his original namesake, he stood in the midst of Paradise touching Eve after tasting the fruit of self-knowledge. Suddenly, he felt uncertain, hesitant as these strange emotions flooded him. His past life was revealed in the complete measure of its emptiness. For the first time, he realized how utterly alone he had been.

As he gathered her to him, primal awareness came to the fore, recognition that she was the missing part of him. Only she could fill that void, assuage this aching need. Was this why the Bible used the term to "know" to describe intimacy? The feel of her arms around his neck, the sound of her soft sigh, the scent of lilac, the shimmering silken veil of golden hair, even the taste of her lips, seemed achingly familiar and right. Though Adam had placed no credence in faith or fate, at that moment, he believed. This woman was meant for him from that first dawn in Eden.

Enchantment surrounded them, creating a space that was beyond the measures of time and place. Together they whirled through the maelstrom of discovery, buffeted by emotion.

Hidden in the butler's pantry, Tante Reina smiled in satisfaction. Lord Damien might seethe like a kettle on the hob, but the lady was confident that his ire would pass once he realized the extent of his sister's love for the Gajo. And from the look on Brand's face, she was certain that the feeling was mutual. Gone was Adam's mask of diffidence, the facade of pride that hid his true self. No need to resort to cards or the palm to see the hand of fortune here.

She sighed softly at the tableau before her as Thorpe purred impatiently. "Peh! You prudish creature! You would have been hissing had they gone past a handshake, I know it," she chided in a whisper, looking down at the animal "That is why the Lady left it to me, eh. Every man is like a tom on the prowl, you think? Well, he is a fine one, Brand. From the caravan days, I know him. Never trouble with our girls, like other Gajos. He knows to treat them with respect. So leave off your whining, Thorpe. 'Tis I who decide when is enough, when the moment is right. "

The tom growled, directing her attention back to Adam and Miranda. The Gypsy's eyes widened.

"Is enough, by Hecate," Tante Reina said, deliberately rattling a pan to warn of her presence. "The moment is right." By the time she made her way to the stove, the two had separated, looking as guilty as a pair of goats in the garden. Miranda's cheeks were nearly red as rosebuds and Adam seemed as dazed as a punch-drunk fighter.

"Hungry, I'll bet," the old woman said, ladling stew into a plate and setting it before Adam.

Her raised eyebrow spoke volumes, giving her words an entirely different meaning. The frown on her face made it absolutely clear that any other appetites would not be satisfied.

"I am starved," Miranda admitted innocently.

"Aye, it can do that, the magic." Tante Reina said, putting a second plate before Miranda. "You must rebuild your strength, child."

"But I did not do anything magical," Miranda protested. "Basically, it was nothing more than jumping into a carriage whose journey was already under way."

"Is not so much the going as the coming back," Tante Reina said seriously. "You struggle against nature of your own soul. She wants to seek her source, you fight to return to the body. Is not same as witch's magic, but is magic still."

"Earth magic?" Adam asked, seating himself at the table.

"Aye," Tante Reina nodded in approval. "Always you learn quick, Gajo. Is one of the kinds of magic that even those who are not Blood, not Gypsy, can summon, but is rare, these things, very rare."

"So Lord Wodesby tells me," Adam said looking at Miranda. "Very few come back from such journeys, according to your brother."

Although Miranda listened carefully, his voice seemed devoid of derision. The sarcasm and doubt that had colored his expression was gone, replaced by serious consideration. Joy welled up in her. "You believe him, then?" she asked.

Tactfully, Tante Reina retreated to the bowels of the kitchen, silently commanding Thorpe to accompany her. As she stirred the pot, she muttered every good luck incantation that she knew.

Adam's face was touched by a self-deprecating smile. "Ironic, isn't it? The naysayer utterly exploded. But if I deny the evidence of my own observations, then I delude myself as much as my father did. I suppose that I never truly understood what would motivate an otherwise sensible man to be possessed by so strong an obsession, to seek on even in the face of obvious deception."

"And now you do?" Miranda asked, her voice just above a whisper. His gaze locked upon her, asking her some unspoken question. But try as she might, there was no reading the thoughts behind that fiery look that seemed to melt her to the marrow.

"Perhaps," he said softly. "My father possessed magic, Miranda, in the form of my mother. Although I was but a boy, there was no mistaking the strength of the love between them. When the two of them were together in a room, I vow, I almost felt lonely. When she died, he spent the rest of his life and fortune trying to regain what he had lost."

"An impossible task," Miranda said, wondering at the change in him. Before, when he had spoken of his father, there had been a brooding resentment, his expression tight with lines of anger. "And entirely wrongheaded. Among witchkind, Orpheus is considered more the fool than the hero for seeking out his Euridyce in Hades. Love is one of the few gifts given to mortals that may survive death. He had only to wait."

"Easy to say. But I suspect that few lovers feel that utter certainty," Adam said, looking down at his plate, concerned she would see his feelings naked in his eyes. "I have begun to think that fear is love's companion. Perhaps Orpheus and my father worried that love might not survive time and separation. Emotions change. And once you have known love, I suspect that it is difficult to survive without it. In a way, 'tis much like your witchcraft. Even myself, though I never really felt love, I yearned for it, if only in my secret heart. Deep down, I envied those few of my friends who had found it, even as I mocked it. 'Tis no wonder that my father refused to let go. Such obsession frightens me."

Even myself, though I never really felt love. Like an echo, the phrase reverberated inside her head over and over again. With all the rigor of a grammarian, Miranda parsed it to fit the framework of her fears. Her mother's instincts were wrong. He had excluded himself from the realm of lovers. That gentle look in his eyes was naught but a friend's concern. And that soul-searing kiss had been nothing more than the combination of his loneliness and her desperation.

Adam met her gaze, puzzled by the sudden transformation in her countenance. Gone was that glowing aura and in its place he found familiar melancholy. Impossible though it seemed after her tryst with death, she was still thirsting for sorcery. How could he tell her that she did not need witchery to weave a spell without declaring himself outright? "I had a friend once, by the name of Robert," he began hesitantly, hoping that Lord Hapbourne would forgive him for revealing his story. "A great lover of music, was Rob, played the piano like an angel. His ship was engaged in battle and Rob was near the mouth of a cannon when it fired. Burned him fairly badly, but worse, it left him deaf as a stone."

"Sweet Hecate," Miranda whispered, biting her lip as she absorbed the import of the injury.

"Indeed," Adam said, his eyes clouding as he recalled Rob's face on that long-ago night. "He seemed to be bearing up rather well, until his sister dragged him to the opera to meet a young lady who, it seems, was willing to ignore his infirmity for his purse."

"A stranger might be excused for her carelessness, but how could his sister be so cruel?" Miranda asked, feeling the prick of tears. "Did she hate her brother so, that she would wish to see him tortured?"

"She was simply an unthinking fool," Adam said, pleased that Miranda had grasped the direction of his theme. "Rob knew full well what his ears were missing. He followed every flourish of the violinists bow, every wave of the conductor's baton, until he could stand it no more and closed his eyes. When the orchestra reached the first crescendo, the vibration chased him from the box. I found him weeping in his coach, a pistol in his hand, ready to put a period to himself."

She hardly dared to ask, yet she did. "What happened?"

"I wrestled it from him. Due to Rob's condition, there were always writing materials at hand. I vow, I have never scribbled so quickly in all my life." He smiled, noting the faint upturn of her lips with satisfaction. "Told him about a musician I'd met in my travels, fellow by the name of Ludwig Beethoven."

"*The Pastoral?*" Miranda asked startled. "*The Eroica?*"

"The same. In fact, Ludwig had just completed his Eroica when we were introduced, wanted to see some of my magic for an idea that he was working on. We became friends. The German is an irascible man, but his temperament is entirely understandable, considering that he had been going progressively deaf since the turn of the century."

"How horrible!" Miranda gasped. "But his music, how—?"

Adam tapped his temple. "In here, Miranda. Ludwig hears it inside. Rob understood that, deciding that life might be worth something after all. But inner music is not enough for him. Last I heard, he was traveling the world seeking for a cure at any pain, any price. I pray that he can reconcile himself to his loss one day, before the quacks kill him. There are people who will hear for a hundred years and not listen half as well as Rob can, even without his ears; just as there are composers who will never create music like Ludwig's though they can detect the drop of a pin."

"Perhaps your friend will find his magic before he loses

hope," Miranda said. "Desperate people can do desperate things."

"As you did?" he asked, his hand stealing across the table to clasp her fingers, twining them in his. "Most of the world lives without magic, Miranda, unaware of its existence and yet content enough in their ignorance, as I was. My eyes were always earthward, denying the stars. But now that I have looked up, I can see that the stars are real."

"Damien can touch them," Miranda said longing in her voice. Despite herself, she felt a tremor at his grasp, like a distant flicker of lightning heralding a storm.

"And you and I can still enjoy their glow and rejoice that they shine," Adam said, leaning forward, squeezing with gentle pressure as if he could convince her with the force of his earnest belief. "There are so many kinds of magic, Miranda."

"Hear him, child," Tante Reina said from her place by the stove. "He speaks the truth."

"But you do not fully comprehend how important it is," Miranda protested, disentangling her fingers as she rose from her place. "Since the time of King James we were hunted. How many died, we will never know, for there were so many accused and condemned for witchery. If you understood, Adam, you would weep at what was lost, forgotten. There are so few true witches now that I had to try. Don't you see? And if I thought there was a chance of success, I would attempt the trip again. Cripple I may be, but I am still a Wodesby. I know what I owe my Blood."

Adam rose, her words wrenching into the core of him. She could never accept him, any more than she could accept herself. Out of a sense of duty, Miranda would doubtless acquiesce to the suitor that her brother had chosen, the man whose affection she doubted. The marquess was honest enough to admit that in the matter of the Blood, he was less than a mongrel.

As the implications of her statement unfolded, Adam realized that his chances of winning Miranda were slim, even if he could somehow win her brother's approval. With a husband who shared her birth, there might be a better chance that her children would possess the Gifts that she herself lacked.

Such sentiments were laudable, part of Society's code that he had hitherto accepted as a matter of course. Ancestry and breeding were paramount.

Yet comprehension did nothing to quell the rage roaring within him. While he could almost accept himself an unsuitable match, he could not abide the term "cripple" coming so casually from her lips again. How could the mate her brother had chosen—a man who, by her own admission, did not love her—come to value her if she did not value herself?

In five strides Adam was around the table grasping her shoulders in his hands. "Because I cannot make music like Beethoven or capture the world on canvas like Turner, am I any less of man? And if you cannot cast a spell, or conjure a ghost, it makes you no less of a woman. So do not dare to call yourself a cripple again, Miranda Wilton, not when there are so many in this world who have far less than you ever shall, who will never know that there is magic." Heedless of Tante Reina and Thorpe, he pressed his lips to hers mercilessly, kissing her with all the frustration of his stillborn hopes. Her blue eyes glistened as he looked down at her. "Sometimes, we are crippled by our own minds, Miranda. Unfortunately, those disabilities are usually the hardest to overcome." Without a backward glance, he headed up the stair.

Miranda managed to hold her tears until she heard the sound of the front door closing above. "He is gone, Tante Reina," she said, sinking down into her chair and reaching up to touch her bruised lips "How he must despise me."

"Despise you?" Tante Reina shook her head as she put a comforting hand on the young woman's shoulder. "So little you know of men, child. Only now has he realized what he feels; it frightens him. To find that he needs so badly is shock to a man. Could I but read your palm, I would tell you what is your future with him, but those of the Blood—"

"Aye, I know," Miranda said, bitterly cutting the old Gypsy off, "my lines of destiny cannot be read by the Rom. Even the cards can be deceiving when it comes to those who inherit the Blood. What good does it do me, this blood of mine, Tante Reina, other than set me apart?"

The older woman's eyes blazed. "He is right, the Gajo. Is

not lacking magic that makes you the cripple, Miranda. Tonight, your man's world is torn apart, much of what he believes turns upside down. Yet he sees your pain, he offers you comfort, he opens to you a window to his soul. But do you recognize this? You think is easy to say what he says? You, who learned to read faces like books did you not see how hard were his words?" She shook her head. "Only yourself, you see; poor Miranda, whom we all must pity. Well, child, my pity is upon you, for Brand was ready to offer you the greatest of magics."

Chapter 11

The swell stood out among the usual patrons of the Thistle like a guinea on the muck pile. Still, there was not a man among those dregs of humanity who was willing to take a chance at him, even with a fat purse for the taking; not with Abel Cole sitting beside him. To the denizens of the Thistle a slow suicide on blue ruin was infinitely preferable to a quick end at Abel's brawny hands. So they did their best to ignore Abel and his guest even as they listened intently.

"I tell yer, she ain't been about fer days," Abel said, smashing his fist against the table "An' them Gypsy people o'theirs don't talk ter nobody, even when I flashed th' ready an arsked fer me fortune, like yer tole me. Scum gives me th' eye like 'twas me who's th' dirt; an shows me th' sharp side o' 'is blade, when I arsked agin. I'm tellin' yer, it 'urt bad, it did, ter walk away when I wanted 'is teeth."

"At least you have some excuse for brains in your guts," Ropwell said impatiently. "Stir them up and we will never get the girl. Perhaps we may have to take her from the house itself."

"Too dangerous," Abel advised. "What wiv th' Gypsies always about. Bide awhile, I'd say. Got ter come out sometime, she does."

Time, however, was a commodity that was rapidly running out for Ropwell. The duns were already banging at his doors. Unless the Wodesby chit located his jewels soon, he was bound for Fleet or worse. Moreover, his lordship had the distinct feeling that Abel would not take kindly to an offer of vowels as promise of future payment. "Well, keep your eyes open for your chance," Ropwell said, letting the last of the cheap gin burn its path down his throat as a vague plan took form. Ironically, his only other hope lay in Lord Brand's hands and that gentleman had shown no sign thus far of fulfilling the terms of his wager before it came to forfeit. If Brand could somehow be prodded, then perhaps the inevitable could be postponed until the Wodesby chit was forced to find the jewels for him.

Lawrence Timmons frowned as the green gown slithered over his nephew's head. "Why is this necessary, Adam?" he said, eying the younger man with concern. "Especially tonight. If you would just wait for tomorrow, I would be glad to go with you to Guttmacher's Hall of Wonders."

"It has to be now, Uncle Lawrie," Adam explained, tweaking the false bodice into place. "The closer we draw to the final date, the more vigilant the false Professor Guttmacher will become. Besides, unless I make my effort soon, I might never be able to show my face at White's again. Rumor has it that I will forfeit without an effort because I have come to believe in witchcraft."

"But you have," Lawrence noted. "Surely you can cease this Inquisition of yours, now that you have confirmed that the phenomena exists."

"To the contrary, Uncle," Adam said, placing the wig upon his head. "'Tis all the more important now to show up the charlatans. With so much falsehood abroad, how can anyone determine the truth? I have never forfeited an honest wager in my life; I am not about to do so now."

"At least wait until I can go with you," Lawrence said, his tones just short of a plea. Nothing good would come of this, not when Adam was acting with such uncharacteristic recklessness. Although Brand's staff was absolutely trustworthy, there was no telling if the counterfeit professor's minions were still on the watch. Changing into costume at Brand House could well be a disastrous error.

"You may go on to Wodesby House in all good conscience, Uncle Lawrie," Adam said, thoughtfully selecting a patch from the box. Supposedly, shape and placement supplied a meaning.

Which one signified a heart that was frozen? "I wish you all the luck in the world in your interview with Wodesby."

"I would speak to him on your behalf, if you would allow it," Lawrence proposed.

"You will not!" Adam thundered, the patches scattering upon the carpet in a black flurry. "You might ruin your own chances to win Wodesby's favor. 'Twould be folly to believe that he would countenance a match with an Outsider like me."

"I am an 'Outsider,' as you call it," Lawrence pointed out.

"'Tis what they call it too." Adam gave a humorless laugh. "The mare that you want is already past breeding. Wodesby might well be content to let her graze on another man's pasture."

"You will cease to refer to Adrienne in coarse terms." Lawrence drew himself up sternly. "If I did not know that you were speaking out of frustration, I would box your ears, m'boy, despite your age."

"I do apologize, Uncle Lawrie," Adam said, shamefaced as a child caught with his fingers in the jampot. He fussed with the folds of the dress and avoided his uncle's eyes. "My conjuring skills deserted me, indeed, if I cannot even hide my feelings."

But Lawrence would not be mollified. "For the past two days you have been acting more the child than the man grown. And know you this, Adam: I am not going to *ask* Damien for Adrienne's hand. I am doing him the courtesy of informing him that I intend to marry his mother, will he, nil he."

"He may turn you into a frog," Adam warned, making a paltry attempt at humor.

"Then his mother assures me that she will be delighted to share my lily-pond," Lawrence declared with a confident smile that faded at his nephew's expression of utter dejection. "When I was young, Adam, I hesitated and lost the one woman that I ever loved. Life offers very few second chances, boy; remember that. Now do me the favor of postponing your confrontation with Bob Taylor until the morrow. Or if you are adamant, I shall send a footman to Wodesby and tell him that I will be delayed and we will face the erstwhile Herr Guttmacher together."

"Nonsense. All is arranged," Adam said, dismissing him with a wave of his hand. "You had given your notice as my abigail and I will do well enough without one, I assure you. Go on and give my felicitations to your lady. I am sorry I spoke so sharply about her."

Though there was a smile on his nephew's lips, Lawrence saw shadows of long-ago in Adam's eyes. The man's look of bewildered loss, the determination to hide the traces of pain were much the same as the boy's had been all those years before. But Lawrence could no longer put his arm around Adam and pull him close, or reassure him. Already, the proscribed boundaries of a gentleman's private business had been breached. He dared trespass no further. "So am I, dear boy," Lawrence replied, making a futile attempt to imbue those few words with the totality of his love and support. "So am I."

For a moment, in the dim shadows of twilight, Miranda thought that Adam had returned to Wodesby House. She grabbed hold of the baluster to steady herself, her heart leaping with hope. But as the man handed his hat to Dominick, the sight of Mr. Timmons's silver hair laid her momentary delusion to rest. She mustered her manners as she walked down the stair. "How are you, Mr. Timmons?" she asked, "and how does your nephew do?"

"I am tolerably well, Miss Wilton," Lawrence said. "However, these two days past, my nephew has been the most miserable excuse for a human being that I have had the misfortune to meet. He is rude, short of temper, and close to utterly impossible."

"It sounds as if he is afflicted by the same malady as the one besetting my Miranda," declared a voice from the stair above.

Mr. Timmons looked up at Lady Wodesby with his heart in his eyes, causing Miranda's throat to contract. Was this what Adam would be thirty years hence, a trim, dapper man with a warm smile and a youthful step? She realized that she wanted to see Adam change, to watch his hair turn from brown to gray, to be able to trace those lines of laughter at the corners of his eyes and know their history.

"I am quite pleased to hear that your daughter shares Adam's lamentable state," Lawrence said solemnly, taking Lady Wodesby's hand and kissing it with courtly affection.

"And your nephew's condition pleases me greatly," Lady Wodesby agreed with a smile. "An excellent omen."

"He is at wit's end," Lawrence added. "When he was dressing for his evening at Guttmacher's, I vow, he was surly as a bear."

"Even better!" Lady Wodesby exclaimed, nodding toward her daughter. "She comes running every time someone knocks upon the door these days."

"Mother, really!" Miranda fumed. "I do not! Nor do I appreciate being discussed as if I were not present."

"Kind of you to greet me, Miss Wilton," Lawrence said, his lip twitching as he resisted the urge to curve it. But the impulse to smile faded as the door to the library swung open. "Ah, the young lion beckons. Shall we beard him in his den, milady?" he asked, offering his arm to Lady Wodesby.

To Miranda's surprise her mother actually giggled as she tucked her hand into the crook of Mr. Timmons' arm. Her mother had fallen in love with Adam's uncle. How had she missed the signs? She watched open-mouthed as the two entered the library, their eyes fixed upon each other. The door closed behind them, then opened again as Thorpe and Angel made their exit, mewling and growling in their disgruntlement at being excluded.

"Private means just that," Miranda scolded, looking at the animals in growing alarm. "Now, which one of you is supposed to be keeping watch over Adam?"

Angel barked.

"What do you mean, 'There is no longer a need'? He is under Wodesby protection," Miranda said, uneasy as she thought of Adam alone and vulnerable. At least he would be among people if he was going out for the evening to . . . to Guttmacher's! "Hecate!" she murmured. Guttmacher was the one who had arranged for Adam to be ambushed. She looked at the closed library door doubtfully, hearing the murmur of voices. If Damien had decreed that the Wodesby shield was unnecessary, there would be no help from that quarter.

She turned and walked back up the stairs to her room pulling her cloak from the wardrobe and stuffing her pistols into her reticule. Silently, she stole out the servant's way, avoiding the curious gaze of the familiars, or so she thought. Halfway down the square, she heard an inquiring "meow" at her heels. "An evening stroll," she replied casually.

Thorpe hissed.

"If you want no lies, then ask no questions," Miranda told him, walking on toward the corner where there were usually hackney cabs to be hired.

"Cor! Nearly missed yer, I did." A hulking bruiser stepped into Miranda's path. " 'Is nibs didn't tell me yer was daft, but lucky yer crazy enough ter talk ter cats, else I would've let yer pass. Wounnent let th' darter o' the 'ouse out by 'er lonesome, I tells meself. Then, I 'ear yer talkin' ter' th' tom 'ere, an' yer didn't sound like no servant."

"I am glad my elocution is pleasing," Miranda said, her fingers creeping into her reticule as the man walked toward her. She would puzzle out his meaning later. At the present, however, there was no mistaking the menace of his stance. It would be a pity to ruin the bottom of the bag, a delightful brocade that matched her walking dress perfectly, but there was no helping it. She cocked the hammer, aimed by instinct and clipped him neatly in the shoulder, knocking him off his feet.

"I have a second pistol loaded," she told him, pulling out the gun with a flourish. "Just in case I need to finish the job."

"Yer daft," he whispered, clutching his arm.

"Then you had best not risk coming after me again, just in case I am mad enough to kill you." She favored him with the most maniacal grin she could manage and he cringed. "My cat will keep a paw at the ready."

Thorpe yowled his objection.

"Yes, you are right," Miranda agreed, taking her cue from Thorpe. A good scare was definitely in order. "It might be much simpler to give his brains an airing, but it would mess the walk and we are in a hurry." She watched from the corner of her eye as the fellow crawled crabwise toward the cover of bushes.

"Dinnent mean no 'arm," he protested.

"Shall I call the Watch, then?" she asked sweetly, keeping him in sight over her shoulder as she walked toward the waiting hackney. Thorpe yowled once again as she shut the door to the cab before he could jump in. "Inform Tante Reina that I am going to Guttmacher's Hall of Wonders to find a cure," she called as the driver flicked his whip. "And tell Dominick to remove that giant slug from the shrubbery and hold him. I want to know who sent him and why." As the carriage careered toward Picadilly, Miranda recalled Mr. Timmons's disparaging description of his nephew's condition. "Surly, rude, miserable, close to impossible." She smiled.

By the time Miranda had paid her fare, she barely had the pound left to purchase her ticket to Guttmacher's Hall of Wonders. Inside, she found the place so gaudy that it made Prinny's pavilion at Brighton seem like a Quaker meeting place. Mirrors and crystal predominated, sending candlelight glittering from the walls to the chandeliers in a series of endless reflections. Rows of gilt and velvet chairs were arranged in a semicircular fashion around a raised platform where an impressive monstrosity sat enthroned amidst a maze of wires and glass. She recognized the Leyden jars from her studies. A magical education required a thorough knowledge of natural forces.

As her eyes adjusted gradually to the glare, she surveyed the other members of the audience. A rail-thin woman coughed agony in the corner while an anxious man held her upright. Consumption, from the sound of it. A young mother helped her son toward a chair; one of the boy's legs was conspicuously shorter than the other. Carefully, she set his crutches beside the seat, ruffled his tow-colored hair in a comforting gesture as she stared hopefully toward the mighty machine. Liveried servants carried in an elderly man marked with chancres, while an old woman in a hideous green dress dozed in the front row, her ancient wig dipping in rhythm with her snores. Every seat was filled with the lame, the halt, the blind, old and young. But with all their myriad ailments, they had one thing beyond hope in common. For the most part, they were obviously well-to-do.

An usher guided her to a seat. Friendly to a fault, he questioned without seeming to pry, worming information that he would undoubtedly relay to Guttmacher. Undoubtedly, the members of the audience would fail to recall those unobtrusive questions and be astonished when Guttmacher pluckered intimate details of their illnesses seemingly from the ether. As she chatted with the usher, Miranda evaluated the charlatan's lay. Obviously the man was a master; all had been carefully planned. A few minutes in the glare of mirrors and lights and the eye would be thoroughly confused. The shining planes of the metal machine mimicked the majesty of the druid's great alter with its velvet-draped table at the center. A silver sickle and mistletoe would have added a touch of authenticity, she thought with a secret smile as she peered around in search of Adam.

Ropwell too, was searching for signs of Lord Brand, but found not a trace. He leaned back in disappointment as it became apparent that the rumors that he had spread at White's had failed to bait the hook. However, the sight of Miranda Wilton entering the room was enough to distract him from his quest. She seemed entirely alone, but her presence was an indication that Brand might well be somewhere nearby. The marquess's interest in the girl had seemed far more than friendly. With any luck at all, Ropwell would have both the girl and his winnings in hand before the night was done. He slouched in his seat, using the considerable bulk of the man beside him as a shielding bulwark.

Adam kept his eyes closed against the glare, opening them at intervals to survey the lay of the land. Favoring the usher with a pinch-mouthed smile, he wondered how long it would take him to be called upon. Their master could not be able to resist the tale that he had been given; an endless list of nebulous female troubles that Bob Taylor could simply announce that he had cured, a potential golden goose for the plucking.

The marquess could barely keep from grinning as he pictured what would happen when he revealed himself as a man. Taylor would be a laughingstock and the Cockney "professor" would slink back to the gutter from whence he came. Eyes shut once more, Adam let his mind float, listening to the mur-

mur of the crowd, hearing the threads of pathetic stories and
aching for these hopeful miracle seekers. Unfortunately, they
would find not magic here.

Magic . . . his thoughts drifted inexorably toward Miranda,
conjuring her face from the fabric of his fantasy even as he
tried to exorcise her from his memory. But he was well and
truly haunted, unable to rid himself of her shade. He imagined
the feel of her mouth beneath his, the yielding softness of her
body; even the sound of her voice seemed to come to him
clearly through the sounds of the crowd.

Adam's eyes flew open. Slowly, carefully, he turned his
head, raising his lorgnette like a dowager of venerable vin-
tage. Seated toward the rear was Miranda, without so much as
a companion to give her countenance. She dabbed her eyes
with a handkerchief as she spoke, favoring the man with a wa-
tery smile that was more dazzling than any of the chandeliers.
What in the devil did she think that she was about? Adam
wondered uneasily. He was in the process of fabricating a
story about his chance-met niece when the crowd began to
stir. Taylor was making his entrance. To the ignorant, he
seemed nearly as German as Blücher himself.

"Gut eefening," Guttmacher began. His long-winded
speech was choked with Teutonic, scientific-sounding
folderol. He spoke of friendships with Franklin and Faraday,
and he named a few Prussian names who had been dead when
Miranda's grandmère had been rocking in in the cradle. His
fakery was so ridiculously transparent that it was difficult to
keep from laughing. However, the serious countenances of the
audience, their nods and expectant expressions, showed their
impressions to be entirely favorable.

Miranda toyed with the possibility of getting up and making a speech in German. To a knowing ear, the man's accent
was obviously as false as his credentials. But she knew that
such precipitate action would only get her summarily ejected.
Somewhere in this crowd was Adam. Though she was no
witch, she could feel his presence and she was determined to
make sure of his safety.

The sham healer started his demonstration with the chancre-
ridden satyr, making the old man's few remaining hairs stand

on end with a dose of simple static electricity before pronouncing his cure in progress. Naturally, the case was too far advanced for one night to render him entirely healthy. However, the old man testified that he was feeling much better and that he would be sure to return.

Adam waited uneasily to be called, but recognized that Taylor was a showman first and foremost. The marquess began to suspect that he was being saved for that grand finale, when the crowd was be stoked to a frenzy. At the point they would accept any assertion, no matter how outrageous, and the line between audience and mob could fade from thin to nil.

"Iss dere a Calvin Hotchkins in mein audience?" Guttmacher asked, his eyes resting on the tow-headed boy. "You cannot valk, yah?"

The audience murmured at this sage deduction.

"Brink him to mein table, fraulein," Guttmacher commanded, "and lay him down, yah?"

Trembling, the young woman helped her boy up on his crutches. Eagerly, she placed him up on Guttmacher's altar, waiting for wonders.

"Votch, fraulein," he told her, "and you vill see the heilig power of mein machine. Pray for your boy, fraulein." Once more the electricity crackled, magnified into infinity by the mirrors.

The characteristic smell was like that of a lightning storm before the rain. Miranda leaned forward, holding her breath as Guttmacher seized hold of the boy's leg and tugged at its bottom until the lad cried out. Before their very eyes the flesh seemed to lengthen. Dramatically, Guttmacher seized the boy's crutches and broke them one at a time.

"No more vill dese be needed!" he declared solemnly.

"Papa will love me now!" the child proclaimed, his face luminous with happiness. "Papa will love me!"

"Stop!" Miranda proclaimed, unable to bear the cruel illusion any longer. Rising from seat she ran to the platform, confounding the ushers. "His leg has not grown so much as an inch, Madame. Just measure it and you will see."

"But I saw it grow myself," the woman protested.

"Yah, as ve all did," Guttmacher hastened to add, nodding toward his henchmen.

"No," Miranda said, backing away. "What you saw was this man manipulating the child's shoe. Measure the leg, I tell you. You will see no difference. Guttmacher is a fraud; he is no more a German than I am an Italian."

"Das poor voman is confused, yah!" Guttmacher said, advancing upon her. "She iss crazy in her head, das is vy dey iss bringing her 'ere. Ve must pity 'er, yah? Ve must help 'er mit a dose from mein machine. A very big dose, yah?"

"Do not lay a hand upon her Guttmacher, or should I say, Taylor?" Brand said throwing his wig to the ground and ripping off his dress to reveal immaculate evening clothes.

"Brand! 'Ow did you get in 'ere?" Taylor exploded.

"Careful of your 'haitches,' Taylor; your Cockney origins are beginning to show," Brand taunted as he leapt to the stage. "Get out of here, Miranda," he commanded in an undertone, putting her protectively behind him. "My coach is waiting to your left, down the street, pair of grays, no driver, in the alleyway. If I do not return, wait until the furor dies down and head home."

"But you need my help," she protested as they retreated in the face of Guttmacher's minions.

"If you do not do as I say, we will both be beyond help," he replied, his teeth gritted as he estimated his chances of getting through the rear door intact. Even if his distraction worked, it would be close, too close.

Miranda reached into her reticule and pulled out a pistol. "I believe that you will find this one is loaded," she said, checking that the muzzle was clean of spent powder before sliding it into his hand.

"Miranda, my love, you are amazing," Adam said, brandishing the pistol. "Get back, Taylor," he warned. "Or else we will see if your miracle machine can accomplish a resurrection."

"One shot, Brand, is all yer got, an' I wiv a dozen men," the Cockney laughed, all traces of his German accent vanishing.

"In that case, I'll reserve it for you," Brand said steadily. "Now you and your men back off."

With a scowl, the false professor signaled to his men, and they retreated to the edge of the stage.

"Stalemate," Miranda whispered.

"Not quite." Brand grinned, pulling a corked flask from his pocket, palming it off to Miranda as he murmured instructions. "An ingenious little bottle this, thin glass chambers separating some simple chemicals. On the count of three, close your eyes throw it to the ground, hard, then use your feet, my love. I go through the back and you take the front way. One . . . two . . ." He raised the pistol and fired at the heart of Guttmacher's machine producing a shower of sparks. "Three!" The magnesium compound hit the floor producing a blinding flare of light and a puff of smoke.

Miranda sprinted for the door, eluding the arms of the momentarily dazzled ushers. One of them nearly caught her, pulling at the heavy chain of her emerald pendant, but the clasp came undone and she snatched it from his grasp. Through the lobby she ran, out the door and down the stairs into the night.

Adam's carriage was exactly where he said it would be. She opened the door and climbed in, leaning back against the velvet squabs to draw a shuddering breath. Her reticule slipped to the floor with a soft thud. Panting, she reviewed the course of the past few moments, wondering if she ought to go back. Had Adam really used the words "my love," or had it just been her imagination? Once might be fancy or the heat of the moment, but twice he had said it, twice. The facets of her emerald cut into her clenched fist as her tension mounted. What was keeping Adam? She set the broken pendant carefully on the seat beside her and reached for the handle of the door.

Just then, Miranda heard the sound of footsteps approaching the carriage. "Adam!" she murmured in relief as the door opened.

"Actually, I expect that Lord Brand is presently occupied," Lord Ropwell said, catching Miranda by the wrist and hauling her from the cab. "Last I saw he was being chased out the rear door; foolishly noble of him to wait until the temporary blindness wore off so they caught sight of him. That was when I suspected you had taken another route and came seeking for his carriage. My second bit of luck tonight."

"Second?" She squirmed, trying to pull herself from his grasp.

"Your friend Brand has just chased the duns from my doorstep. I bet heavily upon his success and the winnings should be substantial. So now, I have money and . . ."

His hand rose. Too late she saw the haft of the dagger in his fist, plunging her into darkness.

"And now I have you." Ropwell laughed as he threw her into the seat of his waiting carriage.

"I vow, Damien, I cannot believe that you were so foolish," Lady Wodesby fumed as the carriage swayed, rounding Picadilly at racing pace. "To remove the protection that I placed without informing me."

Thorpe meowed in agreement.

"Mother, please, must we air our differences before Outsiders?" Damien asked, grabbing at the strap to avoid being thrown into Lawrence Timmons's lap.

Angel barked vociferously.

"No one asked you," Lady Wodesby rebuked. "Lawrence is going to be my husband, Damien—your stepfather, like it or not! So I suspect the poor dear will have to get used to our little quibbles."

"Little quibbles? Like the time Cousin Erasmus set a pair of horns growing from Uncle Walter's head? Or when little Elise Peregrine wove a spell that caused every stick of wood in Gwynnfold to burst into flame, Chippendale included."

"Elise is well past that now," Lady Wodesby declared stoutly. "She will make someone an excellent wife, I am sure."

"One hopes, considering the cost of furniture these days!" Damien snorted. "Welcome to the family, Mr. Timmons. At least we can assure you against a lifetime of boredom."

Lawrence nodded perfunctorily, checking anxiously out the window.

"I am sure that Adam will be well," Lady Wodesby said, her hand reaching across the carriage to clasp Lawrence's. "Miranda is protecting him, you know."

"And who is protecting Miranda?" Damien asked, craning his neck as they approached the Hall of Wonders.

"His carriage will be in that alleyway, there!" Lawrence pointed. "There he is. The devils have him cornered."

"Handy with his fives, I see," Damien said appreciatively as he watched Adam plant a facer. "Still, I cannot like those odds; seven to one is still less than sporting." As the coach came to a halt, Damien pulled off his jacket and swung himself out the door, glancing toward the sky as he heard the sound of approaching thunder. A few moments more and it would be nearly overhead. He grinned, grabbing a bruiser who was about to take Adam from behind. Raising him by the collar, Damien tossed him toward the wall like a rag doll. Whirling round, he waited until Angel's snapping jaws herded his prey into range. His fists joined, Damien drove them like a cudgel into the gut of another of Guttmacher's minions.

Dominick jumped from the box to confront one of the attackers. "Long time since I've had a good fight," the Gypsy said. "I put my knife down, eh, if you stand, Gajo. Do we have a bargain?" His lip drooped in disappointment as the man turned tail and ran.

"Even odds now," Lawrence said, swinging his walking stick to smash neatly across the second man's knees, before leaving him with a well-placed right to the jaw.

"Better than even," Lady Wodesby said, walking up to a fighter who was trying to ward off a clawing, spitting cat. "Allow me, Thorpe," she warned. Instantly, the feline padded off as his opponent stood, awestruck at the diminutive turbaned woman who eyed him with disdain. Hesitation was fatal. With a swift fluid movement Lady Wodesby tugged him by the arm and flipped him to the ground like a sausage in a frying pan. "Peter and I learned that in the Orient," she explained proudly as Lawrence eyed her in astonishment.

"Still want to marry the woman, Timmons?" Damien asked.

"I shall just remember not to anger her," Lawrence replied with dignity. "I see that my nephew has matters well in hand."

"Where is she, Taylor?" Adam demanded, holding the

sham healer up against the wall. "Where is the woman who was up on the stage with me?"

"Dunno!" he gasped. "Dunno, I swear! Lemme go, milord."

"She was not in the carriage where she was supposed to meet me. One of your vermin must have taken her. Now tell me where Miss Wilton is, Taylor, or I will paint the wall with the insides of your head."

"The Tailor!" Lady Wodesby blanched. "Miranda is missing?"

"I found her things in my carriage, but she was gone," Brand explained, tightening his hold upon Taylor's collar. "Now where is she?"

"Back away, Brand," Damien said, his green eyes glowing with a feral amber light.

Adam hesitated, but it was not the savage intensity of Damien's countenance that persuaded him to yield so much as Taylor's reaction. As the Mage raised his hands skyward, the bloodstained sleeves of his shirt slipped to his shoulders, revealing a gold armband decorated with ancient runes. The jeweled ring on his finger emitted a strange light, too strong to be a reflection of the rapidly clouding moon. Taylor began to quiver like an aspic. Perhaps Wodesby could succeed where Adam had failed.

"You are fond of electricity, I hear, Taylor," Damien said, his voice heavy with threat. "So am I." The golden band glowed bright as he closed his fist and the thunder rolled. A shimmering spear of silver came to his hand, like Jove on Olympus. "Where is my sister?" he demanded, his tones rolling like the thunder itself. "Where is Miranda?"

"Dunno," Taylor gasped, trying to melt into the wall. "I swear by the devil isself, yer worship. Ain't seen 'er since she made the lightning come."

"You lie!" He hurled the jagged bolt, barely missing the man's head. "Now tell me where she is!" he commanded once more as the shower of sparks sputtered on the ground.

Taylor fell to his knees, blubbering like a babe. "Dunno, I dunno. Don't let the divvil kill me, please L-ord. I swear, I won't do the healin' lay no more. I'll give the money to the orphans and stop cheatin' on th' missus."

"See that you do," Damien said. "I will spare you for now, but remember, I shall be watching. Help him on the road to redemption, Angel."

The mastiff bared his teeth and Taylor scrambled to his feet and ran, with the hound of hell baying after him.

"Why did you let him go?" Adam asked angrily.

"Because he was telling the truth," Damien replied wearily. "He has no idea where Miranda is."

Adam leaned against the wall, shaking his head. "Then where is she? I had managed to throw them off, but she was not here in the carriage to meet me."

"Perhaps she went searching for you?" Lawrence suggested, pulling a handkerchief from his pocket and handing it to Adam. "Best to staunch that nose, m'boy. 'Tis bleeding something fierce."

"I went back, but there was not a trace of her. Then Taylor spotted me," Adam said, a groan of despair in his voice as he dabbed absently at his bloody nose. "Someone took her, Uncle Lawrie. Her reticule was left in my carriage, and this." He pulled her emerald pendant from his pocket, letting it dangle from his hand.

Lady Wodesby gasped. "Her naming jewel."

Lawrence put a soothing arm around her shoulder.

"You are quite correct, Brand," Damien said, his expression dire. "My sister would not have voluntarily abandoned that pendant. That stone was given to her when she received her name and it has never left her body since. She was taken by force. The question is, by whom?"

Chapter 12

A whirlpool of light, blinding brightness with eddies of glare, like the summer sun on still water. A voice called her name. "Miranda . . . my love . . . Miranda . . ." Adam . . . Adam was calling her from somewhere within the dazzling chaos. She felt fingers upon her skin, in her hair, but it was not his touch. Paper-dry, a lizard's reptilian caress, the touch of Death. The unseen hands wandered to her neck, lingering on the column of her throat, sliding downward. She tried to move, to brush the unseen creature away, but she heard the clink of chains. A manacle held her wrist.

Miranda's eyes flew open. She was lying on a divan, fixed by a length of iron to the floor.

"I thought that might bring you around," Ropwell jeered. "In any case, it was a delightful way to while away the time. No one else here but the two of us."

She tried to get up, only to fall back when the room began to sway. Once more, she closed her eyes trying to still the spinning sensation and steady her thoughts. Recollection returned, along with a sense of dread. It took no witchcraft to determine that Ropwell was desperate and therefore dangerous. Only dire need could have spurred the man to kidnap a Wodesby witch, and witch he believed her to be. Was this the doom that Hecate had set for her, then? To die for lack of sorcery just when she had found true magic? Chained, at Ropwell's dubious mercy, there was no weapon left her.

Save illusion. She nurtured that small spark of hope. If she could use Ropwell's belief in her to her advantage, play upon fear that was companion to his faith in her power, she might be able to purchase some time. A dangerous masquerade, a dance on the razor's edge—the least slip would likely prove fatal, but it was the only chance she had. Her restrained hand slipped to a hidden pocket as she felt Ropwell's breath on her cheek. Brandy . . . if he was somewhat foxed that might prove to her advantage.

"Touch me again, Ropwell and you are a dead man," Miranda warned, shoving him aside with her free hand. The unexpected blow sent him flying off the divan. She rose with languid grace as he got unsteadily to his feet. From the look of it, he had taken a heavy dose of Dutch courage.

"You are in no position to make threats, Miss Wilton. I have it upon excellent authority that iron negates a witch's powers," Ropwell said angrily.

"Some of them," Miranda informed him with every appearance of icy disdain. "However, you are still in mortal jeopardy. Obviously, you have been possessed by some demon, else you would not have taken so foolish a risk. The wrath of the Wodesbys is not usually hazarded unless the stakes are high. You may have thwarted me, but my family will find me. And you."

His sneer was frozen on his lips and while he was not yet trembling, the whites of his eyes had enlarged perceptibly. Fear. She would build on it. "Why are you daring my anger, demon?" she asked, though she could guess the answer. "Answer and know you this: My brother the Mage has never been known to take insult lightly. So even should you prove a satanic shade with powers greater than mine, My brother Damien will pursue you to the very halls of Hades. He has more than a passing acquaintance with the master there."

The image of an angry Lord Wodesby pounding the gates of hell was quelling. It took some moments before Ropwell found his voice. "You did not seem so adept at self-defense when we were in Guttmacher's Hall, Miss Wilton."

She gave him what she hoped was a knowing smile. "I was content to let Brand defend me. Men always prefer to believe that they are stronger, in control. Adam does not believe what I am, and for the moment it suits me so. But you believe, don't you, Ropwell? Else I would not be here. So, tell me what you want or let me go about my business."

Ropwell looked at her in confusion. Her reaction was entirely unexpected, as was her demeanor. Despite her stained, torn, clothing, she had an arrogant air of royalty. "You are the witch," he sputtered. "Why do you not tell me?"

Miranda forced a laugh, her fear tinging it just the right maniacal shade. "It would appear that you do not know as much about witches as you would think, milord. We are not all Seers and Readers of thoughts, but I think I can guess what you are seeking. This." She raised her free hand, plucking at the air above her as if gathering fruit from a bough and threw a shower of coins, silver, and copper at his feet, the entire contents of her hidden pocket. Once more she laughed, this time at his open-mouthed awe. "It always comes down to money with mortals. You wish me to find Felicity's jewels. However, you are mistaken if you believe that you have won my favor with cold iron." She picked up the length of the chain and rattled it distastefully.

Ropwell looked down at the fallen coins, moving one of them with the toe of his boot. "I made your brother an excellent proposal, far more than the original five hundred pounds that I suggested at Lady Pelton's séance," he said, his tones those of a recalcitrant schoolboy.

"You offered him money?" Miranda said, with a throaty chuckle. "Ah, Ropwell, the devil must favor you, for I've seen Damien transform men into mice for lesser insults. As you can see, we have no need for paltry bits of shiny metal. Besides, you should have come to me."

"Then what do you want?" Ropwell asked suspiciously.

"For the jewels?" Miranda tapped her chin in a gesture of consideration. "Firstborn sons are preferable, though Damien has been known to accept a daughter should she prove uncommon pretty. But you are without issue, so you have naught to barter there . . . hmm. I suppose I could ask for your immortal soul."

"You did not ask for Lady Pelton's soul," Ropwell protested. "You would not even take her diamond necklace."

"She was my grandmère's friend and summoning her lord was not a difficult task. Pelton's shade actually wished to see her. However, I suspect that your Felicity might be somewhat reluctant to do anything to assist you," Miranda explained with scorn. "Uncooperative ghosts can be almost as unpleasant as angry mages. When you put that into the cauldron, I doubt that your soul would be worth the trouble, tarnished as it is. Moreover, Damien might consider it forfeit anyway, under the circumstances." She quirked a brow, observing him carefully. She dared not push him beyond fear, back into anger, or she was lost.

"P-p-please, Miss Wilton, I meant no harm. It is just th-th-that those jewels are my last hope," Ropwell told her.

"Very well," she sighed. "I suppose that your soul will have to do, though Damien will be sorely vexed with me. Between Parliament and the Exchange we have had a surfeit of souls come on the market of late. Now, we must get it all right and tight, in contract form of course, before my brother's arrival."

She sounded as if she truly believed it imminent and Ropwell hastened out of the room in search of writing implements.

As his footsteps retreated, Miranda collapsed on to the divan, drawing a ragged breath. From the layer of dust, it looked as if this room had not been visited for some time. She got up and walked the full length of her tether, searching for something that she might use as a weapon, but the tower room was bare, save a small cracked mirror, a warped wardrobe, a plain wooden table, and a bed. Moonlight shone silver through a large window that rose from floor to ceiling. The river winding below was likely the Thames, though she could not be sure. As she tried to puzzle out her location, she heard a curse, the sound of stumbling on the stair. Miranda found herself praying her captor would not put an end to himself before she could win her freedom.

With a triumphant flourish, Ropwell produced a portable writing desk.

"Not quite parchment, but it will do," Miranda pronounced, donning the mask of bravado once again as she pulled out a sheet of yellowed vellum and a quill. She picked up the sharpening knife. "If you will just give me your left thumb."

"For what purpose?" Ropwell asked suspiciously, taking a step back.

Miranda put down the knife with exasperation. "Honestly, Ropwell, do you think I could gut you with a wee bit of steel such as this? All soul contracts must be made out in blood, or else they are invalid. Now, if you wish me to summon your wife, then we had best get on with it before the night wanes. Surely you can spare a bit of claret with a fortune at stake?"

Ropwell stuck out his hand and averted his eyes.

Warm in his place by the hearth, Thorpe opened his eyes as Damien entered the library at Wodesby House, Angel at his heels. Adam stalked across the floor to confront the Mage. "What did you get from the man that Miranda shot?" he asked.

"His employer supplied no name, but from the description that he gave me, we can now be certain that it was Ropwell that hired him," Damien said, looking down at Brand with a forbidding expression that would have stilled the tongues of most men.

Not Brand's.

"A revelation!" Adam said, his voice dripping sarcasm. "How many spells and incantations did it require, Wodesby, to confirm what I posited nearly an hour ago?"

"No sorcery at all Brand, but science," Damien replied, holding up a bruised hand. "Physical force was sufficient and, if I might say, somewhat satisfying."

"But not at all illuminating," Adam maintained, his jaw setting stubbornly. "While you have been scraping your knuckles, I have been to Ropwell's apartments. A crown was all it took to get his valet talking. It would seem that his lordship's man has not been paid for some time now. But when Ropwell left this evening, he promised that the fellow would receive all that was owed him before the week's end."

"Did you find out where Miranda could have been taken?" Damien asked.

"Do you think I would have returned here, Wodesby, if I knew that?" Adam shook his head. "The servant has only been with Ropwell for a quarter. He knows little beyond the fact that his master owns several properties, for his lordship is always complaining that the income they produce is paltry.

My uncle is at White's now, trying to ascertain the locations of Ropwell's lands."

"If he is going to ground in his own burrow," Damien said, slumping wearily into a chair, his head in his hands. "And we cannot even be certain of that."

"Dammit, man," Adam said, grabbing Wodesby by the shoulders. "Ropwell is going to force Miranda to raise a ghost. She may be able to cozen him for a bit, but what do you think her chances will be when she cannot locate those jewels that he seeks?" Like a terrier worrying a bear, he shook Miranda's brother. "Is that all you can do, oh Mage of Albion? What about that much-vaunted magic of yours?"

"Magic has its limitations," Damien admitted, looking candidly into Brand's eyes and seeing his love for Miranda writ there plain. He had wronged this man and his sister both. Fate was not always to blame for misfortune. If Damien had simply blessed the match as his mother had wished, all might have been well.

But he had chosen to interfere and now all his pride and all the power of the Blood could do nothing. "Before history began, the world was filled with mages and witches, our legends say. No different were we than any other men or women in our lusts and greeds. We fought each other in our struggle for power, laying waste to lands and peoples. So it was that Hecate placed restraints on the forces of magic, so that it could not be bent to such horrendous destruction again. When we use our powers for ourselves, they may well go awry. Visions are muddied and vague; a summoning may prove the conjurer's doom, the messages of the cards are oft misleading to those of the Blood."

"So you are saying that your powers cannot help you locate Miranda," Adam stated flatly, his hold relaxing. "Then what is it worth, all your thunder and lightning?" His hand swept the vast contents of the shelves in a dismissive wave. "What is the use of all these books and all your magic, if I lose her in the end?"

Brand's fists fell to his side, tensing into knots of despair, and Damien felt a strong kinship to the Outsider. Indeed, for Miranda, the Blood might prove her undoing, unless . . .

Reaching into his pocket, the Mage pulled out his sister's pendant, staring deep into the crystalline depths. "Do you love my sister, Brand?" he asked distractedly.

"This is scarcely the time to probe my intentions, Wodesby," Brand said bitterly. "Now, if there is naught you can do in the supernatural realm, I am going to begin my hunting in the usual manner. I will find Ropwell somehow and when I do, I might save a bit of his guts for you. But first, I am going to seek my uncle and find out what information he might have unearthed."

"There may be a better way," Damien said, his excitement growing as new possibilities opened before him. Brand's destiny was clearly entwined with Miranda's. Such strong bonds could work both ways and the marquess's love had called his sister back from the brink of the Light itself. "You are not of the Blood."

"Uncommon bright you are tonight," Adam commented, grabbing his hat from a chair. "Nonetheless, Wodesby, I full intend to marry your sister as soon as I find her. She has no need of your consent at her age. If the mage that you have already pledged her to wishes to turn me into a maggot, then let him do his worst, but have him wait until I find her, if you please." He turned toward the door.

"I cannot do magic for Miranda," Damien said, the worried crease in his brow relaxing in relief as the solution presented itself. "But I can conjure for you, Brand, and I will, if you would give me a token."

Adam turned, shaking his head in disbelief. "A token? By heaven, man, she is your own sister."

"It must be for you that I conjure," Damien insisted, his expression inscrutable. "Or else her sanguinity may interfere with my spell. A pledge of some kind is necessary."

"Anything, if it will help me find her. Name it!" Adam declared.

"A dangerous offer, sir, if you would deal with witches and mages," Damien cautioned. "Be wary. For our price is rarely gold and silver and the cost of magic must be in proportion to the service rendered."

"Tell me what you want, Wodesby, and let us be done with

it," Adam demanded, his patience waning. "'Tis your sister's life at stake."

"Not my sister here, but your love," Damien told him smoothly. "A mere matter of semantics though it may seem, it will make all the difference. Very well, my price is my consent to my sister's marriage. You must agree to abide by my decision."

Adam tried to read Wodesby's expression, but no longer was he the worried brother. In the space of a few seconds he was every inch the Mage. By pledging his word, the marquess knew that he would likely lose Miranda to the man that her brother had already chosen. But if that was the price of her life, then he would pay it.

"Done!" Adam replied, his expression gray and hard as granite.

"So shall it be," the Mage intoned, his voice deep as the knelling of a bell. He rolled up his sleeve once again, tucking the folds in his runic band and went to the shelves. "Look for maps, Brand. Particularly London and its environs. 'Tis my guess they could not have gotten too far."

Though Adam wanted to question, Wodesby's brisk professional manner precluded any explanation. Obediently, the marquess searched through the section that Wodesby had indicated. "Here they are—maps. The Land of Hungary, Greece, Genoa, France, Finn's Land, England . . ." He pulled out a series of folios, spreading the volumes of copperplates and engravings upon the library table.

"Now, do exactly as I tell you," Damien commanded, unfolding Brand's hand and placing Miranda's jewel in the marquess's cupped palm. "Hold this by its chain, moving it back and forth above the volumes. Concentrate on my sister and let the motion lead you."

"Dowsing?" Adam asked, looking doubtfully at the pendant. "I have heard of such divining for water or metals, but never for people."

"'Coscinomancy' it is called, but it employs the same principles," the Mage explained. "Miranda has found records of the practice dating back to Greek times, using diverse devices. To find the missing, some personal item is usually the best, but it is not the tool so much as the wielder." Once more, he shifted from forbidding mage to worried brother, fixing the marquess with an appealing gaze. "You must believe, Brand. If ever you have believed anything in your life, believe in your love now." With the tip of his finger, he set the emerald swinging and began a rhythmic chant.

Though Adam could not understand, the Mage's words resonated in his mind, their flavor strange, like a new spice on the tongue. As the incantation echoed, Adam closed his eyes, picturing Miranda's upturned face. He saw her once again for the first time, shy and uncertain at Lady Enderby's party. The chain swung to and fro as he moved slowly along the edge of the table, the motion of the links seeming to tug him along. Miranda in his arms, waltzing, tantalizing him with her nearness. Suddenly his hand was pulled downward and he opened his eyes.

"Horwood's maps of London." Damien seized the folio with a whoop of delight. "He has not taken her from Town yet." With a careless sweep, he brushed the rest of the volumes to the floor. Meticulously, he set out the thirty-two pages of engravings, covering the library table completely with the detailed drawings of streets and alleyways. "Again, Brand, concentrate."

Once more, the Mage began his wizardry as Adam took up the jewel. Letting the swing of the emerald guide him, the marquess filled his mind with thoughts of Miranda. As the chant touched his senses, he pictured her as she had been at Guttmacher's Hall of Wonders, fearless, confronting the charlatan. He felt her at his back, peering over his shoulder, the warmth of her hand penetrating his jacket like a lick of fire. All at once, Wodesby's pitch rose to a mourning keen and though Adam could not translate, he felt the meaning in his marrow. To lose Miranda just as he was beginning to know just how much she meant to him. How could he have been so heedless? He had failed her . . . failed her utterly.

Wodesby's chant changed again to a grieving ululation and a new image came to Adam's mind. Miranda was staring into a mirror. The rounded walls suggested a turret and behind her was a window, framing a reflected ribbon of moonlit water.

Her brocade walking dress was soiled and her bonnet was gone. There was a cut upon her forehead. "She is hurt," Adam murmured, raising his free hand as if to touch her. In turn, she lifted her fingers to touch the wound and he saw the dull surface of metal. "He has her chained!" the marquess roared. "The bastard has her in manacles. I will kill him. I swear it!" The emerald plunged downward and his hand came banging down upon the table.

Adam opened his eyes.

"You must love her very much indeed, Brand, to see her in the present," Damien said softly, shifting the jewel aside. "Greenwich. But where? We shall have to find a map with more detail."

As the two men searched through the scattered topographical sketches, Lawrence rushed into the room. "I have some news, Adam," he said. "Though it may do us little good. Had a private word with the porter at White's. It cost me ten pounds, but old Charlie wouldn't keep his post there if he was one to talk free and cheap. But I gave him a tenner and the man did sing for me. Gave me pause, I tell you, to realize how much he knows about the members, more familiar with our foibles than those of his own kin, I'd wager. If Ropwell has Miranda, Adam, we must find her at once. Peculiar fellow, very jealous of his late wife. Challenged men just for looking at the woman."

"Uncle," Adam said rising impatiently to his feet. "You have run the fox to ground. To the kill, if you please."

"Forgive an old man's tendency to wag on, m'boy," Lawrence said. "According to Charlie, Lord Ropwell owns better than a dozen properties between here and Kent, every one of them mortgaged to the hilt. Unfortunately, Charlie did not know the whereabouts of all of them."

"Any of his land in Greenwich?" Damien asked, dumping his pile of maps on the table.

"As a matter of fact, that was one of the few that Charlie recollected," Lawrence said, brightening visibly. "Ropwell does own a Gothic monstrosity that his father built on the bank of the Thames, not far from David Garrick's villa."

"That has to be it. Thames view and Gothic tower, complete with manacles," Adam said, casting Wodesby a grim look. "Are you with me? You can come so long as you recollect that Ropwell's neck is mine."

"Aye," Damien said, sweeping his sister's emerald into his pocket. "Much as it galls me, I shall cede you Ropwell; you have earned his throat."

"I will join you," Lawrence offered, following them to the front door.

"No, you will be needed here, Mr. Timmons," Damien said, touching the older man lightly upon the shoulder.

"I have found my cards!" Lady Wodesby cried excitedly from the top of the stair.

"Someone must keep her out of mischief and make certain that she does not come galloping after us," the Mage added, with the suspicion of twinkle in his eye. "I gladly cede that task to you, sir, and wish you joy of it." He hurried out the door.

"They were in my sewing bag, if you would believe. Those sly pusses knew how much I detest needlework," Lady Wodesby said, waving the cards in triumph as she descended. "I would not have looked there for a phoenix age, had not the finder's feeling possessed me. Perhaps if Lord Brand will consent, I will read for him and we may thereby gain some clue as to Miranda's whereabouts." She stared at the pair of backs hurrying down the front stair. "But where do they go, Lawrie?"

"They have found Miranda," Lawrence said, putting his arm around Lady Wodesby's waist. As two horses emerged from the stables, Angel shot through the door, loping off after them. "And now, my dear, they are going to bring her home so we may celebrate. For unless I mistake the matter, your son has just given us his blessing."

Ropwell took a long, hard pull at the contents of his silver flask and sighed as he wiped the back of his hand across his mouth. "My finger still hurts," he whined. "You must have took a pint out of me, enough to write a bloody Magna Carta."

"But the contract is all signed and quite legal," Miranda hastened to assure him. Ropwell had rapidly progressed well beyond the bosky stage. She had to get free, before he lost consciousness. "My brother will have naught to quibble about when he comes. Now shall we get on with it?"

"Want some?" he offered.

"Very gracious of you, I am sure," Miranda said. "But I cannot conduct a séance three sheets to the wind. Now if you will undo my fetters."

"Dunno," he eyed her suspiciously. "How do I know you won't turn on me?"

"Why, the contract, of course," Miranda said, pointing to the document on the table. "We have made a bargain. But as you well know, my powers are diminished by cold iron. If you wish me to raise the spirit of your wife, I must be freed."

Grumbling, Ropwell wove his way to the mantel, picking up the key and returning to unlock the shackles. Miranda suppressed a shudder. She had toyed with the idea of knocking him unconscious and picking his pockets. If she had misjudged and accidentally killed him, she might have condemned herself to a slow, excruciating death. Rubbing slowly at her wrist, she seated herself at the table. She had delayed as much as possible, and now she would risk all on a single throw of the bones.

"Well, get on with it, then," Ropwell said roughly. "Night's almost gone."

Softly, she began an incantation, the slowest and most rhythmic she could remember. Like a lullaby, it was, the ancient words of the spirit chant as soothing as a balm. Ropwell's eyes grew heavier, the lids flickering. "Rest, spirit," the Celtic rhyme begged. "Make your peace, oh restless one, and return ye to your source." With her focus narrowly directed, Miranda did not notice the fingers of gray fog that rose from the Thames below, or the three figures in the moonlight making their way to the castle gate.

Damien waved his arm and muttered a spell of unbinding. "Try it, Brand. The lock should open easily enough now," he declared with a superior smile.

Obediently, Adam gave the gate a shove, but it held fast. He cast Lord Wodesby a look of exasperation. "Bolted tight as Farmer George's purse."

Damien dismounted hastily. "Iron," he grumbled. "The lock is made of iron. We will have to find another way in."

"I think not," Adam said, pulling a thin wire from his belt and giving it an expert twist. "A lucky thing that I always carry my own magic. More than once, this little talisman has saved my hide."

"I have never heard of a talisman that can work against iron," Damien said, watching with interest as Brand began to work.

"Doesn't matter if the lock is iron, brass, or steel if you can work this charm," Adam said, carefully manipulating the mechanism. "A pick-lock can outdo magic, Wodesby, in the hands of an expert." He heard a satisfying click and, with a mocking bow, pulled the gate wide open. "You might do well for a few lessons from Dominick's father, Master Mage. Shall we proceed?"

Damien gave a tight-lipped nod. As they entered the cobbled courtyard, he tried to set aside a feeling of acute discomfort. Strange, this feeling of being bested by Outsiders. But the Mage's pique soon gave way to definite feeling of foreboding. Angel whined softly.

"Keep your hound quiet, or bid her stay and wait," Adam whispered, looking down at the mastiff in irritation.

"She is warning us, Brand," Damien said softly, sending his thoughts seeking. "Something wicked is abroad here tonight."

"Aye, we know that already. Ropwell. He is here, Wodesby, and so is your sister. Somehow, I know her presence. Is that part of your magic?" he asked as he picked open the lock to the kitchen door.

"Any sorcery between the two of you is none of my doing," Damien said, handing Brand Miranda's emerald. "Take this; the seeking spell is still upon the jewel. If she is here, as you say, this will help lead you to her."

As soon as Adam took the necklace, the chain began to sway. He turned, letting the movement guide him toward the stairway.

Damien looked up at into the well of darkness, his uneasiness increasing. The presence that he sensed was more than mundane evil, the banal depravity that was much a part of humanity as the smell of the sewer. Sheer malevolence was prowling at the portals, waiting for something, someone to bid it enter.

"Come, spirit, come and seek ye your rest. Find ye judgement and justice and rise to the Light." Miranda's sing-song ended as Ropwell's head sank to the table. Just in time, her hand caught him, following him against the shock that might well have woken him. She tiptoed to the door only to find the key gone. The room grew chill and a wind from the Thames blew up to rattle the window panes loudly, causing the candles to shudder.

"You were trying to trick me."

Miranda's hand flew to her mouth. Ropwell was wide awake. His bloodshot eyes stared at her balefully. "You fell asleep," she said, trying to sound indignant.

"No more of your witch's lies!" he roared, crossing the room and grabbing her by the wrists. "Bring me Felicity now, or you'll share her fate. And by the time I've done with you, you'll be wishing for the Thames, I vow."

"Jaames . . . ," a voice called softly. "Jaames . . ."

"Felicity?" Ropwell let Miranda drop to the ground and went toward the window.

Miranda scrabbled to her feet, knowing that she had purchased only a small respite. Once more, she threw her voice, this time to make it appear to come from the other side of the door. "Open . . . Jaames . . . let . . . me . . . in."

Hastily, Ropwell shoved Miranda aside and fumbled with the key. He swung the door open to the dark. "Show yourself, Felicity," he demanded, the liquor that he had consumed blotting out fear. "Come to me and tell me where you hid those jewels."

Adam heard Ropwell's voice and followed the sound upward, slipping the jewel into his pocket as he took the stairs two at a time. Damien and Angel followed, but the very air seemed to grow thicker around them, like mud, sucking at their feet, hampering their progress. Too late, he realized that the veil to the world of souls had been sundered.

"Beware, Brand," Damien called weakly, but his words seemed to be swallowed by the morass that surrounded him. Feeling like a fool, he muttered the opening words of a warding spell. However, counter measures availed him nothing against the furious incorporeal force. No interference would be tolerated.

The essence of what had once been Lady Ropwell laughed triumphantly as unconsciousness swallowed the Mage and his familiar. Although a small spark of magic burned bright in the mortal who ran toward the chamber, the spirit quickly dismissed him as a threat to her purpose. She had received the summons that she had spurned heaven for, waited for with all the force of her burning hatred. Even a disembodied soul could appreciate the supreme irony. James himself had opened the door and invited his doom.

Miranda was about to make the "ghost" speak again when the air began to shimmer. The room grew icy and she could see the frost of her breath as she panted air. The candles danced and crystals of light coalesced into the wavering figure of woman. "You called, Jamesss, dear?" the ghost asked, her face featureless except for eyes that glowed crimson as the heart of a glowing coal.

"Felicity." Ropwell greeted her with drunken smile. "You make a beautiful ghost."

The ghostly head turned to regard Miranda. "One of yoursss, Jamesss?"

"A witch," Ropwell replied. "An heiress. I intend to marry her, Felicity."

"Over my dead body," Miranda said.

"That comesss later," the ghost said with acerbity. "But you seem a sssensssible child. How did you come to be in league with Jamesss?"

"He kidnapped me," Miranda explained, rising to confront the incorporeal. "He believes me to be a witch."

The ghost cackled. "You have no magic," she said. "Not like the other I have touched tonight."

A frisson of fear ran up Miranda's spine. Who among her kin had the ghost encountered? It could only be Damien, but there was no sign of any trepidation on the spirit's part. What had happened to her brother?

"Of course she has; you have come, haven't you?" Ropwell maintained doggedly, pulling the vellum from his pocket. "I have a signed contract for my soul right here. So you had best show me where the jewels are, Felicity, before the cock crows."

"Cheated the child, have you, Jamesss, with your paltry sssoul? Asss you did me? Then let me lead you to your jussst reward," the shade offered.

"Come, girl," Ropwell said, his hand wrapping round Miranda's like a vise. "We are going to the jewels."

"Yesss," the ghost hissed, beckoning with a skeletal hand. "To the jewelsss."

Miranda looked into the burning core of the incorporeal's eyes and saw into Pluto's fires. The last thin shred of her courage frayed in the face of that merciless promise of eternal torment. She screamed.

Adam heard Miranda's cry and abandoned all caution. He charged through the open door at the top of the stair to confront the unspeakable. A glowing supernatural figure challenged him, shrieking in anger.

"Do not think to interfere, man," she warned with a stormy wail. "Ropwell isss mine. Too long have I waited, too long in the place between the worldsss. I shall finish my busssinessss." The ghost advanced toward Ropwell and Miranda, shadow arms outstretched.

Suddenly, Ropwell began to understand the shade's intent. "Your death was an accident, Felicity, I swear," he said, backing toward the window, dragging Miranda with him. "She is angry. Keep her away from me, witch, keep Felicity away . . ."

"No!"Adam screamed, running toward the manifestation and reaching out, but there was nothing to grab, only bitter cold. "Miranda has done you no harm, Felicity. Leave her." But his words did not stop the ghost's relentless advance.

Ropwell wrapped his fingers around Miranda's throat. "Stop her, witch," he demanded. "Stop her, or else I will take you with me. Stop her, Brand, or else your witch dies, do you hear? She dies."

"Are you so far gone from this world that you cannot discern innocence?" Adam pleaded with the ephemeral creature. "Will you let him destroy again, as he destroyed you, Felicity? Will you kill me too, for your husband's crime? For if Miranda dies tonight, I might as well seek the Light myself and when I do, I swear that I will find you there and seek my justice."

"But she isss no witch," the spirit said scornfully, moving relentlessly forward. "She is powerlesss. Like I wasss. See how she cringesss. But now my hate givesss me power. She hasss nothing."

"You underestimate Miranda, as you malign yourself, Felicity," Adam shouted. "It took courage for you to plan your vengeance, fortitude to hide those jewels. Miranda may not have a witch's powers, but it does not diminish her; quite the opposite. Her wit, her strength, the valor of her spirit, are all the greater because they come from within her, not from the outside source. Even if she could command all the forces of earth, fire, wind, and air, I could not love her more. Miranda is my life, my heart."

The ghost halted and turned once again a tear-like prism of light dripped from those ember eyes. "You love her that much?"

"I love her, Felicity," Adam declared to the spirit. "Surely you remember what it was to love? I am told that it is the only thing that survives death."

"Yesss," the ghost whispered, her tones dropping to the sweetness of a summer zephyr. "I remember . . . I loved you, Jamesss. Do you recall how it wasss? You were handsssome."

"Handsome," Ropwell repeated, his voice rising to an odd pitch. "I was, wasn't I? And you were so beautiful. Men couldn't keep their eyes off of you, but you were mine."

"Alwaysss yoursss, Jamesss," the ghost declared, weaving a siren spell. "Faithful."

"I had to keep you," Ropwell said, a peculiar glassy look in his eye. "The thought of losing you was unbearable, do you understand?"

"Poor Jamesss, ssso you had to confine me." The ghost declared.

Fingers of loathing crawled up Adam's spine at the undertones that lay beneath the spirit's simple statement. His eyes
went to the chain upon the floor in horror.

"You do understand!" Ropwell said. "Who let you loose?
One of the servants?"

"I fasssted, Jamesss . . . fasssted until my wrissst wasss tiny
enough to passs the ring. 'Twasss then that I hid the jewelsss.
Do you want them, Jamesss? Take my handsss."

Miranda quivered as she suddenly understood the meaning
of the manacle in the stone. This room had been Felicity's
prison. She fell to her knees as Ropwell released her, his
hands stretching toward the shimmering conglomeration of
ether.

"I did not mean to kill you, Felicity," Ropwell said. "I did
love you, but they all wanted you, you see, and you were
mine."

Adam plunged into the chill heart of the shade, braving the
dark core of the image in order to reach Miranda. He hoisted
her into his arms and shrank against the wall as the ghost took
Ropwell in her ephemeral embrace. Ropwell was transfixed,
surrounded by the swirling incoporeality.

"I waited, waited ssso he might die in terror, asss I did, but
I will ssspare him from awarenesss for now, for the sssake of
your love, man. For I sssenssse it isss true," Felicity's spirit
explained as she addressed Adam. "But remember thisss man,
hate sssurvivesss death more than love ever doesss. Jamesss
will pay for hisss crimesss and endure my loathing for all of
eternity." The glowing eyes turned toward her victim. "Come,
dear Jamesss, and we shall find the jewelsss together in the
Thamesss."

"Together," Ropwell murmured, turning toward the window, stepping arm in arm with Felicity's ghost toward oblivion.

Miranda buried her face in Adam's shoulder as the glass
splintered, sending moonlit shards falling like tiny shooting
stars into the night. A horrified scream rose, as if in that last
second, Ropwell realized the full magnitude of what hell had
in store for him.

* * *

Adam held her tightly against him, affirming the reality of the woman in his arms. "Miranda," he murmured, not quite daring to believe the evidence of his senses. He felt her body tremble and when she at last looked up, there was a darkness midst the blue, a latent horror. He wanted to chase those shadows from her eyes, wished that there was some way to cleanse away the terror that had touched them both. He whispered to her as he would to a child, promising that all would be well. But he was more than conscious that this was no infant in his arms. His cheek brushed the golden silk of her hair, kindling a nascent spark of desire. "Miranda, my love," he whispered. "My love, you have nothing to fear."

His words were a benediction, stronger than any spell. Miranda's eyes met his and she knew without doubt that he had told the ghost the truth. Adam loved her, loved her enough to defy both heaven and hell on her behalf. He had drawn her back from the Light, shielded her from the Shadow and now, she was at last where she truly belonged. Indeed, all her fears and feelings of inadequacy were banished.

"Adam," she whispered, her fingers reaching up to bury themselves in the dark softness of his hair. His heart pounded beneath her ear, swift and steady as a ritual drum weaving a rhythm that echoed the rapid tattoo beating beneath her breast. She drew his lips down to meet hers, kissing him with a new certainty, an assurance sprung from the pledge he had made, a promise that was far more than any bond or vow. Adam had given her the gift of herself. For the first time in her life, she was more than whole. She was seeing herself not as a witch that might have been, but as a woman worthy of the love reflected in Adam's eyes.

Comfort flowed from her, as if Miranda sensed the sudden need in him. Despite her ordeal, Adam felt the strength in her kiss, an openness, as if she were presenting him with the essence of her being. He tasted her, savoring every second, taking all that she had to give. His memory scribed every sound and scent; his body recorded every nuance of touch, feasting before the famine.

But while Adam received, he also gave in silent adoration,

cradling her with tenderness until her trembling ceased. Without words he told her of the emptiness inside him that was
now filled to the brimming, setting aside his fear of the void
that was likely yet to be. Even as he spoke with his heart, he
knew that he was being a coward. If he had an ounce of in-
tegrity, he would not make these silent promises, oaths that
were bound to be broken. But Adam could not help himself,
any more than his namesake could have resisted the taste of
that fatal fruit. Miranda was offering him full knowledge, of
her, of himself. Though he knew it a sin, Adam feared that he
would be banished from paradise, innocent or guilty. But
when he looked into Miranda's eyes, trusting and full of love,
he traced the line of her cheek, trying to keep the regret from
his smile. She was promised to another man and even were
she not, he had made a binding oath of his own.

The Mage was due his payment. Adam would abide by
Wodesby's decision. He knew what it would be. He did not
care. Miranda lived. That was enough; it would have to be, he
told the remnants of his shattered heart. Magic had its price.

"Your brother is waiting downstairs, my love," he said
softly, taking the emerald from his pocket and fastening it ten-
derly around her neck. " 'Tis time we were bound for home."

Chapter 13

Lady Wodesby swept through the library like a Channel storm. "Were he not your nephew, Lawrie, pon' oath, I would turn him into a toad."

"At least your opinion of Adam seems to be steadily improving, my dear," Lawrence said mildly. "Yesterday, in your rantings, he was destined to be a mouse, and the day before a roach in Tante Reina's kitchen."

"What is wrong with the man?" Lady Wodesby asked mournfully. "It does not take a wizard's scrying to see that he loves my daughter. From all that Miranda has told me, Brand saved her life at considerable risk to his own. Even I do not know if I would dare to confront a ghost bent on vengeance. Damien admits that he was utterly powerless."

"How the mighty fall," Lawrence remarked, pouring Lady Wodesby a glass of sherry. "Your son seemed rather humbled by his encounter with the ghost, actually. Quizzed me a bit about Adam's experiences while traveling upon the Continent. Seems that Damien is considering making a bit of a Tour as an ordinary mortal, trying to get along as most of the world does."

Lady Wodesby accepted the glass with a nod of thanks and a laugh. "Damien without sorcery? That boy has conjured from the cradle. He might as well propose to walk about blindfolded or hop around upon one foot."

"Told him that I believed it was an excellent idea," Lawrence said, filling a second glass for himself. "Magic is not foolproof, m'dear, as your Damien has found more than once."

"Poor Damien," Lady Wodesby murmured, her eyes misting in recollection.

"Poor Damien!" Lawrence exclaimed, setting his glass down precipitously. "Seems to me that you are directing your sympathies toward the wrong individual, Adrienne. 'Poor Damien, his magic failed him,'" he mimicked. "What of poor Adam? I ask you. As I told your son this morning, my fool nephew is packing to set sail for America, leaving behind the estate he has restored from nothing, not to mention the woman he obviously adores. 'Tis clear as glass that your daughter has his soul in a bottle, yet when I ask, he will say nothing more than 'Magic has its price.'"

"That is all?" Lady Wodesby asked, her eyes narrowing as suspicious thoughts began to gather.

"That is all!" Lawrence fumed.

"Miranda is going about as if she spends her hours peeling onions," Lady Wodesby said. "Yet when I question her about what happened she simply bursts into tears. It would seem she has no clue. The cards are close to useless in her case due to her birth, of course. I am at wit's end. That is why I have asked her to join us here in the library. Perhaps you could speak to her, Lawrie."

"What can I possibly say to her, Adrienne?" Lawrie asked. "I have known Adam since swaddling days and I can get nothing out of him."

"Except 'Magic has its price', you say, hmm? What wizardry could your nephew have in mind?"

"Well, should we not ask your son, the resident wizard?" Lawrence asked pointedly.

Thorpe rose from the hearth and meowed.

"Damien? Demanded what?" Lady Wodesby bent down to hear more closely. "Are you certain?"

Thorpe hissed in confirmation.

"No, of course I am not calling you a liar." Lady Wodesby said soothingly.

"Well?" Lawrence asked impatiently "What has that boy of yours done now?"

"It would seem that Damien demanded a price for finding

Miranda," Lady Wodesby replied, her lips compressing to an angry line. "A steep price."

"I knew it!" Lawrence exploded. "I knew Damien must have something to do with it. He has been entirely too humble lately, almost pleasant to be around."

"If you would prefer me surly, I would be glad to oblige," Damien said as he entered the room. "I knew that my ears were burning for some reason."

"'Tis not the only part of you that I would burn, sir. What did you ask of Adam in return for Miranda's whereabouts?" Lawrence demanded, advancing pugnaciously. "His estates? His wealth?"

"That would have been entirely too easy," Damien said, smoothly, "Brand would have granted me his lands or his money in an eyeblink. To effect such magic for one of the Blood, the boon had to be beyond price, a genuine sacrifice."

"He speaks the truth, Lawrie," Lady Wodesby said, putting a restraining hand on her fiancé's arm. "To work a spell of that kind, the cost must be something that your nephew would have hesitated to give."

"What was it, then?" Miranda asked, stalking into the room to confront her brother. "What did you demand of him, Damien? Did you tell him that he must never see me again for the sake of that precious Blood of yours? You know that Adam is the soul of honor and if that was his word, then he will keep it, even if it kills both him and me. Was that the price of life, Mage of Albion? For if it was, I shall never forgive you. I am more than that which runs through my veins. Adam has made me believe that. So if you think that I will forget him and consent to be a brood mare for some Blooded stud, you are sorely mistaken."

Damien shook his head, his brow furrowing in pain as he regarded her steadily. "You believe I would do that to you, Randa?"

"Sometimes I don't know you anymore, Damien," Miranda said sadly. "You are, when all is said and done, the Mage; the good of the Covens is in your hands."

Damien gave her a mocking smile, covering the hurt she

had dealt him. "Your happiness means a great deal to me, Miranda."

"But if it comes to a choice between being the Mage or my brother?" she asked.

"It has not come to that yet, sister," Damien said softly. "And I pray it never shall. Brand had the gall to inform me that he would marry you, no matter what my wishes were, no matter that he believed you pledged to someone else."

"Damien, how could you have deceived him so?" Lady Wodesby said, appalled. "Miranda is bound to no one."

"The notion was not planted by me, I assure you," Damien said.

"I fear that I may be to blame for that false asssumption," Miranda said, her face reddening. "Nonetheless, you might have disabused him of his misapprehension, Damien."

"It did not suit me at the time to do so," the Mage informed her coolly. "And when I required Brand to yield to my wishes on the matter of your marriage, it made his concession to me all the more of a sacrifice. According to my agreement with Brand, my consent is necessary for you to wed. Since I have never concealed my feelings regarding unions outside the Blood, your Adam naturally assumed that I would forbid him to marry you. He also believed you pledged to someone else. I knew that Brand loved you and therefore surmised that the prospect of losing you would be the highest price that he could pay. He agreed."

"For the sake of my life," Miranda said, tears running down her cheeks.

"For your life, my little watering pot," Damien said, pulling a handkerchief from the air and offering it to her. "However, dear sister, the one thing that I did not reckon upon was Brand's cowardice."

"Adam is no coward!" Lawrence protested.

"I would have thought not," Damien said. "Your nephew will fight outnumbered seven to one, he will brave the heart of a banshee, and wear a dress that defies every law of good taste, but he lacks the courage to ask a simple question."

"Perhaps he fears the answer he may receive," came a

voice from the doorway. "But you are wrong on the dress, Wodesby; it was elegant in its own unassuming way."

"Adam!" Miranda ran into his arms.

"About time, Brand," Damien said with a rueful look. "A few moments more and your uncle might have set me upon the stake while my mother and sister piled the faggots round and Thorpe would have brought the torch."

"What choice did I have but to come, with that blasted hound of yours barking beneath my window, then nipping at my heels?" Adam asked, savoring the feel of her in his arms one last time. "Have you Wodesbys ever heard of sending a note by footman?"

"Honestly, Brand, what would you have done with any note that I might have sent you?" Damien asked.

"Burnt it," Adam said, a trifle sheepishly. "Now what do you want of me, Wodesby?"

"'Tis not what I want, Brand," Damien said, with a languid wave of his hand toward his sister "So much as what she wants."

"You are well aware that I love Miranda, Wodesby," Adam told him, clasping her close in defiance. "Just as you know that I shall honor the bargain that we made, for the price of your magic must be paid. Do you taunt us both, then?"

The amused glint in Damien's eyes dimmed. "You too, Brand? Do you think that I was merely saving myself the price of vellum for an invitation to a game of cat's paw, then?"

Adam sent him a searching look. "You have never concealed your feelings, sir, about this unusual heritage of yours. I know myself to be less than favored as a suitor for your sister's hand. Do you refute that?"

"I cannot," Damien said, his eyes meeting the marquess steadily. "For it would be an untruth to say that you are the man that I would have chosen."

Miranda's hand tightened on Adam's wrist, but he could not bring himself to look at her. "Is there any way that I might change your mind about me? I may not have the family's abilities, but I will do all I can to make your sister happy. My estates are extensive, my title, though not dating back to Arthur's times, is nonetheless esteemed. I am a wealthy man."

"Rather conceited fellow, is he not, Randa?" Damien asked. "Are you sure?"

Miranda nodded, her hopes rising once more despite her brother's shuttered look. "I am certain, Damien, more than I have ever been of anything in my life."

"You are aware of what you may be denying your children?" Damien queried, his voice saddened. "Would you chance diminishing the magic in this world, scarce as it is?"

"There are other forms of magic, brother," Miranda said, looking up at Adam. "Magic with the power to last beyond a lifetime, and that, too, Damien, is a rare form of enchantment. Could I deny that to my children? To myself? I love Adam; I would walk on live coals for him or lay upon a bed of nails."

Damien watched his sister carefully, recognizing that it was useless to press her any further. "And you, Brand, why would you want a woman who would risk her footwear or ruin your rest with silly parlor tricks that any nominally trained charlatan could perform?" he asked, the corner of his mouth rising by a fraction.

"I have already told you that I love her, Wodesby," Adam said simply.

"Enough to forsake her without asking a simple question, Brand?" Damien mocked. "Is your pride such that you would run away without my yea or nay?"

"I believed myself certain of your answer," Adam replied, confused by the Mage's mercurial shifts between mockery and solemnity.

"I have learned of late that nothing is certain, milord," Damien said with a look of chagrin that encompassed them all, "especially those things that we deem most immutable."

"Ask him, Adam," Miranda urged him. "Ask."

"Here? With the entire family standing about," Brand asked, puzzled. "That is not how it is commonly done, Miranda."

Lady Wodesby laughed. "Lord Brand, you may have realized by now that the Wodesbys are not part of the common run. Ask, dear boy."

Adam found to his consternation that his throat was suddenly dry. Acutely aware of his audience, he cleared his throat. "Lord Wodesby, I request the honor of your sister's hand in marriage."

"Well, that took you long enough, Brand," Damien said with an expression of exasperation. "May I suggest that you avoid taking the seat in Parliament. It would take the entire session for you to make your maiden speech!"

"Answer him, Damien Nostradamus!" Lady Wodesby demanded. "Give him his answer or I will——"

"Turn me into a frog?" Damien asked.

"Far worse!" his mother threatened. "I will cook your dinner and make you eat it."

"Yes, Brand! You may have my sister and my blessing," Damien said with mock haste. "By The Merlin, Mama, you have no mercy. If you wish to see your first anniversary, Lawrence, keep this woman out of the kitchen."

Miranda went to her brother and embraced him. "Thank you, Damien," she said, kissing him on the cheek. "I know that this is not what you wanted for me."

"I want you to to be happy, Randa," Damien said, hugging her close. "I wanted someone who could protect you and be strong for you."

"Your sister is strong, Wodesby," Adam said, his voice filled with pride. "And if I am ever in need of protection, I could not want for better."

Damien examined his sister's demeanor with a critical eye. The sad, shrinking little girl that he remembered had disappeared and in her place was a confident woman. "Yes, but who will protect you from her, Brand?" he asked, stepping neatly aside to avoid a sisterly poke. "If either of you gentlemen are in need of charms or talismans to shield you from the wiles of Wodesby women, let me know."

"Shall we remove your son, Adrienne, before your daughter does him bodily injury?" Lawrence asked, taking Damien by the elbow.

"If you want something done, do it yourself, I always say." Lady Wodesby took Damien's other elbow.

"If you see a rather dashing-looking frog hopping about

later," Damien called back over his shoulder, "don't step on me."

"I might even grow to like your brother eventually," Adam said as the door closed behind them.

"Hush!" Miranda said, putting a finger on his lips. "Damien is conceited enough as it is. However, I do think that he rather likes you. His taunts are something of a barometer of affection."

"Then it would seem that he esteems me highly," Adam said, clasping her hand and kissing it softly. "He is right, though. I was a coward. These past few days I've done nothing but think about you, envy that nameless man your brother favored. Poor devil. I almost pity him when he is told that you are promised to me."

Miranda reddened. "There is no one else."

Adam shook his head. "But I thought—"

"That there was a man of my dreams?" Miranda smiled. "Only in my dreams, Adam. And since it suited my brother that you believe me out of your touch, he did not enlighten you. I confess that there was someone who might have asked me to wed him, given sufficient coercion. And had I not met you, I might have made the mistake of marrying him, hoping that I could make him into something he was not or dream myself into believing that I was satisfied. I thought that I was worthy of nothing better than Martin. After all, I was no witch."

"The man was a fool," Adam murmured, his fingers reaching up to brush a lock of hair from her eyes, his caress lingering upon the lobe of her ear.

"As was I," Miranda admitted. "I was afraid, afraid to seek for a happiness that I did not believe that I deserved." She looked up at him, trying to make Adam understand what he had done for her. "All my life, my family has judged me by what I lacked. Is it any wonder that I saw myself in their mirror?"

He cupped her chin in his hands. "Look into my eyes, Miranda, and see what I see. Everything that I have ever wanted in a woman, everything that I will ever want in a wife. Without spells or sorcery, my love, you are magic for me, always."

"And you are mine," Miranda whispered. "You called me back from the Light, Adam. It was your voice that I heard that night at Lady Pelton's, drawing me home to myself. So you too must have a magic all your own."

"So now that we have concluded that we are both magical," Adam said, "there is only one thing left to do. Shall we enchant each other?"

In answer, she pulled his mouth down to hers. This was the sorcery that she had been seeking, the bliss of fulfillment in a spell stronger than any witch or mage might dare to weave. His kiss transformed her with its gentle power, changing her into the woman that she had never dreamed that she could be. The woman that Adam loved.

" 'A sea change,' "she murmured, her fingers wandering to smooth the hair from his brow. " 'Into something rich and strange.' "

Adam drew a sharp breath. "That was the phrase," he whispered. "That was the quotation that my mother was supposed to convey from beyond the veil. Before he died, my father said to listen for those words."

"Perhaps your parents are giving us their blessing," Miranda said hesitantly.

Adam smiled. "Only two weeks ago, I would have called it coincidence. There was nothing beyond the scope of explanation in that well-ordered world of mine. But there was also no wonder and precious little joy."

"And now?" she asked softly.

"Now I know that there is something beyond happenstance, beyond understanding. Call it what you will, fate or sorcery, but I know that it has changed me, changed my life. Perhaps that was what my father was searching for, an assurance that there is something that lasts beyond this moment, this hour." He shook his head in awe as the realization struck him. She was his. "And now, I look at you, my love, and find that eternity does not frighten me. For I know that it is not emptiness, but a place where love abides," Adam said, his hand brushing the hollow of her throat where her emerald gleamed bright.

"And magic," Miranda whispered, knowing deep within that she would always feel this wondrous response to his touch. "These feelings reach beyond this life into forever. Together, Adam, we *are* magic." His lips met hers once more in the miraculous alchemy that only lovers share, the transformation of two disparate souls into one.

Thorpe gave a contented purr. Within seconds, the feline voyeur found himself lifted gently but firmly by the scruff of the neck and placed on the threshold.

"For a familiar, Thorpe, I find you decidedly too familiar," Adam said, shutting the door behind him.

In the face of this obvious human ingratitude, there was little the tom could do but ruffle his fur indignantly, twitch his tail, and stalk to the kitchen to seek his supper.